**HAYLEY QUINN** is an internationally recognised dating coach and founder of the UK's largest dating coaching company. She has over 2 Million views on her TED talk and over 100,000 YouTube subscribers.

She is the spokesperson for Match, the biggest online dating platform in the world. She has been featured on BBC1, Sky and Channel 4 and is a regular columnist for Cosmopolitan.

Her first fiction (Harper Collins) and non-fiction (Simon & Schuster) books are due for publication this year. Hayley's goal is to bridge the gap with modern dating and help inspire people to learn to love dating.

# The Last First Date

## HAYLEY QUINN

ONE PLACE. MANY STORIES

HQ
An imprint of HarperCollins*Publishers* Ltd
1 London Bridge Street
London SE1 9GF

www.harpercollins.co.uk

HarperCollins*Publishers*
Macken House, 39/40 Mayor Street Upper
Dublin1, D01 C9W8, Ireland

This paperback edition 2023

1
First published in Great Britain by
HQ, an imprint of HarperCollins*Publishers* Ltd 2022

ISBN: 9780008511043

*For Nanny B & Nanny M*

# Chapter 1

'*I can't believe I'm the one before **The One**.*'

Helen Pines stared at the picture: it had Jonathan's familiar face scrunched up next to a pretty blonde woman, her arms tied around his neck, with a noticeable diamond ring on one finger.

Proposal in Kenya – classy.

She closed her laptop a little more forcefully than usual, and stared around her childhood bedroom: it felt slightly dustier and smaller every time she visited. Earlier, she had even discovered a fossilised glitter lip balm that had come free with *Shout* magazine stuffed down the side of her bed. There were stacks of *NOW!* CDs (that really should have gone to a charity shop years ago) were scattered on her dressing table and her sixth form prom dress still hung in the wardrobe. Her mum, *insisted* on not throwing it away. She had a bad feeling that the only time she could convince her mum to chuck out her prom dress would be when it was replaced with a meringue-shaped dress of a different kind. Walt Disney had a lot to answer for.

The dress was a fussy, puffy, midnight blue creation that sat side by side with a fussy, puffy, lilac dress she'd worn aged six for her local Carnival Queen competition. A bad, niggling memory of trying out for Carnival Queen occasionally resurfaced and still made her feel embarrassed for her six-year-old self. Her mum, in the audience, wildly gesturing for her to curtsy, an underwhelmed group of local parishioners feebly clapping, and Nanny G reassuring her that she'd look good in a bin bag, as someone crowned the pretty blonde girl, Charlotte, Carnival Queen instead. Really, someone should have realised there was something a little irresponsible about traipsing young girls around beauty pageants full stop. But that was parenting in the nineties for you.

Helen sighed and leaned back on her bed, her socked feet dangling off the edge. Today, she had learned that there were few things in life that made you feel more inadequate than witnessing your ex-boyfriend getting engaged to someone else on social media. With added gut wrench for it being in some glamorous (and surely really expensive) destination. Any holidays they had taken together seemed to revolve around his friends. Her strong hints to romantic mini-break destinations had gone ignored, as had crying into his shoulder one night asking why he didn't want to do anything romantic with her.

His answer at the time was that he just 'didn't believe in that kind of thing', and 'he wasn't that kind of guy'; except he was, just not with her.

It had all started so well: it was New Year's Eve when she was invited by a friend of a friend to Jonathan's house party. He lived in a fancy apartment with a terrace overlooking the Thames, and had employed actual waiters to serve champagne to his guests. There were so many glamorous people there, all doing glamorous things: so when she felt his hand touch the small of her back as the fireworks went off, she couldn't believe he was choosing her. It was all too perfect. He said they could meet any night that week for dinner. Then he didn't message. She messaged him instead, and rather than whisking her off into his life, she spent the next two years trying to convince him to like her as much as he had the first moment they'd met, when he didn't have eyes for anyone else. She must have messed it up badly. And now he was with a woman who probably did all the right things, and never said anything neurotic, and was prettier than her. Helen just wasn't good enough to keep him: plain and simple.

So here she was, back at her parent's house in Cornwall, whilst Jonathan and his wife to be were undoubtedly clinking their Malbec glasses to the sight of a bull elephant, gazing up at the stars, and … urgh, it really wasn't worth thinking about.

At her bachelorette pad in London (read: studio apartment in Hackney), Helen had decided that with a total personal wealth of £1,568 (if you didn't deduct her overdue student loan), there was no way she could justify a holiday this year.

So, for Easter break she had decided to 'staycation' with her parents in Cornwall. At the time, she had told herself that it would be great to reconnect with her family, that she would love the walks and fresh air, that she wanted to meet her brother Henry's girlfriend. That would be nice! Wouldn't it? Instead, from the moment she stepped onto the so-crowded-you-can't-move-in-the-aisles Great Western service to Penzance, she was hit with a wave of dread.

She was living in some kind of Groundhog Day of singleness.

The train journey down was a little too much like the trip down over Christmas, which was a little too much like the trip down over Christmas the year before, just after she and Jonathan had split up. She was so heartbroken that year that she had survived the entire six-hour journey on nothing more than a packet of Maltesers. She had intended to be blasé about the split to her parents, and make up some 'cover story' that he was moving away for work, that things had just run their course, yet the second she had stepped off the platform and seen Nanny G, tears had already started to pour down her face. Her mum had just sighed in resignation that Helen had messed it up again.

The following week had been a bad combination of parental sympathy and sickeningly romantic Christmas movies. Her mum had made all her favourite food in an effort to lift her spirits, and she slid from self-imposed starvation to eating an entire tray of leftover cauliflower cheese from the fridge at 2am when she couldn't sleep. Her dad had nobly ignored his daughter's anguish, but when he spotted Helen in the corner of his eye, holding a cushion up to her face to mask her tears during the opening scenes of *Up!*, he wordlessly lifted the remote and changed the channel. Henry had placed his arm around her and pulled her onto his barrel chest for a hug.

That Christmas, she felt like a loser. No matter how many, *I'm not searching for my other half because I'm not a half* memes her two best friends, Elle and Sophie, sent to her in their group chat, Helen couldn't shake the feeling that being dumped shortly before your thirtieth birthday was a bad thing. She didn't feel like slinging on stilettos, marching out to a bar, and starting all over again, so she spent an unhealthy amount of time fantasising about possible ways she and Jonathan could get back together. He was a polyglot, whilst Helen still mumbled through the pronunciation of 'croissant': maybe she would take a language class and then in a year's time bump into him on the Eurostar (she would be on the way to an important meeting in Paris) and impress him with her effortless French? Maybe he would wake up next to his fiancée Katy one morning, and realise that he'd made a huge mistake? He'd knock on her door … take her on a romantic holiday to make it all up to her … slay a dragon to prove his love …

Of course, now that the engagement picture was staring at her out of her phone, she knew definitively that wasn't ever going to happen. A small, embarrassed part of her that was still holding out hope he'd come back, whimpered, and scuttled away into the recesses of her mind. The Carnival Queen dress glinted in her wardrobe. She clearly wasn't good enough.

Helen didn't generally see herself as 'not enough'. Most days, her self-esteem was *okay*, and she made a concerted effort not to feel down when her followers shrunk on social media, or a vlog that she produced limped up to ninety-six likes. However, as the months ticked by, and she met no one that she actually liked, she felt forgotten about – like her thirties were destined to be spent mouldering away in the shade. A feeling probably not helped by her unshaven legs (regrettably down to sheer laziness, and not a feminist statement) and descent into 24/7 loungewear.

She was really starting to worry that there was something wrong with her. Because if there wasn't, *why* was she still single? Her mum would say it was because she 'scared them off', Nanny G would wink and say she needed to forget finding a boyfriend and learn how to have fun instead.

That's not to say she wasn't liked; Helen had always had friends, just never 'real' boyfriends. Her love life was heavy on 'situation-ships' and low on Valentine's Day cards. She considered herself essentially a nice person: she worked hard, she had good friends, and a blogging business with real (if unrealised) potential. But as much as it rankled every bone in her body to admit it, there was something about turning thirty that had changed things, at least for her. A heavy feeling of pressure dwelled around her dates, going out with a totally-not-right guy didn't feel so funny anymore, and she started to notice the month's ticking down to her next birthday.

No matter what her friends said about it being totally normal to be single in your thirties, Helen felt herself oscillating between feeling flat and sheer panic. Rather than being an 'up and coming' baking influencer, she now felt unquestionable pressure that she should have 'up and come' by now. Her best friend Sophie had coupled up with Frank, and they seemed alarmingly happy. Elle was still single but seemed to revel in the role of always being the dumper, rather than the dumpee. 'Treat them mean …' she would say, tapping her false nails on her phone. In fact, Helen got the feeling that Elle thought her desire for a cosy relationship was a little lame. Maybe even weak.

Then there were her parents. Since joining them for Easter, Helen had been dodging questions about her single status like a downhill slalom. Even her younger brother was coupled up; an unfortunate injustice that was always destined to happen. Now, next time they pried about whether she and Jonathan might ever get back together, she would have to spit it out that he was actually engaged to someone else, like some monumental hairball that conceded her defeat.

To be clear, things hadn't ever been bad with Jonathan: in fact, they were really nice. At least most of the time. She had adored him. The only snag was he seemed eternally on the fence about her. He had told her she was the most amazing woman he had ever met, but he wasn't sure they were right together, all in the same day. Helen couldn't quite fathom why, if he thought she was that incredible, he could never fully commit. He kept saying statements that, when placed together in a sentence, seemed to conflict with one another. Towards the end of their relationship, Helen had felt so confused by it all that she hadn't realised just how badly her confidence had been eroded by his lack of certainty.

Her days had turned into a fug of worrying whether he loved her, or not; was he seeing someone else, or not, and who was that woman who had just followed him on Instagram? Etc. She became so on edge that he would walk away and pull the plug definitively on their two-year romance, that she had started to walk on eggshells around him. She tried to be the perfect girl-friend, tried to pretend that she was totally cool with him taking his time, and it had mercifully, eventually, ended when she had given him space to think about what he really wanted, and he had met Katy. Looking back, she had spent years of her life trying to recreate the first moment they met, when all the promise of the romance stretched out before her. When she thought she was The One for him.

As soon as Jonathan had ditched her and found Katy instead, his commitment issues seemed to evaporate overnight, and social media had reliably informed her that her boyfriend, in everything but name, was definitely not hers anymore. Her friends had told her that it would be the same story with his new girlfriend, and that he would never settle. But he just had. Apparently, his total inability to commit was in fact a reflection on her all along. It was because she wasn't enough for him.

She sent a screenshot of the engagement picture to her WhatsApp chat 'Queens xoxo' with Elle and Sophie.

Elle: *That man is* 😵
*I'm so glad you're not with him anymore babe. He never treated you right!!*
*And his new fiancee … Don't know what he's thinking …*

Sophie: *Sorry babe :-( as @Elle says, it just wasn't the right guy.*
*Remember that Instagram isn't real life, and we don't know what's really going on there.*
*Most important thing is that you've both moved on and now that the door is closed, you will meet someone better. I promise! I can feel it*
*Let me know if you want to voice chat later? Xx*

Helen: *Thanks guys* 😎
*I just don't know what went wrong there – or how he suddenly changed overnight??\**
*\*Okay it's been a year but still!*
*Hard not to take it personally :-(*
*How's things with Frank @Sophie?*
*Mum's calling (yes, I might as well be 13 again not 31!)*
*brb! Xx*

Helen sat down at the dining table and was grateful that her parents weren't the kind of people to mention that she'd been wearing the same yoga pants and hoodie for three days now. She instinctively sat next to Nanny G – her favourite grandparent,

7

and officially the last woman left standing of her older relatives. She was wearing her trademark lavender-coloured blouse with diamante butterfly brooch, and was nursing a small glass of port and brandy she'd been warming on the radiator.

'How are you my dear?' Nanny G's voice had the timbre of an old-fashioned wireless set.

There was something about how close Helen felt to Nanny G that stripped her of all her resolve to not make a fuss, and she felt her face growing warm. If she'd fallen over when she was a child, her mum would have said, 'stand up' and Nanny G would have got her a plaster. She inhaled sharply, 'Well, Jonathan has just got engaged. To Katy. I think during a hot air balloon ride over Lake Nakuru.'

'Oh my! Well, he always did like to be the centre of attention – I suppose he let the world know his happy news in a suitably discreet and mature way?'

'He posted a huge picture on Instagram captioned #thisisit.' Helen paused to translate what she had just said into elderly relative speak. 'Instagram's a bit like a photo gallery for showing off how perfect your life is …'

'I know! I opened an account last month, mostly so I could spy on you though!' smiled Nanny G, discreetly prodding Helen's hands with her fork. 'I don't suppose many people are interested in a nonagenarian's life in Cornwall, and I still have to get the hang of hashed tags.'

'Hashtags, Nan … I'll think of some good ones for you later …'

'Did I hear you mention Jonathan?' Helen's mum sat down at the table, and leaned in conspiratorially. 'Don't leave me out! Have you heard from him?'

Helen's brother Henry started rapidly serving the potatoes, and shot her an apologetic look across the table.

'He just got engaged …'

'Oh …'

'I knew it was coming …'

'Well, there will be plenty of other opportunities darling, especially for someone as lovely as you! What about Dean?'

'You mean Dean from uni?'

'Yes! The tall one, nice smile, always very polite!'

'Mum – Dean and I have been friends for over a decade, plus he's gay, so I really don't think there's unexplored potential there …'

'Oh yes, of course, I remember you saying.' Helen's mum paused to digest this reminder. Holding her knife and fork aloft, she gazed upwards as if searching for some divine inspiration to help her daughter's plight. 'Maybe you could try one of those dating apps? I read in *Woman & Home* that they are *the* thing right now to meet people …'

'Unfortunately, Mum, dating apps are really for people who aren't looking for actual relationships …'

'I don't quite see …'

'Just trust me on this, Mum.'

'Well, if you decide to try again, can you set me up a profile as well?' Nanny G smiled. 'There's life in the old girl yet! Would you mind passing me the wine? I think that Helen and I would quite like some.'

# Chapter 2

'So, when are you going to help me make my grand debut?' Nanny G threw the end of her silk scarf over her shoulder with a flourish.

'You mean on dating apps, Nan?'

'Well, only if you think I could snag one of the younger folk! Have you seen men my age? Disgusting!'

Helen coughed into her coffee.

'I'm only teasing. I've probably had my share for this lifetime, but if this is the way to meet people these days, perhaps you could give it a shot?'

A knot tightened in Helen's stomach. Despite her best efforts to muster some willpower, Helen had checked Jonathan's Instagram more times than she wanted to admit yesterday. She fell into bed wired from gazing at her screen, and her sleep had become fractured by uncomfortable thoughts. She'd woken up at the slightest sound, got up to pee at least four times, and her brain kept flashing the alert, 'you're running out of time', like some horrible countdown clock. She'd woken up too early, too hungry, and eventually gave up on the idea of ever going back to sleep.

Grabbing her blanket, she'd trudged downstairs, made coffee, and slumped into a beanbag in her parent's sunroom next to Nanny G (who had only recently realised that it was far better for her knees to sit in a proper chair).

'Not you as well, Nan? I just can't deal with this anymore. I know you, mum and maybe even Dad, are only bringing it up because you care, but it's not making me feel any better. Actually, it's making me feel worse. It's like by me being single I'm a worry to everyone: like I'm a dress on a sales rail that you can't quite shift.

'I know you probably think I'm not trying, but I have. I have *really* tried. I honestly have. It's just not worked out for me and I have to get my head around that. I'm quirky, I get it, there's perhaps not that many good matches for me, and dating just isn't the same as it used to be when Mum met Dad, or you met Grandad.

'Most days, trying to meet someone just feels like a waste of effort. I am tired of going on dates, and being disappointed. In fact, I'm actually *so* done with dating. Rather than focusing on what I don't have, I need to focus on all the things I do have. I have a career I like, and that has *potential*.' Helen winced at her constant need to stress the fact that she was really, honestly doing something with her life. 'I have friends. I have my health, and I just don't think you need to have a man to be happy.'

Helen cringed at just how many clichés she'd strung together in an effort to make her point. The more she tried to express how much she didn't care about being single, the more she came across as someone who cared about this subject very much. Her face had become mottled and pink: a bit like when she didn't get chosen to be Carnival Queen, but had to stand on stage and clap the winner.

'Of course, you don't! As my mother once told me, far better to be left on the shelf than locked in the wrong cupboard,' Nanny G paused and looked Helen straight in the eyes, 'but I do think it's quite all right to say to yourself "I want this or that" and try to find it!'

'Well, maybe dating was easier back in your day …'

'In some ways maybe, but in others certainly not! If you weren't

11

married by twenty-four you were labelled a spinster and all that "no sex before marriage" malarky, what a terrible idea! Nothing worse than marrying who you thought was a man, only to discover he was a boy who had no idea how to treat a woman. The kind that just sticks it …'

'Nan!' Despite herself, Helen couldn't help but smile. 'TMI Nan! TMI! Too much …'

'… information! You know I used to like *Ricki Lake*! Well, this may surprise you but we had our lives back then too, and of course during the war it was all very exciting …' Nanny G's eyes glinted through her glasses, with the flicker of a memory that she had been young once too.

'I thought you met Grandad after the war?'

'I did! But I still had a good war. The parties were fantastic! At the time I was living with my sisters as you know. Beautiful women! Golden locks of hair! But no personality. Looks are overrated I think, and of course they fade … Would you say I'm good-looking now, Helen?'

'You have aged well, Nanny!' Helen said with sincerity as she studied the spiderweb of lines across her grandmother's face, her thin hair curled until it stood on end, and her religious dedication to wearing cerise lipstick. It was hard to think that once, she had fallen in love, fought with her sisters over who wore which dress, and danced into the night.

'Of course, I look just dreadful!' Nanny G pulled her skin taught around her neck and face. 'Maybe that's better?'

Helen laughed and batted Nanny G's hands down from her face. 'You're lovely, so please don't mention a facelift again?'

'Well, even you can't say I'm much to look at now, and the good news is I wasn't even back then. Too thin! But I always had more personality in my little finger than all my sisters put together, and I was the worst flirt the devil put breath into. So, with me in the room they didn't get a look in.

'Not that there was much to get a look at back then. As you can imagine, we were suffering with the selection of local men; with most away at war, we only had the widowers and the farmers left here. Slimmer pickings than you have now, that I can guarantee! Oh, I would have loved one of these dating apps back then. But at least we had the evacuees!'

Helen snorted, 'Err, weren't the evacuees children?'

'Of course, but someone had to bring them all the way down here, and one day on the farm I was minding my own business, and I saw the most handsome man! Initially, I was terribly embarrassed as we were made to wear these ugly brown breeches, quite unfeminine! At the time, as you know, I was working in the anti-vermin squad ...'

Helen frowned, puzzled.

'I haven't told you that story? Another time maybe, frightful business. Not for the faint-hearted. But we did as we had to do. Anyway! On my way to work one morning I was greeted by two new evacuee children and their lovely older brother who had got them down here. Now ... he was a man. Tall, dark, handsome, with those lovely lips! I was quite taken with him!'

'So did you get your flirt on?'

'Most certainly! He was working as a bus driver in London so didn't need to go to the front line, at least not at that stage, but it meant he had to travel back to London the next day, so we only had one night ...'

'... maybe we should skip over the details of what's next, Nan!'

'Oh, don't be so silly: it wasn't like that. Well maybe it was a bit, but not for us, I always thought I'd see him again and so had no reason to rush. Of course, looking back, I was a bit of a die-hard romantic about it all, not unlike you my girl ...' Nanny G prodded her spoon towards Helen.

'Anyway, we agreed to meet later that night in Kynance Cove, you know the one you can walk to over the headland. There was nothing there back in my day, but we had the most beautiful stroll across the beach in the moonlight. It didn't even rain! Which was just as well as I wasn't wearing any nylons. Couldn't get a hold of any, so I'd drawn the line of my stockings onto the back of my legs with a bit of eyeliner; it would have washed right off in bad weather and caused a terrible mess.

'His name was Vernon and he'd bought me two Victoria plums in his pocket; which was quite the thing to get a hold of back then. We sat on the shingle of the beach, and talked until the early hours of the morning. I got quite told off when I finally made it home!'

'What happened, did you ever see him again?'

'Never. He used to write to me once a week from London. I heard from him with the Friday post every week for five months and then – nothing. Of course, I was beside myself at the time, and vowed that as soon as this war business was over that I'd go to London to find him. But then, I met your grandfather, and there was some pressure for me to marry. My mother was worried the men would get called back up, and the thing was, if I was married to a man, I would get a military pension and be quite safe. If he died that is.

'That was all my mother wanted for me: to be safe. Exactly the same as what your mother wants for you, though I know sometimes she can put her foot in her mouth expressing it. So, I married your Grandpa M, and that was that. I don't know what happened to Vernon: maybe he had another woman up there, maybe he was called-up, I really don't know. But I do think of him often: that's the thing at my age; I only have my memories, which is why at *your* age my dear, it is worth making some good ones.' Nanny G gave Helen a little prod in the ribs with one bony finger.

Helen slumped further into the beanbag feeling a little guilty. She was the epitome of nothing to complain about. Her ex had got engaged and put up a stupid post on Instagram: so what? It wasn't exactly comparable to what her nan had been through. It wasn't Britain in the Blitz, and getting to meet the love of your life for only twenty-four hours. Nanny G didn't need to tell her

14

as much, but she got the distinct feeling she needed to buck up her ideas.

'You're right: I'm going to make an online dating profile and go and make some new memories,' she said pulling out her phone.

'Good – just make sure I can have a look at what pictures you're using. None of this down and out look you are sporting right now: choose photos where you're wearing your hair down, and maybe that nice one of you in the yellow dress.'

'Thanks, Nan,' Helen smiled and chose the yellow dress picture for her lead photo. Photos generally made her feel awkward, but luckily her career as a baking blogger meant that if there was one thing she could do well, it was to write.

*Helen, 31*
*Cornish lass, based in London.*
*Makes excellent banana bread.*
*Looking for an old-fashioned romance – or at least a good opening line.*

Sat on her single bed, Helen opened the app and started swiping.

If anything, at least this was entertaining: bad checked shirt (next!), odd angle of photo with cows in the background (next!), proudly clutching two pints at once (double next!).

Then she saw his profile:

*Brody, 37*
*Entrepreneur, surfer, and committed Dachshund fan.*
*Taller than you in your tallest heels.*
*Looking to go on my last first date ;-)*

Brody had sandy blonde hair that framed a strong jawline, and eyes that seemed to look back at her through his profile pic. He had a little dog under one arm, a green smoothie in the other, and was standing against some kind of golden trellised background.

The dog had unusual blue eyes and a shaggy grey coat that matched Brody's slim fitting T-shirt. Helen was not the biggest fan of dogs, especially the small yappy kind, but felt confident she could make an exception in this case. She swiped right.

*You've connexed!* the app proudly announced.

Too good to be true Helen thought. Then a message popped up:

*Banana bread? Any chance you bring a slice to your first dates? B x*

A shiver ran down Helen's spine: like a door had swung open that she was destined to walk through.

# Chapter 3

Helen paused and looked at her phone; she tried to ignore it but a gentle, fizzing excitement was edging out the emptiness she'd felt just hours ago. Now that Jonathan was definitely out of the picture, had that acted like some abrakadabra in the universe summoning up a new romance? A new boyfriend?! She shook her head and focused on writing a witty response:

Helen: *Only for very special people! Do you live in Cornwall?*

Brody: *London – moved to the big smoke 18 years ago – but escape here when I can for the surf mostly. How about you?*

Helen: *Same actually – Cornwall is such a small place I'm almost surprised we've never met?!*

Brody: *I know, I'll have to make a complaint ;)*
*So, I have 3 important questions for you if you're game?*

Helen: *Game :-)*

Brody: *First of all, how do you feel about surfing?*

Helen: *No previous experience but I could be convinced!*

'Outright lie!' thought Helen, waves and sand were a bad combination, especially when they got all in your eyes and up your nose.

Brody: *For a Cornish lass that's truly shocking!*
*Okay question 2, how do you feel about Dachshunds?*

Helen quickly googled 'Dachshunds'. Okay, so Dachshunds were originally trained to smell out badgers and she'd mistakenly been identifying them as 'sausage dogs' this whole time.

Helen: *Sooo cute! Is he friendly to strangers?*

Brody: *Very! Of course, he has excellent taste in people.*
*Final question …*

Helen: *Wait, don't I get to ask you some questions too?*

Brody: *Of course – sorry not very chivalrous of me. Shoot!*

Try to be witty, try to be witty …

Helen: *So, my first question is what's your company? Is it based here? It sounds very exciting.*

Blah.

Brody: *Our mission is all about making it easier for people to choose recyclable alternatives to everyday disposable goods.*
*∧That's our corporate explanation anyway. As cheesy as*

*it sounds, I just want the world to be more switched on
to small changes that can be made and that have a big
environmental impact.
I'm down here at the moment looking to do some
charitable work with Surfers Against Sewage.
Next question?*

Noble!

> Helen: *So, it's not just you in your company?*

Brody: *Not anymore. I'm lucky to hire quite a few people
who are much smarter than me to help get our message
out.*

Noble AND successful.

> Helen: *That's amazing. My job is a little less ground
> breaking; I run a small blog, but I think it could go places.*

Brody: *If it's not too much, can I give you some advice I
received once?
Never dismiss what you do ;-)*

> Helen: *Okay, I'll try :-) Can I ask another question?*

Brody: *Yes, but only if I get to ask my last question straight
after?*

> > Helen: *Deal!
> > So, what are you looking for on here?*

Helen inwardly recoiled as soon as she typed the words. Such.
An. Awkward. Question. She clearly had a post-Jonathan hang-up

about commitment. She may as well have sent him a gif of Beyoncé singing 'put a ring on it'.

> Brody: *Hehe well … let's just say that even if I thought that dating 6 women at a time was a good idea at this stage in life, I don't have the time to do that. I like to focus: in all areas.*

Oh.

> *Was that your subtle way of telling me you're looking for something serious?*

> Helen: *No – well maybe, yes …*
> *Sorry, I just thought I should ask as I'm not much of a dating app person.*
> *In fact, my nan suggested I should sign up …*
> *So, you're actually the first guy I've chatted to.*

Helen Pines! You have NO game.

> Brody: *Well, your nan sounds like a pretty cool lady. So, do I get to ask my question yet?*

> Helen: *Yes of course – sorry!*

> Brody: *Final question: are you free tomorrow?*

> Helen: *Yes, I should be …*

Read: I can fit you into my packed schedule, somewhere between scrolling Instagram and Netflix …

> Brody: *Maybe I can take you for lunch then?*

Okay, that is not a hook-up: it's a proper lunch date.

> Helen: *That would be lovely. I'm near Truro but maybe we could do the coast?*

Brody: *If it's not too far – how about Kynance Cove? There's a café there that does really good avo toast. Might even be up to your standards ;-)*

Oh. My. God.

> Helen: *Shall we say 1pm? I'll get my brother to give me a lift :-)*

Brody: *I'll be there. I've enjoyed chatting to you a lot, Helen. See you tomorrow x*

> Helen: *Me too :-) See you xx*

'Are you okay, Helen?' Henry asked through her bedroom door.

'Yes, why wouldn't I be?' She could feel the heat rising up her neck, and threw her phone facedown on the bed.

'Urm, I just heard you scream and wanted to check you were all right?'

'I'm fine, nothing to see, or hear, here!' Helen picked at her T-shirt; was she sweating?

'Okay then.' Helen heard Henry trudge off slowly down the hall.

She checked her reflection in the mirror, beetroot red. Good job she didn't open the door. She pulled open her dressing table drawer, and reached for her stash of Percy Pigs. After eating three in a row, she felt composed enough to tell everyone about her date. Could it be too good to be true? A very sophisticated catfish? She shook her head, physically erasing the image of Jonathan's engagement. No. She deserved to be happy. It was going to be fun.

Helen: *OMG guys, you'll never believe it but I have such a hot date tomorrow!*

Helen snapped a quick picture of Brody's profile and sent the screenshot to Queens xoxo.

*He's a really successful entrepreneur, 37! We just chatted for the past half hour and tomorrow he asked me out for lunch.*
*But you know what's the weirdest thing?*
*He asked me to meet him at KYNANCE Cove!!*

Elle: *Is that a restaurant? Or a beach thing?*

Helen: *No, it's this really beautiful place (well, yes beach) but here's what's really weird.*
*Earlier I was speaking to my nan, and she had her first date with her one true love there.*
*Isn't it funny that she just mentioned it?*

Elle: *With your grandad? That's weird!*

Helen: *Actually, he wasn't my grandad but anyway, I just thought maybe it's a sign.*

Elle: *That there's not that many date locations in Cornwall? I don't know babe! He sounds great but be careful meeting someone from an app somewhere remote …*

Helen: *I really think he seemed so nice!*
*And anyway, now you have his screenshot you can track me*
*down if you don't hear back.*

Elle: *Yeah, he's cute.*
*Though not sure about men who own small dogs!*
*Oh, did I tell you I went on a third date with that Israeli*
*guy today …*
*He's so keen, he was already talking about going on holiday*
*later this year.*

Helen: *Wow, that sounds great! Nice to see a man who*
*knows what he wants.*

Elle: *I would NEVER go of course, but I'll take the*
*compliment ;-)*

Sophie: *Sorry to be late to the party here!!*
*@Helen that's great news!!!*
*Gorgeous picture and sounds like a really thoughtful date*
*too!*
*Maybe quite nice to date a fellow Cornishman?*
*And you know I believe in the universe, so maybe the whole*
*Kynance Cove thing is A SIGN!*
*Would you be able to see him when you get back to*
*London?*

Helen: *He actually lives in London most of the time. Just*
*doing some charity work down here*
*#swoon.*

Sophie: *Even more perfect then! So whatcha wearing?*
*Send pics xx*

Elle: *You can't go wrong with the black halterneck, skinnies and those ankle boots!*

Helen: *Maybe a bit much for Cornwall.*
*But don't worry I'll send options.*
*Thanks for the support!*
*LU guys xx*

# Chapter 4

The easiest way Helen could describe what she looked like, would be to say that she didn't look like anyone at all. She certainly didn't have a celebrity lookalike. She had never once in her life had someone run up to her and gush, 'Has anyone ever told you? You look just like …!'

With medium-length, thick, brown hair, pale blue eyes, and pear-shaped hips, she looked like an English woman in her early thirties, maybe twenty-eight on a good day. She emphatically did not look like someone you would cast in a movie or who you would see on a catwalk.

She was not attractive, beautiful or striking. At best, she was cute, or pretty – and that was fine by her. She could rest safe in the knowledge that she was never being judged positively or negatively because of her looks: she just was.

Helen actually thought there was a lot to be said for not standing out; it meant you didn't get picked to star in the school play, and could hang out towards the back of the chorus, safe from scrutiny. You weren't disliked for being either too attractive or unattractive; women who had never met you didn't cling protectively to their boyfriends in your presence, and whilst Helen had still had a few sleazy comments in her time, she didn't feel like a magnet for them. She actually quite liked the fact that if they were ever on a night out, men would flock towards Elle, and she could avoid the awkwardness of flirting. Being really 'hot' seemed like a lot of pressure: a lot of spin classes, balayage highlights, and time spent on Instagram.

She was about to go out on a very important first date though. A first date … how long had it been? Well, you couldn't really count that French guy who had weirded her out by asking her why she was still single. So, it had been, well, at least a few months? She couldn't even say she was rusty, more like she was never polished. She'd never felt beautiful, or powerful, or adored on a date. Dates with Jonathan frequently didn't happen, or involved him needling her about past boyfriends, future career plans, and if she really thought the dress she was wearing was appropriate. In hindsight, they felt more like an intense interview process than a romance, one that had perfectly tapped into her desire to please everyone, and made her jump through hoop after hoop in the hopes he would fall as madly in love with her as she had done with him. Tomorrow would be different. She would be herself, but a polished, grown-up, (whisper it) sexy version of herself that Brody would fall head over heels in love with. If it was meant to be of course; you couldn't force these things.

Helen picked up a simple black vest and folded it away again. Having packed to visit her parents she had precisely no clothes that were date worthy: the halterneck Elle had mentioned was hanging safely in her wardrobe in London, and had been trumped by a selection of oversized pastel sweaters and three pairs of leggings.

She sent a picture of herself in cropped skinny jeans and an off-the-shoulder knit to Queens xoxo.

Sophie: *I like that jumper on you!*

Elle: *Cream is a nice and girlfriend-y colour … but are you sure about the Converse?!*

26

Sophie: *Ofc @Elle would never be caught dead in Converse ;-)*

Elle: *Just not my style @Sophie*
*Babe wear whatever makes you feel confident: it's \*just\* a first date!*

'Sis, you ready to go?' Henry was outside her door again.

Despite being four years her junior, he was one of the only members of her family to understand the concept of tact. He never burst through her door uninvited, and instead dutifully knocked every time he wanted to speak to her. He had always been the steadier one of them both. Helen was aware that she had a tendency towards being a little anxious; Henry, on the other hand, had rock-like qualities. He said very little, but always turned up on time, often just where you needed him to be. It was no surprise to Helen that he had found a nice girlfriend who doted on him.

Helen was due to meet her later today; she could tell Henry was quite taken with Nessy because he wouldn't be introducing her over a family dinner otherwise. He was a true stoic and the total opposite of a guy like Jonathan, who'd been all talk and no action. Or if there were actions, they didn't mean anything, and if they did mean something, it was always the total opposite of what you thought they meant.

She remembered how Jonathan had once invited her to see Cirque du Soleil. He told her to dress up, and she had spent nearly £300 she didn't have on a new beige mac for the occasion. She felt like this was Jonathan's way of showing her off and taking a big step towards being officially his girlfriend. Only later on did it transpire that she was in fact not the first person he'd invited, that he'd won the tickets in a raffle and his gesture had a lot more to do with his inability to go to any event alone, than his feelings towards her …

'Yep, yep – coming!' Helen yelled back through the door. After a second glance in the mirror, she put down her Converse trainers and grabbed her black ankle books instead.

They trundled over to Kynance Cove, the sky oscillating between bleached yellow sunshine and hail showers. Helen kept reflexively checking her phone, just in case Brody cancelled. Not that he was going to. She really shouldn't manifest that.

'Here, okay?' Henry asked, slowing his battered maroon Land Rover (or as you would say in Cornwall 'Landy') down into the car park.

'Yes, looks good.' Helen was already distracted scouring for any signs of Brody, somewhere in her mind it was embarrassing if your younger brother was dropping you off.

'So, I'll see you around three?'

'Thanks Henry –yes three is good …' Helen leaned distractedly against the cool car window.

'Okay well … have fun.'

Helen hopped out of the car: why was she so nervous? It would probably be awkward. He may look nothing like his picture, like that last guy she met from Connex in London who she didn't recognise in the pub and then had to make two hours of polite conversation with. But then again, she could walk through that café door and into the rest of her life. In a few short moments, single life could be behind her, and she would be swept into something new and different.

'I need to chill,' thought Helen. She really had to try and not have any expectations. Especially about falling in love. She rolled her eyes at herself, and straightened up, trying to squash the nerves that she was sure would make her say or do something stupid later on.

Helen also recognised that stepping outside of her comfort zone wasn't exactly a strong point for her. Whilst most other children loved being picked up and swung around by adults, Helen had always preferred her two feet safely on the ground.

As she grew older, her natural trepidation turned into a fear of heights, then rollercoasters, and finally surfing. If you grew up in Cornwall, a surfboard, a wardrobe full of Rip Curl, and bleached blonde surfer waves was your passport to popularity, but, unsurprisingly, Helen's fear of waves had definitively outweighed her desire to be cool. So, rather than hanging with the 'in' crowd at school, Helen had kept her few good friends, and had watched the surf break from the safety of the sand dunes with a copy of *Sweet Valley High* instead. She did that a lot even then: standing back, observing, dreaming up a thousand ways that she would be recognised or chosen. Like a princess in a fairy tale. None of which actually happened, probably because most of the time people didn't even realise she was there.

Kynance Cove was a small sandy beach ensconced by rocks jutting out at odd angles from the headland. The sunlight made the shingle beach silvery luminescent, receiving the heavy waves thumping onto the beach at low tide. The rain had cleared and left a fresh spring day, shrunken patches of clover and gorse were emerging misshapen on the cliffs, and for the first time in months the sun felt warm.

There was one ramshackle café on the beach: The Boat Shed. Instead of housing fishing boats, the wooden hut had been transformed into a trendy wood-framed café. The walls were painted a soft yellow with teal awnings, plant tubs were dotted around the entrance, but whatever inhabited them had failed to grow back since the winter storms. Inside were five small, mismatched tables that had clearly been thrown together from neighbours' clear outs and car boot sales. Only one was occupied by a mother and her two small children: a tot dressed in blue dungarees was stabbing the table top with a blue crayon, and a baby started to emit a low grumble, until its mother produced a bottle of milk from her backpack.

Helen made a beeline to the loo for a nervous pee: no sign of Brody yet.

Maybe she was going to get stood up after all?

If so, she wasn't going to own up to it: she would get on the Wi-Fi, eat a large piece of cake, and when Henry picked her up, she would make up some shaggy dog story about how Brody was perfectly nice but just not her type ... then cry in peace and quiet at home over yet another failure. Maybe she would be honest about it with Sophie, but would have to hush it up from Elle; she was sick of her dating 'advice'.

Helen ordered an iced latte with almond milk (was that sustainable??) and opened Instagram. Jonathan and Katy stared back at her, surrounded by Maasai tribesmen in an open and shut case of cultural misappropriation. Urgh. She put her phone down on the table: must appear serene when Brody arrives, she thought drumming her fingers on the table. *If* Brody arrives: he was five minutes late.

'Should have been fashionably late,' Helen cursed inwardly. 'Elle would have never turned up on time ...'

Staring out the window there was no one else in sight, just a mile of shingle beach and foam coming off the sea. Helen tried to imagine what the beach would have been like that night, when The Boat Shed was still just a boat shed. She could imagine Nanny G striding across the beach, her shawl wrapped around her, hair pinned close to her head in tight curls, a splash of cerise lipstick on her lips that were still full and youthful, her drawn-on stockings smudging in the mist ...

Vernon, who would have looked a little like Aidan Turner, with brooding eyes, and his shirt ... No, his shirt would be done up. He was a real gentleman. They would have strolled along the sand, and as they sat down, he would have draped his jacket over Nanny G's slender shoulders. They would have had one of those conversations that engulfs you for hours, as they sat under the clear night's sky, the air unnaturally warm. Lit just by moonlight, Nanny G was more beautiful than ever with perfect translucent 1940s skin. Then, when they kissed, it would have looked like a scene from an old-fashioned movie, pressed against one another before she had to break free …

'Helen?'

'Brody!'

Brody lifted up his hands in a 'guess so' gesture. He was tall, with day two stubble and fine wrinkles around smiling eyes. He had a fading tan, and a firm, lean body made from long days sat 'out back' in the sea on his board.

'You looked like you were daydreaming so I almost didn't want to interrupt you …'

'I know – I was just thinking …'

'Thinking …'

'My nan told me that she once went on a date on this beach – so I guess I was thinking about that …'

'Your nan is making quite the impression on me: you'll have to tell me the story. But first I've got to say sorry for being late …'

'You're late?' Helen feigned 'as if I even noticed' nonchalance.

'Yep. I had an important call and didn't want to lose signal by driving down here. Anyway, I'm glad to see you are still sitting there and that I haven't totally lost my chance,' Brody smiled radiating warmth and sincerity. 'So, to say sorry I'd really like to get you some …' he flicked through the menu, '… no banana bread, how about some avo toast, or whatever you want?'

Helen tried to think of what she could order that would demonstrate how healthy and eco-conscious she was.

Brody touched her lightly on her forearm, sending a shiver of possibility running through her body. 'You're also going to need to swap seats.'

'Why?'

'So you can get a good view of the beach.'

'Oh, okay, but what about you?'

Brody smiled again. 'Well I get to see you …'

As he spoke Helen became more aware of her heart pumping. His eyes wandered over her face. She needed to concentrate. Her blood sugar was probably low. Helen ordered avo toast. Then hot chocolate. Then carrot cake as daylight sunk lower in the window, and she became less self-conscious about her menu choices.

She surreptitiously checked the time on her phone: Henry would be here in twenty, it was all happening too quickly. Helen felt like Nanny G then on her night with Vernon, clinging on to the minutes as they raced by. There was definitely a spark: a distinct, unusual, fizzing, exciting feeling that made her feel light-headed. Partway self-conscious, like she wanted more, but the intensity almost felt too bright.

'So, I have a confession to make,' Brody smirked. 'In fact I'm kind of hoping it hasn't been too obvious so far …'

'Errr no! What is it?' Helen's stomach did a rollercoaster flip. She braced herself for him to tell her that he was actually in some open, polyamorous triad that he'd like her to join. Or something equally disappointing.

'You know … I've never ever been on a date from a dating app before.' Brody paused and waited for Helen's reaction.

'No way!'

'Way. I had a couple of long-term relationships, and when I broke up with my last girlfriend eighteen months ago …'

*No recent exes – tick*! Eighteen months is the perfect amount of time to get over someone –just like Jonathan … Wait, was she actually starting to believe that she was over Jonathan?

'The business was growing a lot and I just refocused on that. I'm also on a personal crusade to not use any form of social media, we have to do a bit for the company, but for me, I'm all about real life. So, I've been working, doing some personal growth stuff, trying to be more present, that kind of thing …'

'I remember you telling me you like to focus …'

'I do! It must be a man thing: I'm more of a mono-tasker than a multi-tasker … Anyway, I saw an old friend yesterday who asked me if I was seeing anyone and I realised that I hadn't even thought about meeting someone for a long time. Long story short, she really arm-twisted me into going on the app, even chose my lead photo. Then after five minutes you pop up: it was really weird. Good, but weird …'

'Just like me. Except it was my nan doing the arm-twisting!'

'Now you're really selling her to me!'

Helen's heart rose like a balloon in her chest. Brody must have noticed the slight pink flush that had come onto her cheeks.

'So, you decided that this was your time to get back into the whole dating thing?'

'Actually …' Brody looked down into his plate and scratched the back of his head. 'I wouldn't say dating. I think something's changed lately; I've been thinking that it's been too long just focusing on my business, I'd like to meet someone. Someone I can share things with, you know?'

Brody had picked up his fork, and pushed the crumbs around on his plate.

'Like your profile said, your last first date …'

Brody shrugged coyly, his eye just catching Helen's and she felt his knee touch hers beneath the table. She drew her breath in quickly, as the atmosphere sparkled between them.

'Well, I wouldn't have thought you'd have too much trouble finding that.' Helen smiled, folding her hands in her lap to stop them pushing across the table towards him. She was being surprisingly composed. Acting like what Brody had just said had absolutely no relevance to her whatsoever.

'How about you?' Brody leaned back in his chair, green eyes looking at her, his knee still touching hers with a heat and energy she hadn't felt in a long time. 'Are you looking just to date?'

'No, I'm looking for my last first date too. Definitely.' Elle would probably have told her not to say that, but it felt good to be candid. Why couldn't all dates be like this? None of the guessing what a guy was looking for? No decrypting his messages for hidden clues? Just a real man, who knew what he wanted. This is exactly what it should be like. The more she looked at

Brody, the more her heart sang, and the image of Jonathan and Katy became pixelated, washed from her mind.

'Okay, bit of a presumptuous question coming up then, and please feel free to shoot me down: are you getting a lift home soon?' Brody asked, stirring the last of his almond milk latte.

'I think my brother's going to pick me up sometime later ...' *Sorry Henry you may end up sitting in the car park for a little while ...*

'Look, I know you've probably got plans but I'm really enjoying spending time with you. Is there any chance I can steal you for an extra hour or two? Maybe we could go for a walk? I can drop you back later too if you need?'

Helen hesitated for a microsecond.

'If that's not too much for a guy you've just met from a dating app? I'm not really sure about the etiquette ...'

'That would be nice actually, let me just text Henry.'

'Awesome. I'll go get the bill ...' Brody subtly pulled the bill towards him and walked over to the counter. Helen rummaged in her handbag and pulled out her phone:

> Helen: *Henry I'm so so sorry but I don't need the lift anymore! Brody's going to drop me back.*

> Henry: *Dude, I'm already halfway there!*

> Helen: *I know!! I'll make it up to you!!*

> Henry: *What about meeting Nessy at dinner later?*

> Helen: *F___k! I will make this up to you. I've already said yes, can't backtrack! Gotta go will grovel later xx*

> Henry: *Fine see you xx*

*Okay not my best behaviour.* But she had to forgive herself. After all those days spent bored and (whisper it) lonely, checking Jonathan's Instagram, and chastising herself for not being happier when Sophie met Frank … she deserved to have some fun! To make some memories like Nanny G said. For her life to have some excitement in it; to not just be work, commute, social media, Itsu.

Today with Brody felt like a holiday; a break in the clouds where for once she felt young, attractive, and free again. It was like time had started to bend and flex so it raced by, and she was clutching on to the minutes they could spend together as they fell through her fingers like grains of sand. Too soon she would be back to London and … well maybe things were going to be different this time.

Brody stood in front of her opening the café door, a slightly shy smile on his face.

This time she was going to hold on to every moment: finally, it felt like her time. Maybe this is just who she had been waiting for.

# Chapter 5

Brody had a nice level of confidence. He didn't seem close to being arrogant, he didn't need to crowbar his achievements into the conversation, or sit up straighter when another good-looking man walked by.

He hadn't even seemed to clock the young mother on the table opposite gazing over at him (before her husband arrived and her eyebrows descended into a frown). But unlike Helen, he wasn't self-deprecating: he didn't embellish what he was good at, but he didn't deny his achievements existed either.

Naturally easy going, he had an optimism that soothed Helen. Helen was, by her own admission, always anxious about something; yet for the few hours she spent with Brody she forgot that her council tax payment was overdue, and that the verruca on her big toe had re-emerged. Instead, she experienced the rare joy of being in the present moment.

Brody matched her pace as they strode across the sand: Helen discovering that Converse trainers would, in fact, have been a far better outfit choice.

'Should have worn my flats!' Helen said apologetically gesturing downwards.

'Well I can't talk. I wear these pretty much 365 days a year.'

Brody lifted up one wirey leg to flash his pair of Havaianas. 'So don't be too embarrassed if I turn up for a date in London still in my flips!'

Helen turned her head away from him to give the impression of admiring the horizon, as she hid her smile into the collar of her jumper. A date in London!

They made their way along the beach at a languid pace, the kind of pace you walk at when you're the last people to leave a very good party. Reaching the car park with no stretch of the beach left to explore, Brody paused next to a black sporty car that Helen vaguely recognised as a Tesla.

'So you didn't go for the traditional surfer VW van?'

'Sorry to disappoint you but I've also never visited Hawaii and I'm not going to make us listen to *The Beach Boys* either …' Brody paused and then looked down at his feet which made a slight shuffle on the sand. 'So I hope I'm going to suggest this in a way that's suitably post #metoo …'

Helen braced herself for a stab of disappointment: here comes the old 'let's carry this on back at mine', 'I have a nice bottle of wine', 'a view of the waves', 'the most comfy couch …' She would most certainly like to go back to Brody's house at some point, if things went well, but now felt too soon. She didn't want to say goodbye to him, and it was getting chilly out, but if all that happened right now, it would feel, well, she'd rather live in this moment a little longer, before all those tricky questions came up.

As much as she wished she could channel Elle and have a moment of passion before turning over to the guy in bed with a devilish smile and say, 'I'm not looking for anything serious you know …' she just didn't have it in her. How her mind worked was very simple: if she liked someone enough to be naked with them, she would want more. In fact, she would expect it, then when it turned out that they didn't see this as the start of some great romance, that they hadn't already started getting used to the tube ride between their flats with a cosy familiarity, then she would feel wounded and rejected.

'Would you like to stop off at Hell's Mouth? Assuming you're okay to get home just a little later? I've looked at the sat nav and it's about halfway back to yours, and forgetting the name, it's actually a pretty cool place to see the sun go down.' Brody paused and reached out to take Helen's hand. Her fingers rested in his. 'I also feel like I should clarify that I am going to be taking you home, and if sitting in a stranger's car on a cliff edge is a bit much for you then I can just take you straight there …' Noticing Helen's pensive expression Brody added, 'I know it's too soon, I just don't want this to end right now.'

Brody smiled, and Helen found herself reaching towards the door handle. Sitting in a (very nice) car with him felt intimate, her mind leapt forwards six months to them taking a road trip, bags packed … The car purred into motion and Helen fidgeted crossing and uncrossing her legs, trying to work out what body language looked the most elegant. As the car pulled out onto the road, she had to bat away the feeling that people would be expecting a much better-looking woman to be sat in the passenger seat.

Hell's Mouth was a gaping hole in the cliff's face that created a deep bowl shape into the sea. If you walked to the lip of the mouth, you could dangle your legs off the edge of the cliff and feel the surging waves beneath. There was a tiny strip of beach beneath the circling gulls, that would be impossible to access from land. The whole place reminded you of smugglers shining their false lights across the rocks, luring ships to wreck.

Brody already had both of his legs hanging over the edge, and patted the rough grass beside him. He was still wearing just a T-shirt despite the strong cool evening air that was roaring off the ocean. His eyes glowed green in the fading light. A silver pendant hung around his neck, drawing Helen's eyes down to the toned muscles of his chest.

Normally Helen would have observed a safe two metre gap from the edge, just in case the cliff crumbled beneath her, but like the gulls on the wind rising up between the rocks, she felt a rare lift of self-assurance within her. Plus she knew that even if Brody was as honourable as he made himself out to be, there was only one real reason why men suggest to women that they watch the sunset together from the cliff tops.

'So you're an East Londoner too? Let me guess, when you're not going back to your Cornish roots you like to drink rosé wine from the Boundary's roof garden, and I bet you write your infamous blog from Fix 126 coffee?'

'Okay, have you creeped on my Instagram to suddenly know this information? Or am I that much of a cliché?'

'No, because you're being very mysterious about what it is!'

Helen paused – her job was a constant thorn in her side when dating. Guys she met usually googled her so much that before date two they knew more about her business than she did. Online she had a slightly kitsch persona and for the sake of personal branding wore a lot of polka dot aprons: little did most people know that out of sight of the camera she usually had her sweatpants on underneath. Whilst her online avatar was also constantly chirpy in the face of a withering shopping budget – or missing a key ingredient – internally Helen didn't feel like that at all. She was totally over guys turning up on dates thinking they knew everything about her after googling her, and being left feeling not in the least bit understood. Not to mention the guys she turned down popping up in her DMs and harassing her thereafter.

The net result of all this, was that Helen had developed a solid policy of being aloof about her work on her first dates.

'It's just I like to get to know someone a bit first; it can get a bit awkward if someone knows more about you online than in the real world.'

'No worries, that makes perfect sense to me, no more questions asked, for now!' Brody playfully jibed. 'So do you want to know how I know where you write your blog from?'

Helen managed a small smirk as their eyes met.

'Well first of all, Fix does the best iced almond milk lattes in Shoreditch, which I know you like, and I know you're an East London girl.'

'Do you go there?'

'All the time. It's right next to my office. Great gluten-free brownies too.'

'So, you're telling me in another lifetime we could have met in my local coffee shop?'

'Hehe, well don't go overestimating me now, I'm not sure I'd make a habit out of chatting up attractive women in my local coffee shop, but if I saw you, well you'd at least get a smile out of me! Guess the real question is … would you smile back?'

'You KNOW I would! Stop digging for compliments!' Helen's smile gave her dimples, and she surprised herself by actually being playful. In Brody's presence she felt like she was occupying parts of her personality that she hadn't known in a long time: like she was throwing open shutters on a room in a house, to recognise that yes in fact it was still there. She didn't need Brody to tell her that she was glowing.

He smiled at her, and held her gaze just a second longer than before. His hand stroked her hair to the side of her face to see how full and deep her smile was. Then he leaned in to kiss her. His lips were soft and lingered after they first touched hers, as if waiting for permission that he could kiss her more. Helen pushed hers back into his and she heard him make a small sound of satisfaction. 'Now, I've really got to get you home …'

Helen sighed and looked out at the darkening sky. 'It has to end here, doesn't it?'

'For now …' Brody looked right at her, his hand lingering on the side of her face, 'but not for long. When we're back in London, you'll be ordering an iced almond milk latte, and there

I'll be. You'll be sick of me soon enough, so I better enjoy this time whilst you're still excited to see me again.'

'Are you asking me on a second date?' Helen looked up at Brody tracing her eyes across his face.

'Maybe a last second date I guess …'

# Chapter 6

'Well, I wasn't expecting that at all.'

Brody leaned against the bonnet of his car. The Tesla's lights were on full beam on a starless night. The car was in the middle of nowhere, halfway down a dirt track, with hedgerows towering either side, pulled up on the verge. Even if you wanted to, you couldn't see where you were. The night was silent apart from the occasional low moan from the fields beyond.

Helen felt moderately embarrassed, she should have known that Brody dropping her back was a bad idea. Now his car had struggled to a halt on the precarious country road that led into an old farming hamlet where her family home was, with the utterly unromantic sound of cows lowing in the background.

'I'm so sorry. I should have explained that we were going to have to cross some Land Rover-friendly terrain …'

'Helen?' Brody turned to face her now, and Helen felt a shiver of intensity ripple through her body as her eyes met his.

'Yup …'

'Can I ban you from apologising? Or maybe we can get you to promise me that you'll limit yourself to just once a day. It's not a problem, driving you back means I got a whole extra hour with you.'

'Should have got that VW huh?'

Brody gave a knowing nod, then shook his head gazing down at the floor.

'Piggyback?' He bent halfway over and gestured for her to hop on.

'No way! Seriously I'll just walk.' Alongside heights, and roller-coasters, Helen also didn't really like the instability of piggybacks. Piggybacks meant him bearing her weight, which meant she would worry about her thighs. She began slowly zipping up her coat, she really did need to go, and was hoping if she took all the actions that added up to her leaving that her feet would finally be compliant and move. Right now, her body still felt like it was locked in Brody's orbit.

He looked down at his feet. 'I don't know, not very gentle-manly of me to not get you to your door, seeing as I promised to drop you home.'

'Well, you got me ninety-nine per cent of the way, and I really should have issued a potholes warning when you made me the offer. Plus, I'm intending to creep in without you meeting my mum.' Helen gave Brody a playful smirk.

'You don't want me to meet your mum?!' Brody gasped in mock offence, and gently pulled Helen into a long bear hug.

'It's *maybe* a little soon …' Helen said, becoming aware that her head had started to nestle onto Brody's chest. It felt right there, like she had found her place.

'What about your shoes?' His voice was softer now, speaking into her ear as they swayed slightly back and forth locked in their bear hug.

'Trust me, I've walked down this lane in worse footwear!'

'How about you take mine?' Brody slipped a Havaianas off his foot and handed it across to Helen. 'Seriously, I can easily drive barefoot.'

'I couldn't!'

'Honestly, I have about three other pairs exactly the same around my house, so I can always find them.'

'No this is silly …'

'Exactly the *same* Helen. Plus …' he held her gaze like he wanted to let her know how important this was to him, '… and this is a big one. If you borrow my shoes it means you'll have to see me again. Can't borrow a guy's shoes and ignore his message the next day, can you?'

'I wouldn't ignore you …'

'Well, I think you should take them anyway, just to be on the safe side, okay?'

'Okay …' Helen's eyes met his. Brody held her arm to help her balance as she changed shoes. Helen felt that exquisite pang of parting loosen slightly; she had his shoes, they would meet again.

'It will also help to salve my conscience for not walking with you.'

'Now it's you who has to stop apologising.' Helen turned in towards Brody one more time, and he ran his fingers gently through the back of her wavy brown hair.

She soaked up those last few seconds, as time began to warp again. Her anxiety fell silent. Thoughts of the next day; that blog she needed to write and Jonathan's Instagram were obliterated. Her mind was silent and her body was alive instead.

She absorbed the soft smell of his clean T-shirt as her hands traced down his chest. His rhythmic breathing helped to steady hers. Her mind carefully archiving memories of his strong hands cupping the back of her head, the last time her lips pressed against his, and then tearing herself away in slow motion. She wandered off into the night, feeling like someone who had just broken the surface of the water, gasping for air, after an interminably long swim.

# Chapter 7

'Has anyone seen the batteries for the remote?' Helen's dad flustered. He bristled past her. It was a rhetorical question, not one intended in any way to acknowledge her existence. There was always something out of place; the Chromecast, Alexa, Netflix, some other phantom household member was always disrupting his carefully cultivated system. She was used to his reaction: wild gesticulations, and doors being shut unnecessarily loudly. Henry just rolled his eyes.

Helen sat at the kitchen counter and kept flicking her iPhone screen open and shut.

Her parents' kitchen hadn't changed in thirty years; they still had the same nineties mahogany units and blue frosted tiles she remembered from her childhood, the same chalkboard to write down what was needed in the weekly shop and the same mismatched mugs. Above the microwave her mum had hung up a sign saying:

*Mother's B&B Services include: laundry, personal chef, chauffeur, psychologist, tutor, nurse!*
*Open 24/7, all year long! Gifts and thank you notes appreciated.*

Henry had bought it for her as a Mother's Day present when they were teenagers.

Henry was in his version of a bad mood. He was even less communicative than usual and answered any entreaties to conversation with a series of grunts.

Helen had made it home, but by the time she floated through the door at midnight, the dishes from dinner had already been stacked in the dishwasher and she had spectacularly missed the long-diarised meeting with Henry's girlfriend.

She knew cancelling last minute on their family dinner wasn't *great* but also felt Henry could really have cut her a bit of slack: all she wanted was some of what he already had in spades, a cosy relationship, domesticity, routine like a metronome.

Now she'd slept through brunch and had walked into the kitchen that morning to be faced with a passive aggressive half-dry scrambled egg sulking in the pan. Mum had folded up the tea towel when she walked into the room and gave her a smile that said, 'I'm not even going to ask.'

Waking up back in her single bed, Helen had felt like the last twenty-four hours hadn't belonged to her life. The memory of Brody wasn't as sharp as it had been when she went to sleep, and the things that he'd said which excited her so much had become hazy, no matter how many times she tried to replay them in her head. She was already starting to feel like they may not have happened, or at least were unlikely to happen again.

They had only kissed twice: once on the cliff tops and a second time gently before she strode off into the night, trying to appear steady in Brody's flip flops. Helen had felt like she was sixteen again creeping back down the gravel driveway, hoping that the crunch of her footsteps wouldn't cause a light to flick on in the house.

As soon as she was safely in her bedroom, too wired to sleep, the details of the date had already been poured over in her Queens xoxo WhatsApp group:

Sophie: *Soooo how was the d-a-t-e?*
*Are you okay?*

Helen: *Sorry I was out wayyy longer than I thought.*
*It was amazing.*
*(I know I shouldn't say that as it's only been 1 date 🙄)*
*We went to a little café by the beach, then we watched the*
*sunset from the clifftops, and maybe had a kiss!!*
*(Or two!!)*
*But he didn't try for anything else like that, if you know*
*what I mean.*
*Main points are that he's been single for 18 months, is a*
*successful entrepreneur (very fancy car) and said he was*
*looking for his last first date.*
*I'll voice note you later with all the details xx*

Sophie: *Seems like a gentleman too to me :-)*
*So I guess you're seeing each other again?*

Helen: *Waiting for him to message me, but we've already*
*planned our second date! :-) xx*

Elle: *He didn't send you a goodnight message?*

Helen: *No but we parted at midnight, so it was technically*
*already the next day.*
*I'm not going to read into it, I think he'll message later.*

Elle: *Okay babe let us know.*
*And keep your options OPEN, remember it's just one date*
*xxxx*

The post-mortem analysis of the date had indicated a lot of
positive 'signs': Brody had been in no rush to seduce her, future

dates were hinted at, he wasn't newly single, he said Nanny G had sounded cool, and then there was the pair of Havaianas still on her feet …

But no notification had appeared on the Connex app saying Brody had messaged her. She dared not open it in case when he logged on it showed that she'd already been online a few hours ago which could make it look like she was either:

A. Talking to other guys
B. Desperately waiting on a message from him

Whilst Elle would purposefully hint on her dates that she was seeing other guys, 'I had dinner there with *a friend* last week actually …' Helen was unconvinced this was a lust-inducing strategy.

Helen sat staring at her phone. On autopilot she opened Instagram, closed Instagram, and glanced again through her WhatsApp messages. Her fingers felt itchy, and lingered over the Connex app. She opened Instagram again and spent twenty minutes unsuccessfully digging through a lot of _brody_, therealbrody, and even a brooody (definitely not right) in an attempt to find him online.

'I must try to be more present!' Helen inwardly chastised herself. She knew creeping on a guy's profile on Instagram (especially one who you'd only had one date with) wasn't 'healthy'.

Helen had noticed that whenever she felt a bit exposed emotionally (like when she'd finally had a date with someone she actually liked) after the initial warmth of the contact evaporated, she was left with a nagging twinge in her gut that told her something wasn't right, or was about to go wrong. No matter how much she tried to push these thoughts out of her mind, the only thing that quenched her thirsty brain was checking something: checking when the guy she liked was last online, looking at his pictures on social media, googling his username on obscure internet forums … the list went on.

She knew this wasn't what you were supposed to do. She also knew that whilst immediately after checking something she momentarily felt relief, like the heavy dread in her gut lifted, she soon felt dirty, as if her mum had walked in on her hiding a wine bottle behind her bed.

(Which for the record she hadn't done for at least fifteen years).

Anxiety was a bird that flew around Helen's mind looking for somewhere to roost: in worrying about a guy, an obscure medical condition, a tax return … Feeling a familiar icky feeling after her internet adventure, she slid her phone into airplane mode and left it facedown on the kitchen counter. She had to distract herself. Instinctively she started pulling out cream cheese, butter and eggs from the cupboard.

Helen loved baking, the rhythm of the kitchen, the smells, the feeling of creating something with care. Cooking was not the same, it was stressful; meat could be undercooked, it could kill you. It was hard to seriously mess up a brownie.

Helen had loved baking since she was a child. One of her earliest memories was licking the big wooden spoon after her mother had helped her dollop cake batter into multi-coloured muffin cups. *Should children eat raw cake mix?* Helen wondered, diligently scrubbing the mixing bowl clean in the sink.

She had got into the whole baking blogger gig circuitously. Academically, she had been okay at uni: she'd studied Anthropology (what arts students choose to study when they don't know what to pick) and despite knowing quite a few facts about teeth in Neanderthal man, had scraped a 2:1. Maybe she could have done better if she'd had cared more, but she had gotten the feeling before the end of her first year at Nottingham that not everyone was supposed to go to university. When she was doing her A Levels, anyone who had half decent grades went to university to while away a few years before having to figure out what they actually wanted to do. Ironically, at the end of her three years at uni, Helen was none the wiser, thousands of pounds

49

poorer, and also found that most of the fancy firms she applied to for an interview weren't too interested in a B grade arts student.

So, whilst Sophie, who had studied Economics, and spoke near fluent Mandarin had sailed into a city job and a studio apartment in Wapping, Helen had drifted around for a year working odd jobs in cafés, museums, and flyering. Her home life in London had consisted of dingy studio apartments, boilers breaking in December and extreme flat shares of seven occupants to one bathroom.

Throughout all of these lows, medium lows, and relationships that she threw herself into in search of an exit route, baking had become her Northern Star, a grounding force to unwind, and reclaim some sense of order.

Her creations were often made of the scant ingredients that were available on a student budget. She also developed an ability to repurpose old ingredients into something new: an early attempt at a coffee cake that had come out undercooked was repurposed into a sticky pudding with maple syrup the next day.

The joke was that Helen's leftovers always metamorphosed themselves into strange new dishes. In her spare time Helen would write blogs about her bakes and, to her wild surprise, one day her Cheap Skate Carrot Cake recipe started to be shared again and again. Eventually it was retweeted by a famous baking blogger and Helen's blogging business was born. She now made her income through endorsements, adverts and writing baking blogs for digital magazines; hopefully one day she would also get the holy grail of a book or TV deal … if she could just get her presenting skills a little less clunky, and her blog traffic a little more buoyant.

Today she decided to make a New York cheesecake which had a lot of fussy processes – blind bake the base, cook the main cake, leave the cake in a cooling oven for twenty minutes with the door open, place in fridge to cool etc – which she hoped would distract her from her phone for at least a couple of hours.

Yet her mobile phone seemed to sing out to her from the counter, like a pop up on a website that refused to close, saying, 'Has Brody messaged yet?!' Helen sighed, seeing only forty-five minutes had managed to wander by since she last looked at her phone. 'Damn it,' Helen thought as she glanced at her homescreen.

Nothing.

She felt a sinking feeling in her stomach. Why hadn't he messaged? Had she seriously overestimated how much he liked her? It wouldn't be the first time. Helen remembered in September last year having a date with a guy called Raphael: they'd met for G&Ts in Exmouth market one Friday night, he'd told her that her love of cooking reminded him of his home town in Sicily, he'd said they should go to his favourite Italian restaurant next week, then … poof!! Nothing!

She'd even sent an, in retrospect, *highly* awkward, 'Would you still like to meet up this weekend?' message with a monkey emoji on it that had never been read. The two grey ticks stared back at her, strongly suggesting that Raph hadn't been mugged on the way home, he just couldn't be bothered to reply to her. A week or so later his WhatsApp picture changed to some artistic shot of him sitting cross-legged on a canal boat. Then finally on the 23rd December at 11 p.m. she got the single word message, '*Hi*'. So much for the spaghetti.

Her friends and memes reliably informed her that this was far from a unique experience; this was just what modern dating was like: stuffed full of zombies, ghosting, orbiting, and a lot of people who couldn't make their mind up.

But last night did feel different. Everything Brody had said rang true, and it's not like they lived at opposite ends of the country; they shared a favourite coffee shop and a home county! She probably just needed to try and be patient and give it more time. Perhaps Brody was playing it cool? Or maybe he was a feminist who was waiting for her to make the first move?

*Do you think I played it too cool and now he thinks I don't*
*like him?*

Helen was panic texting Queens xoxo at 9pm: twenty-one hours and six minutes after their date had ended, and still no word. She'd also checked the surf report which disappointingly said the waves were two feet with an onshore wind (which roughly translated as 'stay at home and wax your board'). Rain had started to smatter on her bedroom window and she'd shoved her old electric storage radiator up to full power which had left the room with the smell of singed dust.

Elle: *No babe! You kissed right? I'm sorry, how much more encouragement does a guy need?! If he wants you, he'll find you, trust me.*

Helen: *So you don't think I should message him first?*

Elle: *Never! Give it time xx*

Helen: *But what if I say something casual like, 'Nice to meet you yesterday' or 'Hope you're not surfing in this weather!'*

Elle: *Could look a bit desperate my love xx*

Sophie: *I think he'll message if you just give it time.*
*If it's meant to be …*
*But if you do decide you want to message him that's OK too. If he's the guy you think he is he'll probably be happy to hear your surf report ;-)*

Helen managed to deliberate for another ten minutes before caving in and opening the Connex app. She went into her messages, reflexively clenching her stomach muscles, like she was bracing herself for ... but there was nothing there?! Her message chain with Brody had vanished and there were no notifications of other matches.

'OMG he's unmatched me ...' Helen felt a surge of embarrassment. Brody had clearly wanted one thing after all and after not getting the right signs from her had dropped her like a rock!! But then where were her other 'likes'? She hit the 'start swiping!' button and instead of showing her a profile of a guy she fancied far less than Brody there was just a white screen.

Her heart rate slowed: it's a Wi-Fi problem! That probably meant Brody had messaged her hours ago and she just hadn't received it! Oh well, at least she'd appear coolly disinterested when she eventually answered. Helen strode out of her bedroom and crossed the corridor with renewed vigour.

'Henry! Are you in there?' Helen knocked at least six times on his door.

'Yup.'

'Are you downloading something? My Wi-Fi's bust! Any chance you can pause it for a second, I really need to check something!' *Goodbye remaining calm, this must be fixed NOW*, said her brain.

She heard a deep sigh through Henry's bedroom door as he heaved himself off his beanbag to open the door.

'Nope I'm actually not ...'

Through the doorway Helen saw Henry and a short, red-haired girl that must be his new girlfriend Nessy, hunched over a coffee table with a half-complete puzzle on it.

'Oh, maybe Dad ...'

'Mum and Dad are out at The Smugglers for quiz night, *remember*.' Henry paused and softened. 'Do you want me to take a look at something?'

Helen nodded quickly.

'I'll be back in a second Ness ...'

53

'Lovely to meet you!' Nessy said overenthusiastically as Henry pulled the door to.

Helen passed over her phone. 'I can't get this app to work, all my messages are gone and the screen is blank when I open it …'

'Hmmm.' Henry closed Connex, opened YouTube and started to play her latest video on pouring fondant. 'Internet seems fine. You tried running an update?'

Helen shook her head. Henry opened the app store. 'Nope it's all updated here. That's strange. I'll reinstall it, give me a minute.' Henry started fiddling on the phone. Helen felt a little sick as he deleted the app, reinstalled it, then opened it again to the same blank screens. 'Nah not that either.'

He then moved to Twitter and went to Connex's feed. 'Ah here you go, that explains it.'

'What explains what?'

'Connex's servers have gone down, they've lost their user data. Well, that will screw them up as a company.'

'What do you mean they lost their data?'

'Here – read this.' Henry opened their homepage which had the following statement on it:

*At Connex we value bringing people together, which is why we're sorry to report that a routine server configuration update has caused an outage across our platform. We understand you want to meet and Connex with people, so our love technicians are working around the clock to get us back online. Whilst we are confident there haven't been any data breaches, we must apologise that any existing data on our app (matches, conversations) appear to have been lost. We will automatically be upgrading all user accounts to premium next month as our way of saying 'sorry we let you down'. Please check back on this page or our Twitter for all the latest updates. We hope you can Connex again very soon.*

Helen's mind went blank. In her myopic vision she couldn't hear Nessy clicking the puzzle pieces into place anymore, and Henry had disappeared from in front of her. It was meant to be easy. Brody had said he was looking for a relationship, it felt right, and she had his flip flops!

In another reality, another Helen was probably messaging him now. They would be swapping voice notes, counting down to their London date, the start of something. Not this endless void of singleness. But she wasn't planning anything. She wasn't glowing warmly knowing in her gut that she'd met her guy. She was right back to where she started, as if fate had just taken a huge eraser to the past twenty-four hours. It wasn't fair.

'Are you all right Hels?' Henry's hand was on her arm, gently pulling it away from the other one where she'd been subconsciously picking at her own wrists. Red marks had appeared in a dirty cluster by her bracelet. 'Maybe you should go lie down?'

On autopilot Helen turned back and walked into her bedroom. She looked at her reflection in the dusty mirror above her dressing table. In the background was her wardrobe, and the prom dress. In her hand was her phone with picture after picture of her and Jonathan on it that she hadn't deleted. She tightened her grip. This was meant to be her time. She would make it her time. She had to find him.

# Chapter 8

Elle: *What! You didn't swap numbers? Or socials?*

Helen: *No, we **just** communicated through the app!*

Elle: *That's a bit weird.*

Sophie: *What a bummer: maybe Connex will get the data back. They're a big company, so I'm sure they're going to try to fix this.*
*I know this doesn't help but maybe meeting Brody (even if it doesn't work out) is a good sign that you're finally opening back up to love.*
*There will be another guy xx*

Helen: *Does it make me a loser to say I don't want another guy?*
*I want THAT guy.*
*It literally feels like I can't ever like someone without it going spectacularly wrong: and finally it goes right and this happens.*
*Sorry to rant, I'm just upset.*
*We had another date all planned: but how can I find him now?*

Sophie: *I've got to go to sleep and Frank's with me (sorry)*
*otherwise I'd call.*
*But will try you tomorrow.*
*Try to get some rest H xx*

Elle: *It is just one guy babe: besides if he really likes you,*
*he'll find you.*

Helen: *How?? He doesn't know anything about me!*

Elle: *He knows where you live, no?*

Helen: *Apart from the fact that's a bit stalkerish, he only*
*dropped me part of the way home.*
*The Tesla wasn't doing so great on the Cornish roads so I*
*walked the last half mile into my hamlet.*

Elle: *Babe – for real he should have carried you.*

Sophie: *Just told Frank I need a minute …*
*@Elle I know you would have made him ;-)*

Elle: *@Sophie No – I don't need to make anyone do*
*anything.*
*If you have the right standards and vibe guys just react to*
*you differently.*

Sophie: *Okay.*
*Anyway @Helen so your home is out.*

Helen: *Well he has the rough geographical area that I'll be*
*exiting in approximately 9 hours when I get the train back*
*to London.*
*Talk about timing!*

Sophie: *What about your business?*
*Surely you're pretty googleable?*

Helen: *You know I don't like talking about my work –*
*I just said I ran a blog … no details. You know the 'be*
*mysterious until date 3' thing we all thought was a realll-*
*lyyy good idea.*
*#sigh*

Elle: *Well I once met a guy at The Ned hotel bar and he*
*managed to find me the next day by checking stories on*
*Instagram tagged in that location … so it is possible.*

Sophie: *How about you just find him and reach out to him*
*on socials?*

Helen: *Already tried. Can't find any users with his name*
*on Instagram. I don't think he uses social media :-(*

Elle: *Okay well what info on him do we have? Other than*
*his name?*

Helen: *I have this?*

Helen re-sent the screenshot she had taken of Brody's profile on Connex. She felt a twinge in her heart as his square-jawed face, and lopsided smile, appeared on her screen.

# Chapter 9

Helen was on the 08:27 to Paddington. In the first ninety minutes she had already demolished the two tasteless bread wraps she'd bought for the journey that morning. Her body felt flat and her mind grey and foggy. She leaned her head against the window as she passed by Dawlish, where the ocean waves crashed onto the line. It was always the same. She was always alone. She noticed a couple ahead of her in the carriage, the man leaning in to kiss the woman's forehead, and Helen looked away sharply like she'd just seen an accident.

The thought 'I really want to feel better' passed across her mind, as she wrapped her jumper around her like a pair of arms. She impassively gazed at her iPhone hoping by some miracle her screen would light up with Brody's name. Of course it didn't. The high pitch notes of Helen's anxiety had dulled overnight. Now, tired after yet another night of bad sleep, her anxiety had retreated to a gentle background pressure in her head, the feeling of wearing a heavy coat she had to drag around all day.

She'd refreshed all her apps, read the news, and favourited a lot of items on Etsy, but the dull feeling wouldn't budge. She decided to eat something, knowing full well that the pit in her stomach wasn't hunger. Helen began the process of unloading her tray onto her lap, flipping up her tray, and exiting the hard aquamarine seat by successfully slinging her leg over the comatose man beside her, who was clutching an empty Ginsters wrapper in his hand.

The air in the carriage felt stale and humid. Students heading back to uni after Easter break, who had run out of seats, cluttered the floor in between the carriages; and seemed impervious to moving as Helen tiptoed past. Making her way to the buffet car she made a mental note of which loos were out of order/lacking loo roll/or had a student using them as a makeshift hot desk. This journey was always grim.

By the time she reached the buffet car she had already added a Twix to her mental wish list of food, as compensation for not only heartbreak, but a really oversold train service. The air felt clammy in the carriage, like she could catch all sorts of viruses by inhaling, so she dug her chin into her roll neck. Her yoga pants also felt sticky on her legs, and she promised herself a long shower when she got back to her studio apartment in Haggerston.

At the front of the queue was an elderly man counting out coins to pay a nervous looking server. Behind him was a glamorous looking blonde woman with a veil of poker straight hair. She was wearing a fedora hat, an expensive looking cream camise, and jeans that Helen could not get away with wearing. Helen also made a mental note that she should try to wear more jewellery. This woman had trendy thin gold bands asymmetrically spread out over three of her fingers that grasped a bright red dog leash.

Helen's heart skipped a beat: at the end of the leash was a fluffy grey Dachshund, with bottle blue eyes peering up anxiously from the side of her ankle boots.

The dog looked exactly like … it couldn't be. Helen opened up her one picture of Brody, clutching what looked like the exact same dog.

'Oh what a cutie!' Helen announced awkwardly.

The blonde woman turned around. She had patrician features: a gently sloping nose and large grey eyes. Her lips broke into a smile – she was an orthodontist's dream.

'Thank you, he's lovely, isn't he?' Where was her accent from? She wasn't Cornish.

'Do you mind if I take a picture for Instagram?' Helen winced as the words came out. If this was Brody's dog she was pretty sure it was behaviour like this that would blow it.

And if it was his dog, who was this woman?

The woman knelt down to hold the dog steady, as Helen squatted down to take the shot.

'Thank you! Does he have an Instagram I can tag him in?'

'Not anymore.' The woman's smile cooled, so Helen slipped her phone away, and made a point of turning her attention towards examining the different flavours of Pringles stacked on the counter.

She stumbled back to her seat, holding a hot chocolate in one hand, a mini tub of sour cream Pringles in the other, and a Twix in between her teeth. She messaged the picture to Queens xoxo:

Elle: *Babe there's probably A LOT of dogs that look like that.*

Helen: *@Elle it's not a Labrador!! It's some extra rare Dachshund, I remember Brody telling me how he bought it as a puppy. That dog has done modelling campaigns for Burberry!*

Elle: *Yes BUT Brody wasn't with the dog, so it can't be his. Also why are we still talking about Brody*

Sophie: *@Elle because it's important to Helen and we're not giving up hope yet!*

61

Helen: *I don't know – maybe I'm hallucinating.*
*Sorry guys just feeling really down right now.*

Sophie: *Did you get a picture so we could compare/*
*contrast?*

Helen: *Yes*

Helen sent the dog picture to the group.

Elle: *Wow I really like her rings.*

Sophie: *It does look a lot like the dog from his profile*
*picture but unless that's his girlfriend and they're*
*travelling back to London together I don't see how that*
*could be his dog. Do you know when he said he was*
*heading back?*

Helen: *We didn't talk about it – was trying to play it cool!*

Sophie: *I think it's probably just a coincidence. They say*
*when something's really on your mind you start to see it*
*everywhere. Like if you're thinking about buying a polka*
*dot dress suddenly everyone is wearing polka dots.*

Helen: *He's definitely on my mind – but not much*
*I can do about that. Who doesn't use social media?*

Elle: *Don't give up on him finding you.*

Sophie: *Or us finding him …*
*His company is in recycling right?*

Helen: *Yes said he was in Cornwall helping Surfers Against*

62

*Sewage – he supplies replacements for plastic products like*
*coffee cup lids, straws, cotton buds, that kind of thing.*

Helen exhaled realising how much she'd hung off his every word, and how she was now telling her friends with pride what Brody did, like he was already her husband.

Sophie: *I'm going to look for their company on LinkedIn –*
*I've got a premium account with work x*

Five minutes later a screenshot appeared: it showed a sandy-haired man in a crisp white shirt smiling into the camera, arms around several colleagues: there was no dog this time, but his lopsided smile was undoubtedly the same.

# Chapter 10

Sophie: *So we now know that Brody is the CEO of True Materials, which is based out of WeWork Moorgate. No personal social media that I can see – and no contact email on his website – they just have a chatbot. BUT the good news is, we know where he works.*

Helen: *First of all, I'm glad this situation has turned into a 'we' not a 'me' – feel much more supported. Secondly, excellent levels of web sleuthing @Sophie. Want to see him again but unsure I can do this without seeming like a total psycho?? (And obvs can't afford office space in WeWork unless someone wants to give me a serious business loan.)*

Sophie: *You don't need to! Just say you're thinking of signing up for office space – they won't know your business is just you :-) Maybe you could do a guided tour or something?*

Helen: *Still sounding a bit stalkerish but appreciate the positivity @Sophie*

Elle: *How about we go to a party instead?*

Helen: *I know I should be thinking of meeting someone new @Elle but I just want to try one more time with Brody.*

Elle: *I mean a party at WeWork. I looked and they have a social this Friday.*
*Looks pretty lame IMO – but we can try.*

Helen: *Do you think we can get in??*

Elle: *Babe, you worry too much*

Helen put her phone away as she arrived at Paddington station; she'd broken her suitcase wheel last Christmas and needed two hands to stop it wobbling off down the platform. She decided she couldn't afford an Uber (especially after that buffet car raid), so took the central line to Liverpool Street, huddled underneath a stranger's armpit the whole way in the crowded carriage. She'd then stuffed herself onto a 149 bus full of teenage boys in their PE kits, leaving her gasping for fresh air and hand sanitiser by the time she got home.

Helen loved shutting her front door: apart from the sirens in the distance, you could pretend the outside world didn't exist. There was something magical about living alone. There was no one there to dress up for, to cook for, or to present a brave face to the world for. Tonight, Helen fully intended to exploit all these facts and eat Itsu (for a food blogger she spent a lot of money on take out sushi), drink wine, wrap herself in her comfiest loungewear, and possibly fall asleep watching Netflix, if she was really treating herself.

But first she needed to unpack. Helen couldn't just joyously slob on the couch, not when something needed to be done. On the bright side, this made her a good starter finisher; on the downside she rarely gave herself a break. She carefully started to unfold her clothes and hang them up in her wardrobe. Of course, before long she was holding the jumper she wore on her date with Brody to her face, as if some essence of him would fall out of it, if she could just clutch it tight enough. Would wearing it to bed be weird? Maybe it was okay just for one night.

Then there were the flip flops. It was funny how two pieces of rubber had suddenly taken on such meaning for her. For a long time, she just looked at them, and let the few memories she had come tumbling back in. The time with Brody still felt so close, she almost felt like if she could somehow peel back her apartment walls, that she could walk right back onto the beach that night.

Maybe there was still some hope. Gosh, what if she saw him on Friday? It would be like a miracle, wouldn't it? Maybe miracle was too strong a word, no, it would be a really nice coincidence. It would be what was supposed to happen; like Brody said, he'd just be there. Helen allowed herself to imagine what it would be like seeing Brody again: she'd be sauntering through the WeWork party, and then she'd walk up to him … No, that was too obvious. She'd be dancing in a way that looked effortless and cool, he'd see her through the crowd, walk right up to her and there she was back in his arms. It could happen. This wasn't like Nanny G and Vernon. It was time for her love story. They would meet again.

Helen neatly placed the Havaianas by the front door, as if Brody himself had left them there. Then pulling on her jumper, *the* jumper, went up to her sofa bed to sleep.

# Chapter 11

'Babe are these the shoes? You gotta chuck them out!' Elle was holding Brody's flip flops high in her hands. Her oxblood red nail extensions twinkled in the light, as she held the shoes precariously over Helen's pedal bin.

'I'm not throwing them out!' Helen gasped as she rushed over to reclaim them like a mother grabbing her tot that was about to topple into a puddle.

'Geez, okay but look, even if you see him again, and he ends up here, you don't want him to think you kept his shoes! Better you forgot all about them in Cornwall.' Elle's (or Gabriella Estevez to go by her full name) hands were on her hips.

'Elle …' Sophie's voice had a trace of warning in it. An undertone of *please can we not go there and make this whole night awkward.*

'I don't want to decide what to do about the shoes just yet, this night already feels stressful enough,' Helen said meekly, looking slightly unsteady in the vegan leather leggings that Elle had harried her into earlier. In Helen's opinion only people who religiously avoided carbohydrates should even attempt to wear trousers like these, but Elle had nodded approvingly when she'd put them on, and told her she looked hot. If there was a committee for hotness Elle would have been on it, but only when it worked with her schedule.

'Fine, but I'm only telling you this because I care. Love, the only reason we're all here tonight is because of you,' Elle sounded moderately annoyed but only in that 'this is how I show I care' way.

'I know, I know ...' Helen fiddled with her bracelets (must wear more jewellery!) And kept running a hair straightener through her hair. It was so thick! She'd be here a while.

'Also, whether *or not we* see Brody, I'm just happy to be spending time with you girls again. It's been too long,' smiled Sophie. Her eyes were a beautiful hazel colour – halfway between her English mum's and her Chinese dad's.

It's true. Girls nights out weren't what they used to be. Shortly after university, during the early years of living in London, Sophie and Helen had met Elle on a night out. They were trying to get into Hyphen, which back in the day was a cool Mayfair club – or at the very least it had seemed cool at the time. All the women wore tiny dresses, and they played the Superman theme tune every time someone bought an exceptionally large bottle of vodka. It came with a sparkler on the top, which in retrospect did seem a bit unnecessary.

They'd been promised that if they turned up early, that they'd be lavished with free sushi and endless vodka cranberries. Admittedly the person doing the promising was a slightly skittish-looking 'club scout' called Ricky who was now loudly arguing with the bouncer about them not being on the list. The bouncer kept flicking through the pages and shaking his head. Helen could feel herself sinking into the pavement beneath her: they obviously weren't pretty enough to get in.

'Oi!' A voice called out from behind them, and there was Elle. Her hair was its natural dark brown colour at the time, and she wore a shimmering green dress with a biker jacket thrown over the top. She queue-jumped right up to the bouncer, and linked her arm in his, as if she'd known him forever. 'I know you are having a hard night amigo, but it's cold out here, and we all want to have a good time, could you please treat me and let us all in a little early?'

The bouncer shuffled on his feet and replied something quickly in Spanish, not making eye contact. Elle beamed her megawatt smile, looked back to the line and said, 'Friends, let's go!' She linked arms with both Helen and Sophie and walked right into the club. Neither of them could work out if she'd turned up by herself that night, and never thought to ask.

They'd had some fun years. Elle had been there when they cried over a boy (to Helen's knowledge Elle didn't cry, she got angry instead), when they needed wine and a pep talk, but recently the shared part of their life seemed to be strained. Like they were all pulling the web that connected them in different directions, until it got thinner and thinner under the strain.

Sophie had slowly turned into the friend you met for brunch, who didn't really do nights out, and Helen was eager to join her. She didn't want to wear her high heels anymore. She didn't want to get dressed up, and toddle around a club. Also, wasn't it slightly embarrassing to be in a club sidled up next to 20-year-olds, expecting Katie Perry or Beyoncé to be played, realising she was a decade too late?

She especially didn't want to have to meet someone, get excited, and then swiftly let down again. She wanted a boyfriend, a shared Deliveroo account and someone who someday she could, you know, start a family with. That really did sound very grown-up.

'I've ordered us an Uber,' Sophie said chirpily.

Helen resigned herself to wearing the leggings and picked up her bag. 'Be calm,' she told herself, though she felt her heart racing as she shut the door.

WeWork Moorgate sat like a huge block of glass behind the back of Liverpool Street station. They could hear cheesy hip hop playing from inside, the kind that you knew all the words to, because the track was big ten years ago when you actually listened to the charts. 'This is going to be fun!' said Sophie, but even she didn't sound entirely convinced.

'Okay so just to recap on the game plan …' Helen paused, Elle was furtively tapping away at her mobile phone and not really listening.

'We're going to go in, have a good time whatever happens, and if you see Brody, I'm sure he'll come and say hi to you, easy peasy!' reassured Sophie, whose chirpiness was straining to conceal her concern that this would turn into another disappointment for Helen.

'Sorry. Sorry. I'm just getting my contact to get us in,' said Elle in slightly stressed tones.

'Who's your contact this time? Another man who has fallen madly in unrequited love with you?' teased Sophie, linking arms with Elle.

'No,' said Elle steadily, 'it's my sister-in-law.'

'Oh cool, doesn't she run that really cool start-up, what's the name?'

'BloomPress …' muttered Elle.

'I would love to get an interior by those guys. I mean, I've got the app but getting my apartment 'greenscaped' is a little above my budget,' shrugged Helen.

'Yes, yes, she's very impressive,' said Elle dismissively waving her hand, 'and there she is. Melody! Over here!'

'Oh, hey guys!' Melody slid her mobile phone in the back pocket of her jeans, as she walked over to them. She somehow looked even prettier despite wearing thick black rimmed glasses, and even heavier Dr. Martens. 'Oh god, I'm overdressed,' thought Helen, as she saw hipster start-up types milling around in trendy trainers, soft jumpers, and backpacks made from recycled materials.

'So, I put you guys down as BloomPress alumni. I'm sure no

one is going to check, but just name check me at the door if there's any trouble.'

'Thank you for helping us out, Melody. Can I get you a drink to say thank you?' asked Sophie.

'Would love to but I gotta get up early tomorrow for spin, then a couple of VC calls, and anyway it's not going to be much of a weekend, but hey I love it. Okay, so I will leave you lovely ladies. Elle let us know if you want to come over on Sunday; Emilio will pick up some of those pastry things you guys go crazy for in the morning.'

'Yeah maybe, thank you Melody,' Elle leaned over and stiffly air kissed Melody goodbye. '*Vamos* ladies!' And the three of them linked arms and walked in together, just like old times.

# Chapter 12

'So, are you guys part of WeWork? I haven't seen you around here before.' A small gaggle of men had predictably formed around Elle at the bar. She eyed them slowly, with the patience of a cat staring at a fish bowl.

'Sort of,' she said, and flashed a tense smile.

'So, what does your company do?' one of the men ploughed on.

Elle exhaled, 'I work for BloomPress.'

'Oh BloomPress, well that's super cool. Who runs that? Is it Melody? She's fierce. I heard they've already raised 2.5 just in their seed round! Anyways, you sound like you've got an accent, are you French?'

Elle's grip on her iPhone tightened fractionally. 'No, we're all English,' she said in her thickest accent gesturing to Helen and Sophie. 'And if you don't mind, we're having a private conversation.'

The men looked uncertainly from one to the other. 'Okay then. Well, have a great night,' and began to move off. The last man to leave brushed past them, and from a safe distance, turned over his shoulder and said, 'You'd be prettier if you smiled more.'

'Yeah, and you'd be less annoying if you kept walking. Ciao!' Elle held her hand up to them like she was swatting a fly, flicked her long heavy ponytail, and took a generous swig of wine. 'Pfff, great party guys.'

'I'm sorry. I knew this was a mistake,' supplicated Helen. From the moment Helen walked through the door, and Brody didn't run into her arms, she had felt herself wobble, like she was a Jenga tower that kept losing bricks.

She hadn't even seen Brody yet. So far, they'd been squeezing themselves around the too busy ground floor of WeWork, dodging drinks being spilled at the bar, and used plastic cups crushed into the floor. Someone had enterprisingly tried to brand the party with 'hustle harder' flyers, which had formed a soggy layer of detritus beneath them; and, not to put a fine point on it, the room did smell of farts. There she said it. Specifically, the farts of someone who ate a lot of vegan poke bowls.

'What an idiot,' shrugged Sophie. 'Perhaps we should crack on?'

Sophie had inherited a generous amount of British stiff upper lip from her mother, and tonight was running a masterclass on 'keep calm and carry on' as their chances of spotting Brody seemed to be getting slimmer and slimmer. She kept scanning through the LinkedIn app on her phone, trying to pinpoint True Materials employees in the crowd. 'I think I need to go to the optician,' she said jollily as she squinted at the pictures on her phone.

Elle had one foot cocked up at the bar, and was picking off the 'h' from a 'hustle harder' flyer from her heel. The flyer gloop was getting mashed up under her nail extensions and you could tell she was clutching tightly the reins of her annoyance that was starting to bubble over.

'Being real with you guys, this party is full of … what's that smell?'

'Farts,' said Helen blandly.

'Well. We need to find this guy soon, or I am out of here.' Elle looked at Helen, and her tone softened, 'I think maybe this isn't the night, babe. If so, there will be others.' She was stroking Helen's arm now sympathetically.

And that was Elle: she could get annoyed with you, the lack of phone signal, a guy daring to suggest splitting the bill, in a heartbeat, but she was also fiercely loyal. She'd grab your phone to stop you texting that guy back, tell you you looked beautiful even if standing next to her you knew full well you looked totally average, and she even once threw a drink in Jonathan's face. He never did get that rosé wine stain out of his shirt.

'I think that might be his CMO over there,' said Sophie, who was noticeably staring at a short blonde woman just ahead of them at the bar. She had too much eyeliner on and was doubled over the bar on her tiptoes to make herself heard by the barman. 'Yeah, I really think it is. Her name's Nicky, and she's been at True Materials for a few years. Perhaps we could talk to her about that?'

Elle rolled her eyes, walked over, and planted herself at the bar next to Nicky. The barman immediately lost all focus on Nicky, locked eyes with Elle, and started rubbing the glass in his hands meditatively. He was probably thinking of a more unique and impressive way of asking, 'So what would you like to drink?'

Nicky turned with meerkat reflexes towards Elle, but before she had time to say, 'Excuse me,' Elle was off. 'My friend …' Elle looked levelly at the barman, 'I think this lady was ahead of me at the bar, so you best serve her first. I think she said she wanted a mar-ga-rita.' Elle pronounced the word pointedly slowly, only just softened by her quick pout.

'Urgh, thank you,' said Nicky somewhat mollified.

'Ah it's so annoying, isn't it? When people skip the queue at the bar. Rude,' Elle emphasised.

'Totally,' said Nicky who probably didn't realise she was nodding along now.

The margarita arrived. 'My friend, please put a little more salt on the rim there for my *amiga* here … that's better.'

Nicky took a gratifying sip of her drink. 'That's good. So, what do you do around here?'

'My sister-in-law owns BloomPress. She wanted me to check

74

out the party, but I'm going to leave soon, not really my scene.' Elle glanced down to Nicky's lanyard. 'Ah True Materials, have I heard about your company somewhere? By the way these are my friends Helen and Sophie.' Elle gestured furiously for them to come over. Nicky waved a polite hi, then turned her attention back towards Elle, who had easily established herself as by far the most interesting person in the room.

'Yeah you might have, I'm CMO actually. We've done some really nice pieces of press recently. I think sustainability is just so now, it's been an easy job to be honest with you.'

'Absolutely,' Elle said, sounding utterly interested. 'So you must have quite a big team now? I'm almost surprised you guys are still at WeWork. Don't tell Melody from BloomPress I said that,' Elle smiled conspiratorially.

'Totally. Well, we actually just have a satellite office here for occasional meetings. We're working towards a full remote working culture, as it's not really sustainable for everyone commuting in these days.'

'And Brody?' God why did Helen just say that. Suddenly the spotlight swung awkwardly off of Elle and onto Helen. Helen wasn't designed to be in the spotlight; she felt a foundational Jenga block dislodge.

Elle shot Helen a look that said, 'you are a dead woman'.

'Oh, do you know Brody?' said Nicky politely.

'Sort of … we're both from Cornwall. It's a small place …' Helen didn't know where to look so her eyes hit the floor. Oh no, was that a 'hustle harder' sticker on her crotch?

'Well, you probably know him better than me. We've only actually met a handful of times; our corporate culture is all Zoom meetings these days. He's delegated most of, well actually all of, the running of the company to his team.' She dropped her voice, 'To be honest, he doesn't do anything. Just came up with a good concept, now keeps swanning off to Mexico.'

'Anyway.' Nicky straightened up. 'He's off pursuing other areas of his personal development,' she motioned the last part of the sentence with inverted commas. 'I came here alone tonight, mainly for the free booze, and to see if there were any cute guys.'

Elle looked to Sophie, who looked to Helen, who felt the final block of Jenga slip out, and her insides start to wobble. She turned towards the bar, and without quite thinking things through, downed the rest of Nicky's margarita.

# Chapter 13

Helen felt a bit sick. It might have been the last whisky sour she'd had, sitting uneasily on top of all those margaritas. It might have been the blaring hip hop, the sweaty dad dancing, the feeling like she really shouldn't do this ever again, and the small fact that she hadn't seen him.

What kind of founder didn't show up at his own offices, and just worked remotely for 'environmental purposes'? How could he not realise she would have tried to meet him?

She wasn't thinking clearly. Elle had left early, after (quite accurately) assessing that the night was a bust. Sophie had loyally clung on, but both of them had eventually given up on making the most of things, of pretending that they were just merrily on another girl's night out. The stakes had felt so much higher than that, and Sophie knew it.

'Are you sure you don't want to stay at my place tonight? I'll kick Frank out?' she'd said kindly as her Uber pulled up.

'No,' said Helen, head blotchy with alcohol, 'no I want you to go and cuddle lovely Frank, and I want to clear my head, it's quite a nice walk home from here.'

'Are you sure you'll be safe?'

'It's central London, I'll be fine,' said Helen and gave Sophie a hug that was stronger than she intended it to be.

'Okay, well text me when you get home then,' said Sophie, her head hanging halfway out of the Uber door. Helen watched the car pull away, then she turned and started walking into the night. Her brain was a jumbled mess of alcohol, and heady disappointment that she hadn't met Brody again. The fresh air, she hoped, would allow the thoughts that were flying around her brain to tire themselves out and settle down for the evening. It felt like all hope of finding 'her person' had all but fizzled out. It wasn't supposed to be this way. They should have been sharing a brownie by now, knees touching under the table.

She crossed through Liverpool Street station that was emptying out, and saw couples catching the last commuter services of the night. People texting their loved ones that they'd be a few minutes late, or calling with an update on their way home. Others jammed at ticket machines, a man in a brown beanie smiled at Helen, and all she could think was, 'much too soon. Much too soon.' Helen zipped up her coat a little higher, stumbling slightly as she exited the station and strode on.

The floodlit streets of the city turned into Shoreditch where juice bars and galleries had erupted, displacing the worn Victorian buildings facades. Only the upper floors had sad, derelict windows and reminded Helen that this wasn't always the trendy part of town.

Her studio was just north of Shoreditch and overlooked the Regent's Canal: a narrow towpath, spotted with tunnels, that ran alongside canal boat moorings. Cyclists liked to hare down the narrow bends of the path at ridiculous speeds, nearly knocking you into the water or a boat called 'broke but afloat', or 'what's up dock?'

She loved how she could get in after a night like this one, and watch the water from her window, checking in to see what new graffiti had been added since the last time she looked. But Brody's shoes would be by the door. 'Perhaps I should at least move them,' sighed Helen, as she flinched at the thought of packing away the last hope of him.

It was somewhere on the canal that Helen started to feel uneasy, like there had been a subtle shift in the air. A cyclist tore past her. The path looked longer and darker than it normally did. Her ankle boots were really rubbing, *did rubbing cause verrucas? No, it caused blisters!* Gosh she really was a little tipsy still. The more she focused on it, the more the discomfort in her left pinkie toe grew. Maybe she could adjust her sock?

She stopped at a bench alongside the canal, slung her bag down, and unsteadily started yanking her sock out from her boot. The dark water was eerily still, it was a clear night. Somewhere behind her she glanced movement, what was it? 'It's a bird, Helen,' a bossy voice in her head reprimanded her. Sometimes, when her anxiety woke up with a jolt, her rational mind felt the need to slap it down with excessive force.

Helen tried walking again: nope that hadn't done it, the sock was still rubbing. She slowed again, and became aware that a second set of footsteps slowed at the same time behind her. Her heartbeat was louder now, her blood started pumping so loudly in her ears it felt like they were closing over. She turned around, and saw a figure behind her on the path, just exiting the shadows of the last tunnel.

She felt her chest tighten. It was probably nothing, but if it was, would she even be able to scream?

'Hey,' said the figure.

Helen's eyes focused on the man behind her, he had dark small eyes, and was wearing a brown beanie.

Hadn't she just seen him? She definitely had. Her stomach started fastening itself in knots, she looked forwards, she needed to get off the towpath, to the well-lit street ahead. She walked quicker now. The lights bobbed in front of her, their shape bouncing off the water. She felt dizzy. An intense heat had started to creep over her back, where she could feel his eyes fixed on her.

The footsteps were quicker now. Louder. Behind her.

Oh god.

'Lucy!' A voice called out.

It wasn't behind her though, it was in front of her now.

Three metres ahead of her on the path was another man. This was it. She shouldn't have walked home. No, she shouldn't have gone to that party. Or thought that anything good was going to happen to her.

'Lucy,' the man repeated, he sounded like he knew her, and was waving both arms above his head. 'You donut! I've been looking for you!'

Helen checked back over her shoulder. Who was Lucy? She saw brown beanie. He was a little further back on the path now, his dark eyes went from Helen, to the other man, back to Helen, and just like that, he turned on his heels and walked swiftly in the other direction. She heard his feet break into a jog, until his footsteps faded out into the night.

'Hi! Hi!' the guy in front of her called. When her eyes met his, he seemed to leap back like a cat that was spooked. His gangly arms were raised above his head, like someone was arresting him.

'Lucy … err sorry I actually don't know ya name.' He had an even northern accent. 'Look, I don't want to wig you out even more, I just saw that guy, you know, the one with the hat? I cycled past ya and I dunno. He looked a bit odd, that fellow, so I stopped …' The man pulled a battered yellow bike out of the hedgerow. 'And anyway it might have been nothing, but just to be safe and all, you know …' His voice trailed off, and he looked down self-consciously at his body, and shrugged his backpack across his shoulder.

Helen squinted at him, and felt her feet were glued to the floor. She needed to text Sophie.

'Look. How about I just cycle a bit ahead of you until you get on the main street? I swear down I won't follow you, just want to make sure, well you know?'

'Okay,' said Helen slowly, and pulled her mobile phone out of her handbag.

'Yup, good plan to have that out, and for the record I won't be nicking that either,' said the man and gently started stepping up the path rolling his bike along beside him. 'I'm Ish by the way. Don't need to know your name though,' he said brightly.

'I'm Helen.'

'Well Helen, nice to meet ya. I live just over in London Fields. I like this area, all the history, but at night, yeah …'

'I like it too,' ventured Helen. 'I don't know who that guy was but I'm sure I saw him at Liverpool Street station. He smiled at me. You don't think he … do you?'

'I dunno, well, maybe, but he's gone now and I'll get you home. Well not *home*, but safe, wherever you feel comfortable.'

'Thanks. I feel … better … comfortable. Well, actually I have a blister coming, and I'm a bit, not tipsy, but anyway, apart from that I'm okay. Comfortable.'

Ish stopped and patted the front of his jacket. 'Here ya go.' He fished a plaster out from his front pocket. 'I'll just leave that here for you.' He placed it on the bench in between them. 'You can pick it up …'

'I get the concept Ish, don't worry.' Helen felt herself smiling, since when was she so confident? 'It is Ish, right?'

'Yeah Ish, Ishan to be correct. So what do you do around here, Helen?'

Helen took a deep breath, 'I'm a blogger.'

'Oh right, fair enough, me too actually,' smiled Ish. 'I do history stuff. I look at major historical events, mainly in London at the minute, like Britain in the Blitz, the Black Death, Jack the Ripper, oh shit, sorry, probably shouldn't have brought that one up! Sorry! Anyway, I make short videos about it, like educational, for kids, tweens, that kinda thing,' Ish cleared his throat.

'I'm a baking blogger. Well, blogger/vlogger really. I had one

big hit video that went viral, it was about cheap carrot cake …
and anyway that's my job.'

'Ah cool. Good, isn't it, working for yourself? But hard to get
the whole thing started. Bet it must be annoying when people keep
asking you to bake cakes for them too? Ya probably like a good
takeaway when you're not on camera,' Ish chuckled to himself.

'Yeah, it is a little something like that,' Helen smiled. 'Well this
is my street, it was nice meeting you, Ish.'

'Yeah, you too. I'm @Ishtory if you want to follow us on Insta.
No pressure though! You take care of yourself, all right?'

'I will. I will this time.'

# Chapter 14

'Squeeze that juice … mmmph! I'm here as your conduit. I'm here to transport you. Release yourself to me and … warrior two, triangle, reverse triangle, side angle pose, and flow!' The lithe instructor barked into his headset, tattooed arms raised to the ceiling.

Helen thought he would make a great Jesus at Halloween.

Helen was at yoga, hoping that by doing something spiritual and calorie burning she could counterbalance the night before. She felt guilty. Guilty for trying to find Brody. Guilty for drinking far, far too many margaritas. Guilty for not getting a cab home – but why shouldn't she be able to walk home? *Because strange men try to attack you Helen!* Her thoughts kept tumbling out in a tangled mess.

Mainly she felt guilty for limping in through her front door, too tired to sleep, more upset than she wanted to admit, and trawling social media for trace evidence of Brody's life.

She'd gazed at her screenshot of him from Connex (could she recognise anything in the background??), had looked at small pixelated images of him on the True Materials site, and still wanted more. She peeled off her too tight leggings, took some leftover chicken satay sticks out of the fridge, and spent hours basking in the glow of her phone, mind whirring.

Deep down she knew what she wanted to find: she wanted proof that they could never be together.

A picture of him on social media, arms around another woman, an incriminating comment on some gorgeous Instagram model's post, a discovery that he was with someone else right now …

If she could just get the proof she needed it would be over, and she could retreat back to being normal, hopeless Helen. It was better that way, better than feeling like she could have almost been happy.

By 3am she had rearranged her pillows, drunk a large glass of water, squinted at her smudged make-up in the bathroom mirror, almost fallen asleep, needed to pee, and flicked her phone back open. She sat uncomfortably in the darkness, her mind persistently awake. She felt down her legs, 'what are they?'

Helen switched on her lamp and examined a field of small red bumps running up her inner thigh; it didn't look normal. Her skin had developed a mottled red tone. She had chorizo for legs.

Was it itchy? She speculatively gave it a scratch. It certainly wasn't *not* itchy.

Quickly she googled, 'rash on legs.'

Flea bites?

Helen sat slightly less comfortably on her bed.

Eczema?

No, her mum had that and was always sending Helen close-up pictures of the latest.

Shingles … Could it be shingles?

She pressed her hand to her forehead, not too warm, but maybe a little warmer than usual? This wasn't good. Perhaps she had somehow gotten so stressed with the whole Brody saga that she'd triggered something in her immune system? The train! She knew she should have stayed in her seat.

She was feeling a little run-down earlier … Oh God why had she been so stupid to go out drinking alcohol when she was not well?

It wasn't just a drink either, it was a lot of drinks, each one gently blotting out part of the red-hot jolt of disappointment she'd been feeling, that was now seeping back through her.

It was almost farcical to think that someone like Brody would like her anyway.

She could at least admit it to herself, it wouldn't have worked. She was too nothingy, too average, definitely too pear shaped, and probably had some kind of autoimmune condition that she'd only just discovered.

'What happens if you let shingles go untreated?' her fingers typed rapidly.

'If left untreated, some complications of shingles can be fatal. Pneumonia, encephalitis, stroke, and bacterial infections can cause your body to go into shock or sepsis.'

Helen felt a little sick. Should she call 111? No, bad idea, the last time she'd done that they had been well, a bit dismissive. She'd call the doctors first thing tomorrow. She set a reminder in her phone. Not that she would need a reminder, she just needed to look at her legs. Her disproportionately short, muscular legs, that didn't fit perfectly into any jeans, and now had a rash all over them.

She took a picture and texted her mum.

*This is what my legs look like, do you think I should be worried?? Xx*

She fell back into bed, and into a confused sleep, as the glow from her phone told her it was 03:41.

Predictably, she'd woken up with a headache, and had about twenty glorious seconds lying in her bed before her memories of the night before came rushing back. There was an empty glass of water on her bedside table, a dull humming sound from the bathroom where she'd left the light on, and her faux leather leggings hung limply on the radiator.

She checked her phone, which displayed the reminder: 'Call docs!! Ask about shingles. Poss autoimmune issues?!' Then read the one message she'd received from her mum:

*Good morning darling, you were up quite late, are you all right? That looks to me like a heat rash, you haven't been wearing those dreadful leggings again, have you? Can we talk later?? x*

Helen looked down at her legs; they did look a lot better than the night before. The scaly red rash was in fact a few small innocent looking bumps. She was also relatively confident that her fuzzy head and nausea were a result of alcohol and disappointment.

She took a long exhale, watching her mobile phone rise and fall on her stomach.

What was wrong with her?

To Helen's surprise a long slow tear rolled down her cheek. It was just all a bit much. She couldn't handle the disappointment, the anxiety, the highs, the lows. It was time to put this whole dating thing behind her. If it happened, it happened, but she wasn't going to go chasing it anymore.

She sat upright, and pulled open her blinds to let the glow of mid-morning sun come through her window. She really needed to change. To get fitter, to get focused, to try and actually achieve something for once.

She was going to throw out those leggings that didn't suit her, and you know what? She was chucking out those Havaianas too. Grabbing both items she marched over to her pedal bin, and only hesitated for a nano second before dropping them into the bin with a satisfying plonk.

Pulling on a comforting pair of sweatpants from the airer, she padded slowly into the bathroom and looked in the mirror. Her natural frizzy curls had formed a halo around her head, slowly ousting the perfectly smooth blow dry Elle had been fussing over last night.

Helen felt her shoulders drop, it was going to be okay.

Her phone buzzed, there was a DM on Instagram from @ishtory.

*Get home safe in the end? Have you had any leftovers yet?*

She followed him back, half typed a response, then put her phone away. This wasn't the day to get lost on social media. She needed time away from her screen, a good yoga class, and to take her bins out.

# Chapter 15

*'Jack the Ripper is an unsolved crime*
*Where at least 5 women lost their lives*
*In autumn of 1888*
*The police couldn't crack the case …'*

The camera shot panned to show @ishtory jumping in and out of shot, as he rapped, dressed in full Victorian costume.

Helen smiled coyly to herself; he did look a little bit silly. However, it went to show that even someone like Ish was far ahead of her on social media. He had fifty-two thousand followers ranging from school kids, 'Thanks man, helped me get that A grade GCSE!' to their mums, 'Another helpful video, Ish, we're really hoping you do Britain in the Blitz soon!' Some mums even sounded moderately flirtatious, 'You look very charming in that hat!'

By comparison, Helen's latest video, the first in her 'Easy Baking Challenge', was a flop. She'd scraped three thousand views so far and most of the comments revolved around her outfit, which certainly hadn't been her intention.

*CakesInMyTummy: Great vid, and nice dress Helen, checks really suit you.*
*EveryAdil: Heart-eyed emoji*
*Dk1113: Nice bobs.*

She needed better styling, better video editing, more personality, and probably a few airbrushed Instagram pictures of her in a bikini.

Annoyingly, the baking bloggers who were doing painfully well at the moment were usually the yummy mummy type; brandishing a toddler in one arm, and a cutesy slotted spoon in the other. They always wore unfeasibly low-cut white tops (surely the least practical colour for baking?) and tolerated a lot of online commentary about their 'bobs'.

The intro reel to their videos would always show some pristine family home, with a cute baby on the floor, and really expensive fridges: the American kind with built-in ice machines. It was like everyone on social media lived in some mythical fairy land without bills to pay, glowing with eternal youth and handsome husbands that posed gushingly on camera.

Helen just couldn't compete. Her niche as a student baking blogger clearly wasn't working anymore, and not a day went by without her seeing yet another new blogger explode overnight, eclipsing her 'success' with just a few viral videos.

'What are you watching?' Sophie sat down next to her and peered over her shoulder.

They were doing post-work juices on Helen's insistence that she was on a health kick. Helen had even come straight from a spin class and was intermittently dabbing her cheek with a damp napkin to look less flushed, and more glowing. She adjusted her posture to be more upright, and feel more at one with the £7.65 revive juice she'd splurged on.

'How are things with Frank?'

When Sophie was really happy, she smiled like a cartoon character exposing all her teeth. 'He's lovely really.'

'That's good. What are we doing for your birthday by the way, it's only two weeks away, we need to plan wine!'

Sophie inhaled. 'Actually Frank's booked us a surprise trip! Well, obviously, he knows where we're going, but he's just told me it's going to be hot, and he's only going to reveal the location at the airport,' Sophie's smile lingered expectantly. 'I have a feeling it will be somewhere we're meant to go together ... but we should definitely have drinks when I'm back! Whenever that is!'

Sophie looked hopefully at Helen. Helen knew this was her cue to express her happiness for Sophie, but instead she just about managed to croak out a 'that sounds great' before her voice trailed off.

Somewhere in her stupid brain she couldn't quite compute that someone else's happiness was not in conflict with her own.

Her phone flashed with a message. It was her mum again. The only person ever to double text her. Helen turned the phone facedown on the table.

'Hola!' Elle joined them at the table, in a lilac jumpsuit that only she could have pulled off, and started flicking rapidly through the menu. Predictably the waiter made a beeline for them the second she'd sat down. 'Can I have a glass of rosé?'

'I thought we were doing a health kick?' ventured Sophie.

'You do you ladies, but I stick with the wine. How are we all?' Elle crossed one leg over the other, and looked somehow like she was conducting an interview.

'Well, my latest YouTube video flopped, my favourite jeans don't fit, and I'm running up a huge Uber bill taking taxis home after the episode with the brown beanie guy.'

'I still can't believe he followed you home! I knew I should have gone with you,' said Sophie shaking her head.

'What a creep. What about that other guy, was he cute?'

'Elle!!' Sophie's eyes noticeably widened.

'Sorry, jeez I was just asking.'

'I didn't really notice but he is a viral YouTuber so I'll stay in touch for work stuff …'

'Well on a positive note, at least you're over this Brody thing.'

'I wouldn't exactly say *over*.' Helen tucked her hair behind her ear, and looked down into her juice wondering if she could taste the 'energising kick' of ginger.

'Well, his flip flops are at least in the bin. I know you liked him but, you can't keep chasing these guys. They have to come to you.'

Sophie's voice went up half an octave, 'Maybe this isn't the best time to bring this up, Elle?'

'*No tener pelos en la lengua.*' Elle folded her napkin daintily in front of her and reshuffled her words into English. 'I mean it is better to be hit with the truth, than kissed with a lie.'

Sophie's eyes squinted long and hard at Elle like she was trying to send a telepathic message to shut up.

'It is because I actually care that I'm the only one who is being honest here,' Elle exhaled noticeably loudly and looked levelly at them both.

Helen felt the blotchiness increasing on her cheeks again and started dabbing furiously. She needed to ask the waiter if she could upgrade to kitchen roll.

'I don't think it's fair to say that Helen always chases guys.' Sophie was sitting more upright now. You could imagine that behind her five foot two inch stature and hazel eyes that Sophie Wu was a force to be reckoned with in the city.

'I think it probably is fair,' shrugged Helen, brushing a strand of recently dyed hair off her shoulder that no one had noticed.

'What about that Italian guy? The one who disappeared after the great date. I was the one who had to do 'surveillance' on his Instagram stories.' Elle's eyes flicked from left to right. 'Or what was his name? Freddie, no Teddy! Very English, tall, and in my opinion, quite boring. We all went to that lame member's bar in

West London, and I had to flirt with his friend. Am I the only one that remembers this?'

'Maybe it's just something in your energy, that you're not attracting the men you deserve,' Sophie said and laid her hand on Helen's arm with trembling sincerity.

'You're both right, honestly I struggle, I know I do.' Helen wanted to say that she was proud to actually care about what people thought of her, that she didn't want to take people for granted like Elle did. She wanted to tell Sophie, 'Thanks but maybe it's not my energy, maybe I'm just not as lucky as you,' but instead she started to shred the napkin she was holding into tiny strips.

'Helen, listen to me, you are a beautiful woman, you are kind, you are fun, you are a great friend, I just don't want to hear you sat here heartbroken over someone you went on, what? One date with! He's not the man of your life. You need a man who will make a real effort for you!'

'That's nice to hear Elle but if there are guys like this out there, I'm certainly not meeting them!'

'Open your eyes love! A man asked you out on the street a few days ago …'

'… technically he just stopped me being harassed by another man, then followed me on Instagram …'

'And look …' Elle flipped open Helen's phone, '… just look at all these guys messaging you on Connex; some of them are actually quite hot.'

'Really?'

'How about someone like this?' Elle thrust a picture of a hand-some olive-skinned guy in Helen's face. She couldn't help but think he looked a bit like a male version of Elle. 'He sent you a sweet message, I'm replying!'

'What?! Elle I'm not ready, I don't want to meet some random guy …'

'Well babe, if you want to fall in love, you're going to have to meet some 'random guy' at some stage.' Elle shook her head and reticently handed the phone back to Helen.

Helen glanced at her screen, another message from her mum, this one clearly read:

*Darling, I've been trying to reach you all day! Is everything all right? Sadly, all is not well here, Nanny G has taken a turn, I don't want to worry you, but can you please call me back?! x*

Nanny G's 'turn' was in fact pneumonia.

Not the phantom symptom of chronic shingles that Helen had wasted a whole night googling, but the real deal.

The kind that left you struggling against breaths that grew shallower and shallower, that had confined her beanbag-loving, Chablis-sipping nan to bed. The kind that had a mortality rate of thirty per cent for severe pneumonia, or at least that's what the NHS website had said.

There was no question of what Helen had to do; for once it was obvious. Not like when it's obvious with a guy you like and it turns out the summer you'd been fantasising about spending with them was all a joke because they were just, well, not that into you. It was actually clear what Helen should do.

She needed to get on the first train to Cornwall tomorrow, and be with Nanny G. Like Nanny G had been with her all those times when her mum had seemed too preoccupied to notice she was there. She needed to pack up her expensive, ridiculous and upsetting life in London and go to be with the people she already loved, and who undoubtedly loved her.

# Chapter 16

Helen's parents' old garage had been converted into Nanny G's annexe six years ago. Despite some significant protests that she was 'perfectly all right thank you' living alone, Nanny G eventually moved in after Grandpa M had died. They hadn't exactly been madly in love, more like just mad at each other.

Nanny G would pull the plug whilst Grandpa M was washing dishes in the sink. Grandpa M would leave confrontational post-it notes around their cottage: 'Immersion heater works between 7–8am and 6–7pm. DO NOT RESET!' It had all come to a head one day when Grandpa M had particularly annoyed Nanny G (by taking in his washing off the line, and leaving hers out to get soaked in the rain) and she'd tipped half a pint of milk over his head.

When he died, she'd cried almost constantly for a day, and then went about packing all his clothes away into boxes. She said she didn't like the clutter, but it seemed like she was erasing all the memories of him. Helen's mum had sentimentally gone back through all the boxes, pulling out his walking stick and flat cap as keepsakes, much to Nanny G's chagrin. When Nanny G had attempted to restack all the boxes in their appropriate order, she had badly hurt her lower back and, being unable to march off, was moved into the family home.

Nanny G never quite regained her full mobility, so after several heated debates (at least on Nanny G's part with Helen's parents being as diplomatic as possible) they'd converted their garage as a compromise option, to give Nanny G some independence.

The annexe now looked like Nanny G's old house in miniature, with a lifetime's worth of knick-knacks, decorated plates and old volumes of books stuffed and stacked into every corner. Nanny G lay on her sofa, feet propped up on a pile of cushions at the end. Helen could see how thin her ankles were, with thick blue veins trailing up into her pyjama legs.

An old Christmas cake tin over spilled with ginger nut biscuits, and there was the constant fuzz of Netflix in the background, which Henry had recently converted her to. Someone called Shaena was on the screen in a tiny lime green bikini, talking about how Col had, 'turned her head.'

'Helen, you look …' what have you done to your …' Nanny G stopped short as a deep cough made her curl forwards. Helen noticed the pile of crumpled tissues at Nanny G's bedside and how her spine was so much more curved than it used to be: gradually coiling into a C-shaped ammonite.

'Oh this …' Helen picked loosely at the ends of her balayage, a recent splurge to make her feel, well, more attractive.

'Your lovely natural hair.'

'I thought I could do with a change up, to be a bit less boring.' Helen sat down in front of her on the floor like a five-year-old.

'Rubbish! There's nothing boring about you,' Nanny G faltered to take a gulp of air. 'I always said you'd look lovely even in a bin bag,' the last words struggled out of her mouth, and her hand traced down to her side to pick up her oxygen mask.

Nanny G had been a real doer. Conditioned from decades of raising children, washing dishes by hand, and working the farm, she couldn't sit still for a minute. But today she just couldn't get going. Once upon a time she had been a headstrong farm girl, who would walk fifteen miles a day without thinking about it.

It had taken her a long time to realise that the powerful muscles in her legs weren't there anymore. That her already thin lips had receded into her mouth. She felt like a marionette: brightly animated one minute, then flopped forwards the next.

'Are you feeling okay, Nan?' Helen's hand was on her shoulder.

'Well, no I'm not. The truth is my girl, I'm finished.'

'Oh Nan, don't say things like that!'

'It's just the truth! It can't be argued with. You know I liked the version of myself who could walk across the cliffs for miles, or at least be helpful to your mother. You know how much she worries! I am not wedded to the version of me who is confined to this couch. Out with the old, in with the new, that's what I …' Nanny G stopped to breathe deeply into the mask.

Helen felt pressure in her ears, like they were actively trying to close themselves off to hearing anymore.

'Now don't look so worried. I'm not afraid of dying. I've had a good run, very few regrets.'

Helen clambered back into the conversation, trying to ignore the feeling of having a gaping hole where her stomach should have been. 'I think there's already so many things about my life I'd like to change.' Helen paused, remembering again that life actually wasn't all about her and her petty micro-dramas. 'Is there anything you'd do differently?'

'Well, we all got married terribly young. We had to be a virgin, no question about it, and I think it might have been quite fun to have some different experiences, maybe some different men …' Nanny G managed a wry smile, '… because that's all you have at this age. Memories. Boxes and boxes of memories to flick through, to keep you going.'

'Do you miss Grandpa M?'

'That's like asking me if I'd miss my left foot. He was just always there. Until he wasn't.'

'What about … was it, Vernon?'

'Oh Vernon. I wouldn't say I regret not seeing him again. It's just that chapter was never closed. I suppose you learn in life that things don't always have neat endings, but yes, I do think of him often. I wonder what his life held for him.'

'It would be great for you to see him again,' ventured Helen.

'Ah well, that would be something to get out of bed for. But I suspect that I might have outlived him! I have had a nasty habit throughout my life of outliving everyone I knew. My parents, my sisters, Grandpa M.' Nanny G glanced down at the scrunched-up tissue in her hand. 'Yes, I suppose it is my time to go.'

Nanny G stopped trying to lift her head off the pillow, and let it flop to the side. Helen guessed this was what it was like, by the time you reached 'the end', you didn't resist it. Maybe it opened out ahead of you like a gateway back to all the loved ones you had lost. Helen moved to tuck Nanny G in, and pulled the blanket up around her shoulders.

# Chapter 17

'How's Nan?' Henry leaned his oversized frame against the back of the fridge and popped open a can of Fanta. He'd always liked sugar.

'Worryingly calm, I'd say, it's like she's accepted it's the end.' Helen bit hard on her lower lip. 'I just don't know what to do to get her to hang on.'

'I love Nan, too, Hels, but maybe it's just her time. I know mum will find it hard …'

'Yep.'

'We all will, but what can you do? We've made these last few years good for her I think.'

'That makes her sound like a rescue cat, Henry.'

'Right. Yep it does. I mean, just put yourself in Nan's shoes though; how would you feel if all the people you'd known growing up were gone? Mum and Dad, Sophie and Elle, me and Nessy …'

'Nessy? Getting serious huh?' Helen managed a quick jab to Henry's barrel-like ribs.

'Well yes probably,' said Henry; he was incapable of being playful. 'But you see what I mean, she's just got memories.'

'She's got us.'

'I have a feeling it's not the same … Oh,' Henry stopped and pulled out a wodge of paper from his back pocket, '… I found these letters earlier when I was doing a bit of a clear out of her room. She told me to give them to you. You know how funny she is about throwing things out.'

Henry passed Helen a small bundle of letters: they were cream coloured, tiny envelopes with swirly fountain pen writing on them that reminded Helen of being at school. Most had been ripped open by eager fingers unable to wait to read their contents.

Helen gently pulled open one of the letters. In it was a tiny card with a black and white drawing of a barn on the front. Inside was a poem:

*In this breast, the thought of thee waits, hidden yet bright;*
*But it must never, never come into sight;*
*I must stop short of thee the whole day long.*

*But when sleep comes to close each difficult day,*
*Then night gives pause to the long watch I keep,*
*And all of my restraint falls apart.*

*Many happy returns for your birthday.*

*With love,*

*Vernon*

'OMG, these are love letters!'

'Yep I guess you could call them that. Strong stuff.' Henry's hand scratched the back of his neck nervously.

'They're beautiful.' This is the love I want, Helen thought. Not a, 'Hey how's your weekend going?' message on a dating app, I want the real deal. The kind that travels endless distances, or lingers through time, to find you.

'I know, I think about Nan, you know, carrying them around

for years. Nearly a century actually.' Henry scrutinised the Edward VIII stamps on the letters.

'She must have really loved him.'

'I think he loved her too, read this one ...' Henry pulled out a letter from the bottom of the stack.

*Gladys, my dearest,*
*I know we cannot meet, but please forgive me for writing to you again. If I had the strength to turn my back on us, I wouldn't be human.*
*Don't you realise what you did to me that wonderful night in Kynance Cove ...*

'Geez, I didn't think they were allowed to do that stuff in those days ...'

'Henry! It's romantic!'

*Was I weak to kiss you then?*

'See, it's just *kissing*,' Helen cleared her throat.

*I can't be the same man again that I was before you kissed me. Since then, I have been yours and will remain so.*
*It is best that we never meet again perhaps, but is it weak to want to be with you again? To joke with you, to walk with you, and to kiss you?*
*I hope our moon can rise again.*
*I am linked to you now, and that link can never be comfortably cut, even though we can never set eyes on one another again. But I believe we shall! I love you too much and have so much admiration for your courage, frankness and kindness. One day, on Faith's will, we will meet again.*
*This isn't what I intended to write to you, but it is all the truth. Goodbye my darling and may God bless you.*
*Yours,*
*Vernon*

'What do you think he means by 'I hope our moon can rise again'?'

'Sounds pretty sexual to me,' shrugged Henry.

'He's probably just being romantic,' said Helen carefully folding the letter up again. 'Just think what it's like to have kept these letters all this time, and they never met again …'

'Well at least Nanny G met Grandad, and we were born,' offered Henry.

Helen rolled her eyes. 'But she can't have loved him, not like this! In fact, I'm not sure if they even liked each other.'

Helen wanted to be loved just a fraction of what Vernon had felt for Nanny G. Finding love was so hard, how could they have allowed time and the war to pull them apart?

'Perhaps he's still out there?' Helen was leafing feverishly through the letters now.

'I doubt it Hels, Nanny G outlived pretty much everyone.'

'But it's not impossible right?' Helen was circling around the kitchen counter gaining momentum. 'Maybe if she could just have one last meeting with him …'

'It would be a FaceTime at best, but carry on …'

'Don't you think that would be so special for her? That they'd be reunited at last?' Helen wanted to see Nanny G smile again, to be that young woman with the dark red lips, and the wind running through her hair, as she marched across a moonlit beach. That would be a reason to live, to know not everyone she knew and loved was gone.

A secret part of Helen, untouched by the cynicism that modern dating had ruined everything, also wanted to prove that love could still conquer all. That when someone truly loved you, that they could always find a way of coming back.

# Chapter 18

Helen was sitting on her parent's sofa scrolling Instagram to try and numb the queasy feeling in her gut every time she glanced in the direction of Nanny G's annexe.

Sophie and Frank were on holiday in Tulum, faces squeezed next to one another. Sophie was wearing a wide brimmed hat, clutching a coconut water in one hand, and a bottle of factor fifty in the other. It had been applied in white splotches to Frank's face which had turned that particular shade of red unique to British tourists. She was always so sensible, even when it came to love. Frank wasn't charismatic or exciting, and deep down Helen wasn't sure she could settle like that. That's probably why Sophie had a boyfriend, and she didn't.

She gave it a like and kept scrolling. There were a few pictures of baking influencers in microscopic pinstripe aprons extolling the virtues of their 'guilty pleasure' vegan brownies which Helen was convinced they never ate. She liked the posts anyway because she wasn't bitter.

Jonathan and Katy were stood outside a stately home #weddingplanning. Would Helen seem more or less over it if she liked the photo?

Then there was a video of Elle twirling in the mirror in skin tight leggings she'd been #gifted (link in bio). Regrettably, Helen knew the truth that Elle's incredible figure was the result of a solid diet of calamari, rosé wine and iced lattes. Some things in life just weren't fair. She continued flicking through her feed, her eyes falling on a familiar face.

*In 1940 we had the Blitz*
*Evacuating London's kidz*
*The Germans dropped bombs by the ton*
*But the Brits kept calm and carried on*

This time Ish was in some kind of tunnel with an old-fashioned lantern, casting shadows on his face like someone telling horror stories around a campfire. His followers seemed to love it though, and were already eagerly anticipating the next in his 'London Ish-tory' series.

London. History. Helen looked down at the address on the letters:

*292 Lionel Rd*
*London*

Ish! Ish! He could help her. She clicked on his profile to send him a DM. There was a message in her inbox already from him, unanswered.

Damn it. Why hadn't she responded? Hopefully he wouldn't hold it against her:

Helen: *Ish! Sorry I thought I'd responded to this already.*
*Thanks so much for your help that night :-)*
*Would it be really cheeky for me to ask for your help again?*

Helen just had time to go and make herself yet another mug of tea when her phone buzzed with a response.

Ish: *Can't knock a chancer!*
*How can I help?*

Helen: *Okay I know this sounds crazy but my nan is very unwell and I'm hoping to track down a lost love of hers. I have a London address from the 40s and a first name, any good?*

Ish: *Sorry to hear Hels …*
*Great plan though, I'm all up for matchmaking some oldies.*
*And yes I should be able to work with that :-)*

Helen: *Amazing!*
*I'm back in London tomorrow. Maybe we could grab a coffee?*

Ish: *Come to mine?*
*Not like that ^^^!*
*I just have all my gear at home and it will be easier for me to help ya.*

Helen: *Okay sounds like a plan.*
*Thanks Ish!*

# Chapter 19

Helen's train home was later that afternoon. Her mum had promised her that she would let her know if anything changed, and for once Helen wasn't in a hurry to leave. There was nothing for her in London. It was just a gloopy swamp of bad dates, humid tubes, and overpriced everything. If she stepped outside her front door, she'd always end up spending at least £20. She'd have to get better at staying in, actually focusing on her work, and being organised. She was going to read that book Sophie had given her for Christmas, *The Magical Art of Folding* or something like that.

No more distracting herself with expensive lattes, Uber rides, and haircuts; she fiddled nervously with the tips of her balayage, which probably didn't suit her anyway. She needed to stop living like some high-flying executive, on a woeful freelance budget, it was embarrassing. Some of her friends were even buying houses! Sophie would probably get married soon. Elle would get married as soon as she decided she couldn't be bothered being single anymore; and Helen would be left on the shelf in an overpriced Hackney studio …

Nanny G would never live long enough to see her settle down, have children, or make a success of herself. Not that it was at all likely that she was ever going to do any of those things. Helen clenched her face to stop a tear from sliding down her cheeks; she wasn't going to say goodbye to Nanny G like this! She rubbed her eyes furiously with her jumper sleeve, she really annoyed herself sometimes.

Her nan was still very ill. Their local doctor had been shuffling in and out of her parent's annexe nervously every day for a week now, and when Helen passed him, he'd hold his breath, avoid eye contact and clutch his doctor's bag across his chest, like any form of communication would wound him. Helen's mum had long since pronounced him useless and had been hitting the NHS website hard for alternative solutions.

She'd got a humidifier whirring in the already too-cramped annexe and had piled cushions behind Nanny G, leaving one on her lap for her to coil over. It didn't look very comfortable. Helen was trying to quietly clear the pile of plates that was accumulating on Nanny G's bedside table from her mum's many attempts at getting her to eat something other than ginger nut biscuits, or semolina.

A fork nervously clattered against the side of a neatly cling-filmed plate.

Nanny G's eyes fluttered open, and she managed a faint smile. 'Helen?'

'Hi, Nan. Sorry I was tidying away, get some rest.' Helen reached over and pulled the blanket back around her shoulders.

'I'm sure I'll get plenty of rest where I'm going.' Nanny G's smile broadened. 'I'd like to talk to you before you go, you're the only person I can speak to … your dad and Henry never say more than two words, and your mum, well, she keeps fussing over me.'

'I think you should let us fuss over you, Nan.' Helen took Nanny G's hand. 'I got your letters by the way.'

'Good. I wanted you to have them, I know you'll keep them safe.'

'Nan … Do you think Vernon was 'The One'?'

'Unfortunately, my girl I believe in 'The One' about as much as Adam and Eve, or the tooth fairy.'

'Nan!'

'I know my mother would have told me off for blasphemy for saying that, but …' Nanny G took a long pause. 'I've never been one for fairy tales. I would have liked to have met him again, and those lips! But do you really think there's just one person out there for you? If so, I wouldn't like those odds! I just can't believe it. I suppose Vernon to me was about being young, about still having some adventures, about still believing romance could be around every corner … and I'm just not young anymore, and I've made my peace with that.'

'I'm going to try and find him for you, Nan.' Helen's grip on Nanny G's hand tightened.

'Oh Helen, you need to focus on your life, not mine! You've still got all yours to live!'

# Chapter 20

Helen watched the country fields slowly turn into low-rise identikit houses. These turned into industrial train yards, which themselves turned into the backs of towering old Victorian houses leaning over the train tracks into Paddington.

The journey had been predictably bad. Helen hadn't wanted to leave, and had cried as soon as she sat down on the train. A snotty-nosed tween boy had sneered at her over the top of the seat in front of her, as she prayed no one would sit next to her for at least the first few hours.

She ate her normal assortment of stodgy unsatisfying snacks and kept being pulled back onto her phone. Every time she thought about Nanny G laying down in her annexe, she scrolled Instagram furiously until even the app had to tell her she was 'all up to date'.

If her mind drifted to the limp oxygen mask hanging in Nanny G's mottled hands, she would read through the entire contents of News App: a toddler had died from swallowing a battery, babies were being sold in the Middle East and scientists were predicting a climate change apocalypse by 2050. At least Nanny G didn't have to see all this.

Finally, Helen swapped to Connex and saw she had three new likes:

*Carl, 32*
*Pro cuddler.*
*Currently in Amsterdam.*
*What's your favourite bagel?*

*Saf, 36*
*Looking for a partner in crime.*
*Who can make up a good lie for how we met? ;-)*

*Eddie, 41*
*Travel. Tennis. Tequila.*

It was so depressing, she didn't even want to think about reading their messages. She opened her inbox anyway and tried to will her chat with Brody back into existence. She could still recite big chunks of it, like lines from a secondary school play. In a sea of Eddie's, Saf's and Carl's it had been so … perfect.

Well, she'd been incredibly awkward as usual, but he was just so different to the other guys with their staged puppy photos, and inane 'how are you finding it on here?' first messages.

The train lurched as it pulled into Paddington. Helen put her phone away and grabbed her decade-old carry-on case with a wonky wheel that ricocheted as she tried to walk in a straight line towards the ticket gates. As usual, she had packed too many clothes that wouldn't fit back into her case this morning, so she'd ended up wearing three jumpers and had her long fluffy cardigan tied around her waist. She was pretty sure it wasn't a 'look'.

People poured towards the gate and Helen squeezed up between a university student with a large backpack and a city worker talking abrasively on their hands-free kit.

In the jumble of frustrated limbs, oversized bags, and the smell of damp coats, she saw a pair of white AirPods sailing in the other direction. As the momentum of the crowd pushed her through the gates, she realised who she was looking at: grey cashmere sweater, white trainers and Ray-Bans, walking purposefully down platform nine, destination Penzance.

Brody.

Helen couldn't think. A box in her mind that she'd been trying to close sprung open, and she was back on the cliff tops breathing him in. In a flash of memory, she was kissing him goodbye, vaguely tracing the Tesla's bonnet with her fingers. Why did she throw away his shoes? And why was she wearing three jumpers?

One annoyed passer-by after the next jostled past her, slurping from reusable coffee cups. It was like her feet were rooted beneath her. Then came the wash of adrenaline, as she gripped her luggage tightly and walked back towards the ticket barriers. She had to try and talk to him.

'Ticket please.'

'I don't have one, but I need to get back onto the train,' Helen said remarkably assertively, balancing her wonky carry-on between her legs as she wrestled off the first of her three jumpers.

'Please stand aside.'

'I've actually lost something very important on that train.' She could still just see the outline of Brody as he walked down to the far end of the curving platform.

'And what is that, Miss?'

'My … passport.' At least she sounded desperate. She yanked her scrunchy out of her hair.

'You'll have to wait for the cleaners to return. If they have the item, you will receive it then. You will first have to register the lost item online, you can do that now.' The man prodded her mobile phone.

'Can't I get it?'

'No, you can't. Once you have disembarked the train you may not re-embark. Now please stand aside.'

Brody's silhouette had slipped out of sight.

'Okay, look it's not my passport, it's my … boyfriend. He's on that train and I need to speak to him!'

'Can't you call?' The hand prodded her mobile again.

'I don't have his number.' The man's moustache bristled as he physically exhaled in response.

'We met on a dating app. The dating app broke and now I've lost his contact details and I need to get them back!'

'So, what you're telling me is, he's not your boyfriend.'

'Technically no, but things were … things were definitely heading in that direction.'

'May I give you a word of advice Miss? Leave it. If he wants to see you, he will, and by the looks of things he doesn't. Now please stand aside.'

The train on platform nine shuddered to a start.

Helen was not a risk taker. She pretended she'd sprained her ankle on her first (and only) ski trip to avoid having to attempt ski lifts, and anything icey-mountainy. She developed a love for hot chocolate instead.

Yet she found her hands letting go of her case, and her legs moving beneath her. As the case clattered to the ground her hands clamped down on the gate ahead as she swung her legs forwards over the barriers. Just like hurdling at school: but more successful. She started to run down the platform. Heart beating furiously. Cardigan shimmying down her hips. Calling 'Brody' as she sprinted.

He was going to hold her. It was going to be such a big surprise. Sophie would say that it was fate how they met again. What were the odds? She would show Elle that it was for real. She would have a date with him in London, their legs glancing each other under the table of a dimly lit cocktail bar. She wouldn't be the last one left … She would …

She was going to … not make it. Just like a movie, her hands planted onto the train doors just as they clenched shut, and the train mockingly pulled away. Her hands fell onto her knees, hot

111

and sweaty. Why hadn't he seen her? How could she not have caught him? She had jumped the ticket barrier!

Blank faces stared at her through the carriage windows, and an old Twix wrapper blew around at her feet. She knew she looked blotchy, red and stupid. Why didn't Brody see her? Was it him? It was definitely him. They were destined to meet again; she could just feel it.

The knowledge that he still existed made Helen feel a bit sick. As the days had passed since she last saw him it had been easier to pen Brody off in her mind, a 'no trespassing' zone that she tried to avoid thinking about, which millimetre by millimetre was receding into the distance. That night with him had taken on a dream-like quality, every time she dredged it up from her memories she remembered the colour of the evening sky differently, and the words he said morphed and shifted around until all she was left with was a feeling. The sensation as he kissed her.

Now he was right in front of her again. It was like she could still feel the warmth in the air where he'd walked. The carefully constructed barriers in her mind were tumbling over and she felt if she could just concentrate hard enough it was like he was here, right here with her now. But he wasn't. He hadn't even seen her.

'Miss, please return to this side of the ticket barriers: we will be required to log this as an incident.'

# Chapter 21

Elle: *Love, you know I don't think you should be chasing guys but that stunt today?!*
*Wow.*
*That was CRAZY even for you.*
*I'm going to listen to this voice note again!!*
*Made my day :-)*

Sophie: *Are you okay @Helen?*
*Sounds quite stressful.*
*Are you going to receive a fine??*

Helen: *Could have been fined £1000.*
*So basically my life savings.*
*But luckily they took pity on me.*
*A poor woman with a broken case, wearing all the clothes she owns, and chasing after a guy she doesn't know.*

Elle: *So you're actually convinced you saw him??*
*You know that last time you thought you saw his dog.*

Helen: *I DID see his dog.*
*This time it was definitely him.*

Sophie: *Maybe this does mean something …*

Elle: *Yep, that Helen needs to get over Brody already.*
*Can we maybe have a new rule where we never mention*
*him again?*

Sophie: *@Elle not kind!!!*

Helen: *Actually that sounds like a great idea.*

Helen locked her phone and rested it down by her side. She looked around the same four walls of her flat: she knew every crack in the ceiling and misplaced tack where a previous, more domesticated tenant had hung a picture.

She was bored with herself. Her neediness. Her desperation. She had been over this a thousand times but this really was the end of her chasing men. Chasing Brody, or at least the idea she had of him in her mind, that was becoming blurrier by the day.

Imagine if she'd been fined? Imagine explaining this one to her mum who was already increasingly concerned about Helen's obvious spinsterhood. Imagine that this was the last piece of news Nanny G learned about her?

Time to change.

Helen wiped her eyes and marched briskly about her small flat. She put a wash on, took a shower, and threw together a tiramisu that she hoped Ish and his roomies would like. She was going to become that kind of organised, grown-up woman who always chose the right outfit, and bought the perfect gifts. Finally, she took out all of Nanny G's letters and organised them into a clear folder, ready for tomorrow. She went to bed early before any more thoughts of Brody could creep into her mind.

The last thing she needed right now was another dream about a handsome man who wore Havaianas.

Helen woke up slowly, spooning an oversized toy dog that she'd had since she was eight. Sleep was so nice, it was like a little break from being herself. She wearily put on a loose summer dress (the yellow one that Nanny G always liked) and made herself eat a bowl of sugar-free granola which bore an uncanny resemblance to the food Grandpa M used to give to his budgerigars.

Ish lived five minutes from Helen in a six-story Georgian house that had been spliced into maisonettes. The stone would have once been golden, but it had been covered in a Dickensian layer of London grime and soot. It felt out of place in the Victorian brick and warehouse maze of East London. She stood on the black and white tile doorstep and rang the buzzer.

'Hi! That Helen?'

'Yep, it's me.'

The door buzzed open and Helen walked up the twisting staircase. It had a faded red carpet with golden fleur de lis that once might have looked presidential. The door to apartment three was slightly ajar and she nervously pushed it open. On the left was a small bedroom, a guy wearing an Xbox headset nodded solemnly as she walked past. The whole apartment smelt vaguely of incense. She was surprised that anyone still used that.

The open plan living space had a samurai sword hanging off one wall, another sported a mandala tapestry swaying psychedelically in the breeze. Strange succulent plants were stacked along the window ledge, and all the sofas had all been pushed to the sides of the wall to make way for a heavy black sports mat in the centre of the room.

'What's that?!'

'Y'all right Helen? Nice to see you!' Ish waved awkwardly at her from behind the breakfast bar. It was almost as if his arms were too long for his body like a human-sized Mr Tickle. 'Well, that's a jade plant, easy to keep; and that's erm well, that's our Ju Jitsu practice mat. But sometimes we do a bit of yoga, meditation, you know that kind of thing. Anyway, can I get you a drink? Then let's crack onto those letters.'

Helen perched on the edge of the sofa, Ish's apartment had 'man cave' written all over it, 'Just a water is fine, thanks.'

'We have options, you know. Not those kinds of lads to just have half a pint of milk in the fridge. I actually don't even drink dairy these days. Sorry I'm ramblin'. How about a bulletproof coffee, cacao maca smoothie, or …' Ish drummed his equally gangly fingers on the kitchen counter, '… maybe a classic matcha iced latte, got some lovely coconut milk to put in that?'

'Dealer's choice?' shrugged Helen and accepted a long green drink with a faint hint of pineapple to it. 'I actually bought you a tiramisu, but you're dairy free?'

'And caffeine free. But as it's the famous baking blogger's dessert I'm gonna try some.' Ish pulled a spoon out of the drawer, and went to eat the tiramisu straight out of the bowl.

'You're not sharing then?'

'When it's this good, Mark and Raj are going to have to fight me for it!' Ish winked in the direction of the mat. 'Unless you wanted it?!' He dropped his spoon, eyes widening.

For the first time she noticed how his eyes were warm and deep.

'No, I'm fine thanks, had some already.' Helen lied, patting her stomach.

She pulled out her folder, and spread the letters out on the mat. She had to admit the weird green drink also wasn't so bad. She noticed Ish had given her a candy cane coloured reusable straw and put a pineapple chunk on the side of the glass, and was already ferreting through her stack of letters with enthusiasm.

'So, what we got? Ooh, I love an old postage stamp, me!' Ish gestured towards Nanny G's birthday card, he'd sat opposite her on the mat but kept his distance, tucking his long limbs under one another like a yogic octopus. Helen pushed the pile of letters towards him, and Ish started examining the front and back of each letter. 'This one's Deco!'

'How do you know that?'

'Did a bit of Art History. Moderns isn't my forte but I can recognise a classic little piece like this!' Ish cleared his throat. 'Sorry I'm buzzin' – vintage excites me way too much.'

He had a warm accent, the kind of voice that makes you want to sit down and put the kettle on.

'So, what do we know about our Vernon apart from his address 'ere?'

'Well, he met my nan when he took his brothers and sisters away to Cornwall to be evacuated, during the Blitz …'

'Ah, so 1939 then? Same year he wrote all these letters?'

'I think so …'

'Mint. If Vernon lived at 292 Lionel Road in 1939 then chances are he would be on the 1939 register. They took it for ration cards and all that, so we know where everyone lived. Good timing for him to have a bit of a flirt with yer nan.'

Ish pulled out his laptop and started typing away. 'I've got a subscription to Ancestry so this should be easy … Right there you go.'

Ish spun the laptop around and Helen read the record:

Address: 292 Lionel Road
Schedule: 101
Surnames & other names: Vernon F Newman
M or F: M
Birth Day: 20 May
Birth Year: 1918
S, M, W or D: M

'Give over. Well, that bit's interesting …' Ish pointed to the 'M' and raised an eyebrow.

'Does that mean …'

117

'Yep, our Vernon was a married man. Explains why he disappeared off and never came back. Looks like he had quite a few kids too.'

'It just doesn't make sense, why write all these letters, if you're married??' Helen felt herself shudder, what was wrong with romance at the moment? It felt like the possibility of true love kept being trampled on by unfaithful husbands, and dating app server failures.

'You're a nice woman, Helen.'

'Why do you say that?'

'Only seeing th' good in people. Look, we dunno, maybe he was unhappy, maybe he had to stay married, maybe he was just cheating scum, but the records don't lie.'

'Any idea if he's still alive now?'

'If so, he'll have got his letter from the Queen! Sorry not the time for a joke …' Ish's thumbs accelerated around one another nervously '… well we can search death records, they're not released until over a hundred years after someone was born, and to be honest often take longer than that.'

'Ish?' His deep brown eyes met Helen's for the first time that day. 'Are you moonlighting as Sherlock Holmes in your next video by any chance?'

'Ha. More like Watson.' Ish sat more upright and ran a hand through his thick, dark hair. 'So, what we can do is take a look and see if he still lives at that address now. Plenty a dodgy internet company that will tell me who lives at any address for a £15 a month subscription.' Ish made a grimace and began typing away again.

Helen tried to sweep that disappointed feeling that had settled in her stomach to one side. Why did Vernon have to turn out to be one of those guys? And why wasn't she in Brody's Tesla driving down the Amalfi coast? Or at least having a coffee with him? Because really what would someone like Helen be doing in a sports car on the Amalfi coast anyway?

She felt a pat on her hand. 'Don't be down now. It's only one bad bloke.' Ish studied the laptop screen. 'So he doesn't live there now, by the looks of things, so he may well be dead. If that'll cheer you up?'

Helen felt that restrictive feeling in her throat again and a tear (why was she always crying lately?). She turned to the side and tried to wipe the corners of her eyes with her dress sleeve.

'Hels, Hels, look if you weren't a strange woman in my apartment, I'd offer yer a hug.' Ish's hand resumed gently patting hers like she was a tiny forest creature. 'Best I can suggest now is we take a drive over to Ealing, chat to some neighbours, see what's what; and if anyone remembers anything maybe it will be a funny story to tell your nan. Plus, the good news is the person who does live at his address shares Vernon's surname, so we've got a hot lead right there.'

'You've got a car?'

'Yep, nothing fancy. Parked outside. Like to drive home and see me mum on the weekends like a good boy.'

'And the famous vlogger @Ishtory has nothing better to do today?'

'Well just some editing but it's a nice day and I like a bit of spontaneity.'

Someone with Vernon's surname? It had to be a relative, probably a descendent? Maybe they'd inherited the house after Vernon had died, or maybe he was in a nursing home nearby? It was *possible*. Even if she couldn't catch Brody before he got on the train, maybe this smaller wish could work out? Hope squeezed in Helen like a sponge.

Ish had a small, black Golf parked just on the street outside his apartment block. Squeezing into the (not untidy) car, Helen ducked under the various rosary beads that were dangling down from his rear-view mirror.

'Are you Catholic?!'

'No, I just like vintage crucifixes. Hopefully, many years of

119

good vibes and prayers in that,' said Ish, unravelling the beads from the mirror and throwing them on the back seat. 'So, apart from chasing around after hundred-year-old players, what else can I know about you? How's the business?'

'I think calling it a business may be a stretch. It's just me. It's going okay.'

'Ah, very insightful. We'll leave that topic there then. But I'll just tell you right now, I often feel the same ...' Ish smiled. 'Favourite food?'

'Hmmmm, peanut butter and jam sandwiches.'

'A classic! Not the same on gluten-free bread unfortunately. Star sign?'

'Libra.'

'You're indecisive?'

'You know about astrology?'

'Only when it comes to saying the odd corny chat-up line.' Ish faintly smiled. 'How's the love life?'

'Oh God.'

'Okay ... Well sat nav says forty-five minutes so what are we going to chat about until then?'

Helen shrugged and felt her stomach grumble.

'How about a game of I spy? Come on, it'll be a laugh. I'll start, then you can think of the next one. I spy with my little eye something beginning with 'B'.'

Brody?

'Building?'

'Nope.'

'Brick?'

'Nope.'

'I give up.'

'Ya only had two goes, are you sure?'

'I'm sure.'

'Beech. As in the tree.'

'That's hard, Ish, you can't go level eight difficulty on our first round of I spy!' Helen twisted in her seat and swatted Ish on the arm.

'Okay next game: first person to name five types of dinosaur wins.'

'A don't-even-go-there-saurus.' Helen swatted Ish again, but noticed she was smiling in the rear-view mirror.

'What about a you're-not-even-trying-rex?' Ish's eyes met hers in the reflection.

By the time they got to Ealing, Helen had managed to remember seven.

# Chapter 22

Lionel Road was a stretch of houses made from little red bricks, with even smaller little green doors. Apart from some double glazing, not much looked like it had changed since 1939. Helen could just imagine Vernon stepping outside of the front door, brushing past the limp daffodils outside his door, and tipping his hat to his neighbours. He'd be suspiciously charming like that.

Helen and Ish leaned against his Golf and eyeballed the door to 292. Net curtains hung in the living room windows. A prim white planter sat on the doorstep, with a few loose stalks hanging out of it.

'So, are you going to knock?' Ish nodded towards the door.

'I can't knock! I don't know them. What am I going to say?' Helen hissed.

'That you're on the hunt for a (probably deceased) man that your nan had a wild fling with in 1939 and can they help you with that.'

'It wasn't a fling … at least not for Nanny G.' In reality, Nanny G probably wouldn't object to that word, thought Helen.

'All right then.' Ish stepped forwards and knocked loudly on the door of 292.

'Ish … you can't do that! We don't *know* them.'

'Well, we will soon … Hi!' Ish smiled awkwardly at a little old lady who only half filled up the door. She had small, shrewd, pale blue eyes, and tributaries of wrinkles over her face. Her little remaining hair was folded into neat curls close to her head, clipped close with bobby pins.

'We're looking for a man called Vernon, he lived here, well a long time ago …'

The woman's eyes narrowed. 'And how do you know Vernon?'

'It was my nan who knew Vernon. During the war …' Helen looked hopefully at the old woman.

The flicker of a smile moved her thin lips. 'Oh well you better come inside then,' said the woman in an unexpectedly gravelly voice.

She stepped back from the door and manoeuvred slowly through the narrow corridors of her house, gently tracing her hands along the walls for balance. The living room was dominated by an old dresser. The shelves had collections of snow globes on them, miniature porcelain figurines of children dancing, and a fake bowl of fruit next to an even faker potted plant with large purple tinged leaves.

Helen and Ish sat rigidly in her sitting room, the sound of a carriage clock persistently ticking away in the background. The chairs reminded Helen of Goldilocks and the Three Bears: one was far too hard (Ish had sat in it) and the one Helen was in was far too soft, her thighs were being absorbed by the memory foam cushions like a dinosaur trapped in primordial goo.

Through the serving hatch, Helen could see the old woman moving around the kitchen and there was the sound of rattling china. She brought them a small tray of custard creams and tea, and sat primly in her chair revolving her thumbs in small circles around one another. She took a half pint of milk and poured it into the cups, Helen's eyes widened noticing the milk was two months out of date.

'Don't worry love, it's been frozen. You have to have a system when you're my age and you live alone.' The lady straightened her back. 'So you want to know about Vernon?'

'Yes, we do. Is he … still alive?' Bad question, Helen! What if this woman was mourning him? Ish looked like he was about to choke on his custard cream. She was always so …

'No,' the woman smiled coyly, 'he's not. Died in 1958, heart attack. Not really surprising. So, I suppose you want to know who I am? I am Vernon's daughter. His second daughter. Violet Joyce Muriel Newman.'

'Ah, yes we saw your name on the 1939 register; you've lived here this whole time?'

'I do hope this isn't one of those scams?' Violet's eyes narrowed.

Helen thought any con man would have his work cut out getting anything past her.

'No, no. My friend Helen here, her nan met your father in 1939, and …' Ish scrunched his eyebrows together looking for the right word, '… they had a brief liaison, they exchanged some letters … we were just seeing if we could finish the story.'

The old lady let out a guttural chuckle. 'Oh well, you've definitely got the right Vernon. My father was a terrible womaniser. Too good-looking, too much time on his hands. He never really worked; it was all my poor mother; anyway, not a week would go by without another woman's name being mentioned in this house. Even I was christened after two of his mistresses, can you believe it? My poor mother here, ill in bed after giving birth, and he comes home after registering me, oh so pleased with himself to have given me their names!!'

'Was he really all bad?' Helen winced.

The woman chuckled again. 'My dear he wasn't bad at all, that was the problem! He loved women. Loved spending time with them, speaking to them,' Violet dropped her voice, 'taking them to bed. And they loved him too. We all did. He was fun and exciting, and well it was the war. Times were different then. Of course, my mother suffered having to stay with him, but you couldn't leave in those days. He was born in the North …'

'Where all the best lads are from …' Ish paused awkwardly. 'Sorry.'

'Then he was a sailor. Covered in tattoos under his dress shirts.' Violet reached onto her coffee table and leafed open a photo album. She opened it like a box of chocolates and turned to a page with a large black and white photo on it, showing a rangy man with thick black hair, a smirk, penetrating eyes, and a huge tattoo of a moon rising on his chest.

'Well, that's the full moon rising,' thought Helen. Proof that Vernon's shirt (at least) had definitely been off. She gave a small shake of her head to get rid of the unhelpfully graphic image her brain had conjured up. Why was she such a prude? It was *the war* after all. No wonder she was so horrible with … Helen, do not make this all about yourself again!

'I know this is probably the wrong thing to ask but would I be able to take a picture of that? It's not for the internet or anything, just for my nan – she's not feeling too well, and I think she'd love to see him …'

'Bit of eye candy, our Vernon,' winked Ish.

'You see, she still talks about your dad to this day.'

Violet let out a whoop and slapped her hands down on her knees. 'Oh he did a good job on her didn't he? And that was our father, spends a day dropping his evacuated youngest in Cornwall, and walks away with a girlfriend. Of course, you can take a picture.' Violet twizzled the album towards Helen who awkwardly snapped her photo like a self-conscious tourist taking pictures of pigeons in Trafalgar Square.

'Anyway, then he was a bus driver in London. After that, did a bit of what he called 'security work' whatever that meant. I had to put that down as my father's profession on my marriage certificate in 1942 so that's how I remember. I wore a lovely A-line skirt, shortened to the knee. Not much fabric around back then. Rations and things. Anyway … my father's work … to me that was a way of saying that he didn't do very much, and what he did was done at night, with alcohol. Any easy excuse to slip off and visit Violet, Joyce or whoever was flavour of the week back then. And as you can imagine all those good times, and good women, eventually caught up with him. I found him at the bottom of the stairs there one day, dead as a dodo. Poor sod. It finally all caught up with him. But he was a lovely man. He was a good father, and I miss him terribly.' Violet dabbed the corner of her eyes with a pocket hanky.

Helen could see the initials VFN sewn into the corner. The polished wooden stair banister leaned ominously in the background.

'I have some letters he wrote … he wrote to my nan every week for months. If you'd like to see them?' Helen slipped out the folder and handed Violet the letters. Violet gingerly began leafing through the folder, the smile of a distant memory creeping back onto her lips.

'He wrote to her? Ah he only did that with the special ones. I imagine your nan was a lovely looking girl, just like you,' Violet said with surprising warmth. Helen noticed Ish was smiling too. Was he standing up straighter than usual?

'She wa-, she is. She's still lovely.'

'So what's the matter with her?'

'At the moment pneumonia, but she's had her fair share of things …'

'I know how that is. First it was my hip. Then my knee. Then glaucoma. I take it she's told you it's no fun being old?'

'Something like that …'

'Well send her my love, I've enjoyed reading these …' Violet handed the folder back quickly, like if she held on to it for too long, she wouldn't want to let it go.

'Thank you for all your help, Mrs Newman,' said Ish.

'I don't get many visitors, and well this has been wonderful.' Violet folded the handkerchief back up gently into her pocket.

'I'll post you copies of the letters if you like?'

'I would like that very much. Just when you think life doesn't have any new surprises, something like this shows up.'

# Chapter 23

Helen was plaiting the ends of her hair on the bus. Last night there had been some talk of her and Ish grabbing drinks after their adventures in Ealing, but Helen felt tired from the day. She'd wandered back to her apartment like a zombie, all the energy had drained out of her. The excitement of *maybe* meeting Vernon had plastered over the disappointment of not catching Brody before he got on his train, but now that feeling was soaking back through. She wasn't in the mood for social drinks, even with someone as nice as Ish.

Plus, from now on she was trying to be more responsible. The kind of person who went to bed early, and sat at her desk (read: kitchen table) by 9 a.m. ready to work. She'd even stopped procrasta-cooking herself elaborate breakfasts and had a two-day hot streak on the sugar-free granola.

Life felt a bit deflated; there was an empty space in her mind where Brody used to be. But she would have to get used to that, and eventually (as in by the next month at the latest, and definitely before her next birthday), force herself back onto Connex. She wanted to meet someone. She would meet someone. Carl, Saf and Eddy probably weren't *that* bad.

Besides, she'd already woken up to a text this morning that was better than any one guy could send her:

*Helen. Nanny G here reporting for duty! The doctor has
finally said I'm getting better. He actually made an affirm-
ative statement about it! Your mother still has me under
house arrest but I can feel I'm on the mend. I've tried
looking at your Instagram but there's never anything new
these days? I do hope you're okay. I will look forward to
speaking in a week or two once I've gotten my breath back!*

Helen smiled thinking about how she was going to spring the
young Vernon photo on Nanny G, like some 1940s Chippendale.
She should wait to do it in person, Nanny G's face would be
priceless. She put her phone in her bag and went back to making
braids in her hair. The rain had stopped, giving the streets a watery
sheen and for once Helen had remembered both her umbrella
and her sunglasses. It was going to be a good day.

Helen was on her way to meet Sophie and Frank.

There had been a zippy urgency in Sophie's messages lately.
She'd been using a lot more emojis than usual, and had booked
a catch-up with Helen for the day after she got back from Tulum
(despite the fact they would still be jet lagged and Frank would
undoubtedly have a red nose.) Sophie had fudged some excuse
about spare holiday days that didn't sound quite right; and why
bring Frank at all? He was lovely (of course) but in a kind of
dependable, dutiful (okay boring!) way. The kind of guy who
would sit on the 'man seats' whilst you went shopping, or go
along to karaoke, and not be able to tell you one song that had
been played.

They'd decided to meet in the city as a halfway point between
Helen's Hackney studio, and Sophie … no, Sophie and Frank's
two bed in Wapping. Helen paused for a second to consider the
luxury of having a spare second bedroom as an office, or maybe
not having to sleep in the same room as your dishwasher.

She pushed the doors open to the bar in the city: it was all
marble-tiled floors, and golden metal rimmed tables. Her eyes

immediately saw Frank with his arm around Sophie, and zoomed in on a huge diamond ring nestled on her finger. Of course. How Helen zeroed in on that detail so quickly she didn't really know, it was becoming a reflex as people around her started gathering up rings like magpies. It gave her time to prepare the expression on her face, so she could tidy away the emotions on her face into a smile.

'OMG Sophie you're *engaged*! Congratulations!' Sophie stood up and gave Helen a hug. She always felt tiny when she hugged her, Helen wished her bones were smaller sometimes. It would be nice to be petite. 'Frank, good man! I knew you'd do it!'

'Well, I couldn't let this one walk away.' Frank never gave a witty response to anything.

'I wanted to tell you in person before posting anything on socials.' Sophie squeezed her eyes slightly and spoke with an edge of tension like she was trying to deactivate a bomb.

Be nice Helen. Be positive. Why wasn't she gushing about the colour scheme, the bridesmaids' dresses? Why, in moments like these, did she miss the simpler days when Sophie was equally, perilously single, and they could fall asleep spooning after a night out in uncomfy high heels? Helen was big spoon of course.

Why was it so disappointing that Sophie no longer sent her play-by-play screenshots of messages with guys that she liked, that were soon to be proclaimed 'neverminds.' That when she did go out with Helen it was for an increasing amount of brunches, and apologies of 'I should go home, prosecco really goes to my head.' Where had the Sophie she knew gone? The one who had once got tipsy from eating all the fruit floating in a sangria jug? Where had the dancing to Britney songs in the noughties evaporated to? How could that be over a decade ago? How come Helen didn't have her flat keys anymore?

'It was so romantic, I just didn't see it coming. I mean the trip in itself was such an amazing present, honestly Helen you have to go, you'd love it there,' Sophie spoke so rapidly she was starting to sound out of breath, Helen leaned in and forced eye contact to look more attentive as her knees started an uncontrollable jiggle beneath the table.

'Anyway, we had one of those villas with a pool that led up to our room, and the evening of my birthday Frank had scattered a path of rose petals from the pool to the beach. That's where he got down on one knee! I honestly didn't have a clue what was going on. No intuition at all! But anyway, he said he didn't want another day to go by without me being his wife!'

Frank looked down into his orange juice. Helen looked down at her hands. Sophie looked down at her ring.

'Honestly, this is the best news.' Helen pressed her abdomen into the table like it would somehow keep all the pieces of her together. Breathe Helen. Breathe and smile. Fight that uncomfortable balloon of feelings that's rising in your stomach. She gave herself a shake.

Sophie and Frank were back to holding hands expectantly; Helen needed to say something more to acknowledge the gravitas of this occasion. She needed to ask questions about whether they were going to have a summer wedding, had they thought about venues yet, did they want her to bake a cake … The words were lodged stubbornly in her throat though, and Helen worried that if she even started to speak the smile would fall off her face and be replaced with … envy? Was she really jealous of her best friend?

She should be happy. She was happy. This was true love! She looked at Frank, and her mood softened. Okay so it wasn't quite like the fairy tales, but it was beautiful in its own way.

'So does this mean I'm invited to the wedding?' Helen smiled. 'Or if you need someone to bake a cake …?'

'Of course, you are!' Sophie cast a relieved look at Frank. 'It won't be for a while. Lots to plan and organise, but we're actually thinking of doing an engagement party soon.'

'Oh that will be fun!'

'Drinking, dancing, excellent Chinese food …' ventured Frank. 'You're welcome to bring a plus one of course.'

Sophie winced for a millisecond.

Helen gazed around the walls of the café. Just breathe Helen. You've got this. It was one of those cafés that had been created specifically to look good in Instagram pictures. All pastel walls, hanging plants and a very distinct golden trellising on either side of the bar. Helen did a double take. 'Sorry, I don't want to be rude, I just need to check something.'

Helen fumbled through her bag for her phone, and scrolled back a month through her pictures. Gold trellising. There was Brody holding his dog under one arm, a green juice in the other, standing against a gold trellis background.

'This is the bar where Brody's profile picture was taken. Sorry I know I'm not supposed to be talking about myself, I just never knew where it was …' Helen's mind drew a mental map and realised WeWork was about a five-minute walk away.

'That's so spooky! Can you imagine Frank, we chose this café out of all the cafés to meet Helen in, and it's the one!' enthused Sophie unfazed by Helen hijacking her engagement announcement to talk about that guy that she'd been on a date with once.

'I'm sorry.'

'We need to get you a sorry jar, Helen the amount you use that word,' Frank chuckled, looking at Sophie to check if his joke was appropriate. She put a hand gently on his knee.

'What do you think this means?' Her eyes were fizzing again.

'That I should probably delete this photo and turn myself in as a stalker?'

'No there must be a *reason* … have you searched this place on Instagram? For that picture?' Sophie already had her phone in her hand.

Helen opened up Instagram and searched for James & Jim Juice. There were a lot of posts. Instagram types with heavy amounts of lip liner and too white smiles, leaning over iridescent juices. Then there it was: Brody's picture. She thought he didn't have socials? Helen clicked through to the account @aliceimagines.

Alice?!

*Hanging out with this cute one, and the owner's okay too @jamesandjimjuice.*

It wasn't Brody's account. It belonged to a woman with a sheet of silvery blonde hair, and lots of interesting rings on her fingers. Oh. God.

She scrolled through the pictures.

Skiing in Courchevel last Christmas.

A loo selfie at Shoreditch House.

On the beach in Tulum (had everyone been there except Helen?!)

Alice had been everywhere. A bit like the fictional character. She even had the blonde hair and penchant for hair accessories to match.

Helen scrolled to see if she could see any more pictures of Brody. He appeared occasionally with his dog who Helen now knew was called Bean. He was with her in Thailand in locust pose about to go on a ten-day silent retreat. He stood covered in dust wearing a feathered fedora and goggles next to her at Burning Man. And yes, he'd been to Tulum.

None of the posts were that romantic, but look at her! She looked like Grace Kelly to Helen's … well Helen didn't look like anyone. Alice had great style, an enviable travel budget and really nice hair. The sleek, perfectly straight kind Helen always envied on girls at school. She started unplaiting her braids. She just needed to wash and blow-dry her hair more often, then it wasn't that bad.

'I wouldn't say that it looks totally romantic … I mean yes there's a lot of pictures of Brody but none are sort of couply photos, what do you think?' Sophie was rotating Helen's phone in her hand, her diamond ring blinking as it twisted in the sunlight.

Helen thought of Vernon. 'I'm not sure … I mean it's definitely not #couplesgoals like your pictures from Tulum.'

'Why don't you message her?' Sophie gestured to the messaging feature.

'What if she's his girlfriend?' Helen pushed the phone away from her on the table like it could explode on contact.

'I'm sure Elle would say he deserves to be caught?' Sophie paused. 'Though maybe that's not very kind?' Her voice had a funny upwards inflection every time she considered doing anything 'naughty'. Sophie was incredibly law-abiding, the sort of person who wouldn't dream of being 'unkind' and who actively informed her accounts department that she needed to pay more tax on her bonus.

'You don't think it looks desperate? How do I explain that I found the account?' There was no real good way of saying, 'So I've been following your movements for weeks and I was excited to finally have a break in the case …'

'I'm sure we can work out a way to put it across, if that's what you want Helen?' Sophie's hand was now squeezing her knee.

'I'll think about it.' Which really meant she had some googling to do.

# Chapter 24

Helen was now a serial stalker.

Lines had been crossed in her pursuit of Brody, and the latest was creating a fake Instagram account to follow Alice's stories and posts. She'd even set up alerts. She was no better than Helen's social media stalker Dk1113.

She'd recently learned that Alice had attended one of those Pilate's classes with the scary machines, drank unearthly amounts of kombucha (which no one actually likes) and was a songwriter. As far as Helen could tell, being a songwriter roughly equated to being photographed in cool places with cool people and having a seemingly endless budget.

Helen had googled Alice's work, expecting to find that she had some kind of trust fund paying the bills with song writing as her cover story, and felt bad to realise that Alice had in fact written quite a few really good songs. All by herself. A successful, self-made woman, with perfect hair; Helen struggled back the urge to dislike her.

Elle: *She wrote 'Light Me Up'. I LOVE that song. We should make friends with this girl!*

Sophie: *Gosh that was actually on our short list for wedding songs. How weird?!*

Elle: *'Light me up, up, up, like a firework! Show up, up, up, with what you're worth!' That song is all me.*

Sophie: *So, what does this all mean?*

Elle: *NADA.*
*You guys always have to find meaning in everything! It's just coincidence.*

Helen: *I think I want to see him again.*

Elle: 😑

Sophie: *Are you going to contact Alice?*

Helen: *I actually had another idea. You promise to tell me if I'm being crazy?*

Elle: *Are you going to try and jump a train again?*

Helen: *No but … I saw they were going to a festival …*

Sophie: *How do you know? Are they following it?*

Helen: *Alice's friends keep tagging her in posts about it. And in her IG stories there was this picture.*

Helen sent a picture of Alice holding Bean in matching diamanté chokers with the hashtag #shipwreckedready. If you searched the hashtag you could see enthusiastic posts from hipsters trying on their outfits and packing up their backpacks.

*I mean she's not going with Brody's dog*
*right??*
*She has to be going with Brody.*
*The festival is in Cornwall too, so I think it's 90% likely*
*he'll be there.*

Sophie: *It certainly sounds like he'll be there …*
*But are you sure it's good for your mental health to go all*
*the way to a festival in Cornwall to find him?*
*Of course, I'll support your decision whatever happens, but*
*I worry!*

Elle: *What's wrong with just sliding a DM?*
*Are you sure Brody isn't in her followers?*

Helen: *He's definitely not on there …*
*I know it sounds mad but I think if I could just see him*
*again it would be better.*
*I don't know if they're a couple or not.*
*I don't want to be chasing him.*

Elle: *Babe you are chasing him!*

Helen: *I thought if I saw him again.*

Sophie: *It's really romantic.*

Elle: *It's really a lot more effort than a party at WeWork …*

Sophie: *I just don't want you to get let down. Have you got*
*a link to the festival?*

Helen sent them a link to the festival's homepage:

*Ship/Wrecked Festival*
*There be magic in these coves.*
*Magic. Community. Wonderment.*
*Expect the unexpected.*
*Polveath Cove, Kernow.*
*June 20 – June 23*

The website had a swirling cartoon in pastel colours of pirate ships on huge waves, treasure boxes exploding with fireworks and strange technicolour gnomes. Helen wondered what art period Ish would sum this up as.

Of course, Helen wouldn't precisely call herself a festival lover. Again, at the plight of her being in any way cool, she'd dodged ever actually attending a real festival. She'd been to a day festival once just outside of London and her main memory of it had been long queues for everything, a lack of toilets and picking small flecks of glitter off her body weeks later.

The core issue with her not really being 'up for' festivals in the past was probably that Helen was chronically unable to 'go with the flow'.

She didn't get 'playing it by ear' or 'let's just see what happens.' She liked to know she'd be sleeping in a comfy bed, that a fridge full of food was just there, and there was absolutely no chance of her getting cold.

Donning welly boots, a skimpy floral dress, and braving the elements like an ingenue Kate Moss was never going to happen.

Had she just described Alice?

She really needed to stop following her as soon as she met Brody again.

But she couldn't go alone. It was one thing to casually bump into him again at a festival in Cornwall (I mean, she was Cornish after all …) with a group of cool friends, looking cool, and absolutely not like this moment meant everything to her. It would be quite something else to have to turn up by herself, and start a conversation with him when he would probably be there with Alice, and his other cool friends, anyway. She couldn't do it. She would wither in front of someone like Alice. It would be just like when she sent Oliver Hamilton a love poem in year eight, and he and his friends had run around the school corridors singing phrases from it after her.

'*Oliver you make my heart beat, it's you one on one I want to meet …*'

She was not going through that again.

Helen messaged Sophie one to one. This was hard enough anyway without Elle scoffing something like 'who attends festivals in the UK anyway?'

Helen: *I know this is a big ask – but can you come with me?*
*We can stay at my parents, then head over on Friday to Ship/Wrecked?*
*I'm not a festival person either but maybe it could be fun?*
*Though Cornwall has more cider than sangria?*

Sophie: *I can't.*

Helen's internal Jenga tower of feelings wobbled.

Sophie: *I feel so bad.*
*Frank's parents are in London that weekend … wedding planning stuff.*
*But honestly you should go!*

Of course Sophie couldn't traipse over to some random festival with her, because Sophie was now a real grown-up, with a fiancé, family commitments and a house deposit. Helen took a moment to hold her phone to her chest and breathe.

Helen: *I can't go alone!!*

Sophie: *What about Elle?*

Helen: *Can you see Elle at a festival? She's going to make me feel \*this\* small for even wanting to go.*

Sophie: *Henry? You guys were always tight?*

Helen: *He'll think I'm crazy … besides you know Henry, he's so square he's a cube. At least I'm only a 2D square.*

Sophie: *Anna?*

Helen: *Haven't hung out with her in ages. You're the only person I can ask.*

Sophie: *I'm so sorry Hels.*

Helen: *It's okay, I understand.*

Helen didn't understand. She couldn't process how she was the last woman left standing; her singleness had become an island. All her friends had sailed away on earlier boats whilst being single was still fun, and left Helen stranded, the water rising, with the little parts that made single life actually enjoyable gradually evaporating.

Helen's phone buzzed again.

Ish: *Hels – how are ya?*

Helen: *Hi Watson ;-)*

Ish: *Yeah that is me isn't it? What are you up to?*

Helen: *Whole lotta nothing.*

Ish: *Not even baking?*

Helen: *I'm on strike.*

Ish: *Ah that's a shame because I had some ideas for your videos …*
*Thought maybe we could get a drink next week?*
*Whenever you're free?*

Helen: *How about tonight?*

Ish: *Should I get used to this level of spontaneity from you?*

Helen: *Definitely not!*

Helen dragged on some blue jeans, a white T-shirt and her beloved Converse trainers. The sun was still warm in the sky, she really should be working … The problem was that she had blogger's block. Which she could probably re-name as Brody block. Every time she sat down to write a post, the words didn't flow. She could focus for about fifteen minutes at a time (provided she had some Lindt chocolates or a Diet Coke on hand), after that her attention would drift off. Like some virtual reality simulator, her brain ran through a hundred different scenarios of what meeting Brody again could be like, helpfully zeroing in on any obscure eventualities ('the festival loos don't have proper locks and he walks in on me!') that would leave her humiliated. With all that creative brain power on diversion towards anxiety, it was unsurprising she wasn't feeling creative in her work. After an hour of trying, all she'd come up with was some woefully humdrum comments.

'It's delicious alongside sliced apples, carrots or even pretzels!'

'So easy anyone can prepare it!'

She'd gone from being borderline cool, or at least a passable writer, to churning out lines that made her sound like some overly chipper, cardigan-wrapped judge on Bake Off Britain.

All her analytics told her that her follower numbers, engagement levels, social media reach were down with scary percentages like minus 276 per cent. Was that even mathematically possible?

If there was ever a time to meet Mr sixty-seven thousand followers (thank you very much) it was now.

Plus, Ish was just Ish: nice, non-threatening. He didn't make her feel awkward. She didn't have to worry they wouldn't have anything to talk about. Or that he'd suggest a flimsy reason to go back to his place, 'I have this samurai sword …' He would just be pleasantly normal. He could even give her his man-pinion on the whole Brody drama. And mainly, Helen really felt like now was a good time to cave in and have a glass of wine.

Helen: *Where do you want to meet?*

Ish: *Your first clue …*

Helen: *Ish I just want a drink!*

Ish: *Don't worry I kept this easy for ya!*
*Difficulty level 4 at best …*

Helen: *Okay*

Ish: *Start where I left you a plaster for your foot,*
*Look across the river for something covered in soot.*
*Follow the sherbet houses down,*
*It's in an Ivy House where I'll be found.*
*PS Don't use Google Maps – you got this! ;-)*

Helen liked planning; Ish liked playing. Everything was a game to him. It wasn't a bad characteristic, it was nice to hang out with someone who wasn't prone to overthinking everything, but at other times Helen wished she could just have a serious conversation with him. Why had he written a riddle for a Monday night drink?

Helen set off to the bench on the canal where Ish had left a blister plaster the first night they met. Looking at the old towpath, Helen was pleased to notice she didn't feel afraid. She didn't remember the brown beanie guy lurking one foot out of the shadows; that memory had been obscured by the thought of Ish and his yellow bike. His jacket with too many pockets, and the plaster left at the halfway point between them. She sat on the bench and looked at the skyline, and felt her lips curving into a smile.

Loaning her the plaster was sweet of him … She felt a twinge of affection for Ish. With Sophie out of action on account of being in love, she could do with a new confidante. Someone to drink rosé wine with, and someone who would sit there patiently as she unravelled the whole Brody saga in front of them.

She saw The Shard in the distance. She'd met Jonathan there for dinner once, dressed up and excited to see him after he'd been blanking her for a couple of weeks. She remembered spending hours perfecting her make-up, and choosing the right dress, thinking that night would be their reconciliation … then they'd fought over dinner. He'd wanted to take a picture of them both to send to his family, Helen had felt too nervous to do it. After two weeks of not hearing from him, it felt forced, fake. He'd paid the bill, stormed out into a black taxi and left her standing on the street. She didn't hear from him for another two weeks after that …

Had it been her fault? Had he picked the fight? Her memories of him were so muddled it was hard to tell. She felt a familiar pinch in her gut thinking about him, and an even

143

bigger squeeze knowing he had found true love, and she had lost hers.

She shook slightly, hoping the memory would evaporate off her like drops of water. Helen looked back at the skyline: graffiti marching up old brick buildings, a skeletal gasometer, and a row of old factories across the canal.

Factories = soot?

That sounded about right, surely Ish wouldn't make her walk all that far? Helen walked over the bridge and around the corner to a row of old factory buildings. They'd been painted teal, yellow, pink, and now housed trendy coffee bars, bike shops, and an Apple Mac repair store. She followed the corner around past the pink building to see a wall of Ivy. On the wall was a metal placard that read, 'The Secret Garden'.

Helen pushed against a heavy metal door. She knocked and a slat opened.

'Hi, is this the Ivy House?'

'Name?'

'Helen Pines, I'm here to see Ish?'

'Come right on in.'

The door opened onto a courtyard garden. Bees clung to lavender stalks coming out of old ceramic pots. Fairy lights were just blinking on as dusk fell, criss-crossed above them. Ish was sitting at the back near a large honeysuckle plant; wearing a slim cut blazer and Chelsea boots. Helen wasn't used to seeing him in anything other than fancy dress, staring down at her Converse she'd clearly missed the memo on what to wear.

Seeing Helen walk through the door, Ish stood up, shaking the table as he tried to extract his long legs out from beneath it.

'Ish, this is so nice!' Was it too nice? Helen brushed the thought aside and knotted the end of her T-shirt so it looked like she'd made some kind of effort. She never managed to nail the dress code for anything.

'Ah well you know … so how have you been? Spoken to

144

Nanny G yet?'

'Not yet. I actually think I'm going to go to Cornwall next week so I'm saving it up to tell her in person.'

'Ah nice – I think I'll go home that week too. Any special occasion?'

Helen paused, picked up the drinks list in her hands and pretended to look very interested in what a hibiscus fizz was. She had planned to tell everything to Ish, like she'd just met up with Elle and Sophie for a catch up; but looking around at the fairy lights, the cocktails, it suddenly didn't feel quite so much like two friends catching up.

But she should be honest, shouldn't she? Not telling Ish that she was going to Cornwall in the hopes of seeing Brody would feel a bit like she was keeping her options open. It would be a bit like Elle, wouldn't it? Maybe even a bit like Jonathan … She liked Ish as a person, but she wasn't ready to give up on Brody just like that, and if she lied about it, wouldn't that be leading Ish on?

'Well, I think I'm going to go to this festival called Ship/ Wrecked.'

'I've heard of that, can't say I imagined it being your kinda thing though?'

'It isn't,' Helen took a deep breath, the Brody story edging its way out of her mouth. 'There's a guy I like who's going. So, I thought I'd meet him there.'

'Oh really?' Ish shifted slightly in his seat. 'How long have you guys been seeing each other for?'

'Well … the thing is …'

'Try me Hels. Remember I never judge anyone … I'm your friendly neighbourhood Ish.'

'Well, we met once, a month or two ago, on a dating app. Have you ever had that before where you've met someone and just felt like "okay this is going to be my next serious relationship?" Like an instant connection?' Helen paused searching Ish's face for a sign of recognition. 'Anyway I really got that with him, and I'm pretty sure he felt the same but then the app crashed …'

'Ah yep, Connex server failure, that was all over socials …'

'So, I lost his match and I've been trying to find him ever since. In a nutshell.' Helen knotted her fingers in her lap and looked up at Ish.

'That's you all over I think, always on the hunt for something …' Ish leaned back slightly more in his chair. His arms were gently folded now.

'Honestly, my life isn't normally like this!'

'Are you sure?' Ish looked right at her.

Helen thought about her relationship with Jonathan. It wasn't really comparable. She'd made more effort than he had, probably? No, she definitely had. It was like she turned up to be with him month after month, and there was always something that got in the way. He was stressed with work, he wanted to give it more time, he was still hurting from his last break up …

She should have moved on sooner, finally stuck up for herself and been the one to walk away: but she couldn't. In her mind somewhere, Jonathan loomed high like being with this smart, successful guy was an achievement worth grasping for; that if he liked her then she must be worthwhile? That if they could just be together, the credits would roll and everything would be perfect.

But Brody was different to Jonathan: nicer, humbler, a better kisser …

'I don't know, maybe?'

'Just ya know they say that happiness is the path, not the destination …'

'Is this something you learned whilst buying your samurai sword?' Helen smiled and felt her leg brush up against Ish's under the too-small table. She quickly pulled it back towards her.

'All right, all right now. I think it was Buddha: but I want you to listen to my point. It's like you could be searching … searching for something to show yerself you've finally made it. Meeting some guy, getting so and so many followers, whatever, to make you happy, but that's just perception. What gives you the potential for happiness could be right here already. You know, in the present.'

'Is this my Ish pearl of wisdom for the day?' Helen couldn't help but smile.

'Well, I was also gonna let ya know your video editing needs a little work …' Ish grinned as Helen kicked him under the table.

'Okay, one last serious point and then we can talk shop. Go to any festival you want if it makes you happy, but don't try to chase one idea of happiness too much, all right?' So, Ish could be serious.

'Does this mean you're not going to use your @Ishtory knowledge to help me think up the perfect costume? Or come with me …?'

Ish smiled at Helen like he knew something she didn't. 'This might be one goose chase I'll leave it down to you to figure out.'

# Chapter 25

Helen woke up feeling warm and optimistic, like she'd just stepped out of a deep bath. Ish had walked her home last night. If it had been a date, she would have described him as the perfect gentleman, apart from the part where he suggested they play a game where they had to think of an animal for each letter of the alphabet.

'I know how this goes. It's all fun and games at Aardvark and then I'll get frustrated by the time I get to the letter I ...'

'Impala?'

She gave Ish another poke in his ribs for that. He was such a strange person: so fun and also so deep all at once. Helen also smiled thinking about how long it had been since she'd met a guy friend, as in a guy you could actually really trust.

He'd also given her some ideas for her work: a couple of changes to her videos, some kind of optimisation software, and how she needed way better thumbnails. He hadn't been critical, he'd been helpful. He seemed to actually think her content was pretty good. Again, a dim memory of Jonathan flicked on, watching her YouTube videos on repeat, pausing whenever Helen said something stupid, or pulled a silly face ...

So anyway, she had some ideas of things she could do

differently to breathe life back into @HelenBakes and it was nice to have someone showing interest in her work again, like it could actually go somewhere. Ish had even apparently baked her famous cheap skate carrot cake.

They'd also brainstormed a 'video collab' where Helen could appear in one of Ish's videos talking about popular Victorian cakes, to help her get a few new followers. It could be the start of something better. She felt a tiny flicker of belief again that maybe she wasn't past it.

Helen's phone pinged: another story posted from Alice.

She tried to hesitate but who was she kidding? She slid open her phone to see a photo of Alice in one of her festival looks: the video kept looping to show her pulling open her kimono to reveal sparkling butterfly wings. Pink streaks had appeared in her hair.

#5days.

If Helen was going to actually do this, she needed to plan fast. She needed festival tickets, festival outfits, witty things to say and someone to go with. She could go by herself? Was there any way that could be cool? Brody seemed to be into all things mindfulness? Maybe she would seem confident going solo?

But then there was the camping, the stormy Cornish weather, the fact there were only three 'water stations' (and showers?!) on site. It sounded like a war zone. A noisy, messy, tundra with people who were too cool (or too high) to care about biting winds, loo roll and whether their kebab was cooked through properly.

'Be realistic Helen, even if you took a full medical kit, fisherman's galoshes, and enough cereal bars to last three days it will be a disaster going by yourself. You're going to not sleep, get worried you're getting hyperthermia and be calling home by the end of the first night,' her inner critic droned on and on.

But if she was going with anyone – there was only one person left to ask, who didn't have an office job, a steady boyfriend or any lack of confidence. Elle. But it was so not her scene and Helen didn't want the confrontation of 'Babe, really? Come on, let's go to my friend's party instead …'

Her hands hovered above her phone before calling Elle. It was that much of an ask, that it seemed to warrant an actual phone conversation. Not a WhatsApp. Not even a WhatsApp voice note …

'Babe – you're calling, are you okay?' Elle sounded more surprised than annoyed.

'I'm fine, I just wanted to ask you something and thought it was more of a phone call conversation …'

'This sounds deep, but okay …'

'You know that festival. The one I think Bro-'

'I do read our WhatsApp, Helen …'

'Look, I really want to go, you know Sophie can't because of …'

'Yeah, she's basically married already …'

'So could you come with me?'

There was a pause on the line. Helen could imagine Elle running her manicured nails through her hair, lying luxuriously on her sofa, staring up at her ceiling.

'Of course, babe.'

'Really?!'

'Look, I'm not going to pretend this is my kind of thing. It looks a little … hmmm. But you're my girl. I know you want to see this guy and I want to see you get over this guy; so we can go. I can plan some outfits for us, we'll spend some quality time …'

'We're also probably going to have to camp, they only have those tree tent things left …'

'I have camped before *Helen*,' irritability flared into Elle's voice. 'Look, the point is it may be shit, but we're friends. We don't just always do fun things together, you know? We're friends that can call each other when we need help. We do things together …'

'Elle, you've never once needed help.'

'I have love, you just don't remember. When I met you girls, I'd just moved to London. You were my first friends, you put it out of your mind that at that time I didn't speak the best English, or have the best job …'

'Just look where you are now! You're basically famous. Famous for being hot and cool on Instagram. It's the dream job!'

'I know … But the facts are, we go back to a time before any of that. You were there for me, and I'm still here. You can count on me.'

'Thank you so so much, Elle …'

'Stop thanking me, geez this is just what friends do. Real friends. Now hang up and send me your outfits.'

# Chapter 26

'Morning, babe …'

Elle's 'beauty sleep' eye mask was pulled halfway up her face, as she sat cross-legged in a camp bed on Helen's childhood bedroom floor. They'd actually made it. Helen had bought festival tickets, they'd booked a train and Elle had given plenty of 'constructive' advice on Helen's outfits. Now they were camped out at Helen's house in deep festival-prep mode.

It was like Helen was sixteen again, inviting one of the popular girls at school over for a friendship-affirming sleepover. The kind where they'd eat Häagen-Dazs, watch *American Pie* movies, rate the boys in their school year by who was the best kisser, and who (by rumour alone) had the biggest …

They'd travelled down together on the train yesterday and for once the journey to Cornwall wasn't dotted with memories of the break-up with Jonathan, and eating bags of Maltesers not recognising the taste after the first bite. Elle had bought them take out sushi and iced almond lattes at Paddington; she'd also insisted they travel first class as the tickets were only £30 more expensive, and, well, Elle didn't really do coach. As the train slipped out of the station, Helen looked once more at the spot where she'd seen Brody, where her feet had been planted to the floor, perhaps he'd sat in this same carriage …

'Helen, smile, come on, we're going on a holiday!' Elle slung her legs over the side of the seat. 'Would you like to eat? I've got cupcakes too? Help me with these?' Elle pushed a tray of iced synthetic looking cakes towards Helen. 'And can you take a picture of me holding one in this seat?'

Considering the ask of Elle to drop everything to go to a festival with her, Helen could forgive being her unofficial photographer.

Elle had regaled Helen the whole journey down with tales of her recent dates: a hot twenty-five-year-old Abercrombie model ('I really gotta stop choosing these younger guys, but the … wow'), a doctor who had taken her to brunch at The Ned, ('He's smart, I'll see how it goes …') and a rapper who had noticed her at a party ('I don't take him too seriously, you know?')

Helen was in fits of schoolgirl giggles as they met her family at the station, they probably didn't know what had gotten into her. This was obviously how single life was supposed to be though. Single life wasn't meant to be a monochrome silent movie of falling into your pillow crying, or running after a man who turned, shook his head and walked away. It should be like Elle's life: full fat and technicolour. A joyous ensemble of interesting characters, amazing sex, last-minute vacations and …

'Dude friendship is so important, for real. I am so excited to spend some time with your family today and finalise our outfits.' Elle was shaking her hair out of a ponytail. 'We also really need to braid our hair today.'

'Braid our hair?'

'Babe, haven't you read the website? They have like three showers there, let's be real here, they are going to be *nasty* after day one. We braid our hair and take dry shampoo.' Elle let herself flop back on the bed. 'You know, I'm actually getting quite excited for this!'

'You're not nervous?' Helen pulled her My Little Pony duvet a little closer, she'd given Elle the more 'mature' lilac one with stars on it.

'No babe and you don't need to be either. Remember, if we see Brody, cool, if not we still have fun okay?' Elle offered her pinkie finger up to Helen. Helen interlocked hers with Elle. 'I promise.'

Her mum was downstairs making a special 'we have a visitor' breakfast for them. Helen loved her mum, but she was easily impressed by things like Elle's huge Instagram following, 'well she really is quite famous, isn't she?' She could imagine her mum mining Elle for details on which fashion blog she'd recently done an interview with, then chirpily reporting (and embellishing) these details back to her friends at the tennis club, despite no one there really knowing what Instagram was.

When they'd arrived yesterday, her mum had hugged Elle with surprising warmth; she seemed genuinely happy that Helen had brought someone home, even if it came in the shape of a good friend rather than a suitable boyfriend. Henry had taken one look at Elle, and taken two steps back, like she was some kind of wild animal, and Helen's dad was too busy worrying about why his recently installed smart lighting system wasn't working to really notice there was another person in the house. Nanny G had also been well enough to greet them at the front door, perched up with the help of a stool and Grandpa M's walking stick.

Helen opened her phone and looked at the photo of Vernon, she couldn't wait to show her.

'Hmmm what about this?' Elle had yanked Helen's old blue prom dress out of her wardrobe, and was bunching up the twinkling organza next to her face.

'I don't think that look is very festival-friendly, Elle!'

Elle rolled her eyes. 'Not the whole dress *obviously* but we can take this material and make butterfly wings out of it, you know, like the ones you showed me Alice was wearing.'

'I don't know … maybe I shouldn't try to be too Alice derivative, I mean she does have better hair, better skin, a better figure …'

Elle threw the prom dress onto the floor. 'Babe, are you listening to yourself?' Helen shrugged and looked down into her hands.

'When are you going to start to actually rate yourself? I know you English people go in a lot more for 'false modesty' but you have to stop running yourself down. If you don't look at yourself in the mirror every morning and recognise how much you have to offer; how is Brody, or any other man, supposed to see that?'

'I guess I've just got used to seeing myself that way, and it's not like anything in my dating history tells me that I'm going to be any good with men …'

'That isn't true …'

'What about Jonathan?'

'Don't start me on Jonathan, before you met him you didn't feel this way about yourself. He put you down. He wasn't even nice … or hot …'

'He was who I wanted to be with …'

'No you didn't. When you first met him, he was the one chasing you, that night at his party. Then he started to lay it on thick …'

'When he actually wanted to see me …'

'Let me finish! Yes, he was unreliable, but whenever you met, he did something to keep you on the hook … There were the nice restaurants, he talked about the future, got you gassed about being with him, then he took it all away. No. Sorry. He was *not* the man of your life. He was just a man, and you know what? Before you had those years with him, I never heard you worry once, not *once*, about whether you were going to meet someone "in time".' Elle used her quotation mark finger gesture again. 'Seriously, my love. Seriously. You have to start to change how you talk about yourself. Be proud of the business you've created …'

'It's not going that well, Elle …'

'See! Here you go again. You have your *own* business. You get to make cakes for a living. Think how many people would love to do that! Plus there's always guys who like you, you just don't like *them* …'

'Like who?'

Elle's hands went to her hips. 'Ish!'

'Wait … How do you know Ish?'

'I follow him on Instagram! Did you even see his stories earlier this week?'

'No …?'

'Well, he was tagging himself in that place you went for drinks. He *likes* you, Helen …'

'He's never said anything?'

'Babe, he helped you out with something for your grandma, of course he likes you!' Elle shook her head and looked up to the ceiling.

Maybe Ish did 'like' her, and maybe she did like him, a bit … Was that disingenuous to Brody? No nice people liked more than one person at once, did they? Every time she tried to conjure up a possible scenario in her mind where she would fall into Ish's arms, the reel cut and she was back, fitting perfectly into Brody's chest, her head tilting upwards expectantly for his lips. Even when she'd met Ish at the Ivy House, it was like the phantom of Brody was sat at the table next to them … Helen realised she was staring out the window.

'Look, even if you don't like him, at least take the compliment. Now tell me something good about yourself.'

'What?'

'Tell me something good about yourself, like what you have going for you …' Elle gestured for Helen to continue.

'I'm nice …'

'Helen, what kind of word is nice? You're a writer, come on, tell me just one thing about you that's good. No, that's more than just good. Something you can be proud of!'

'Okay, I'm a loyal friend, considerate …' Helen watched Elle's eyebrows arching. 'Okay, I'm a domestic goddess, I take things seriously which I actually think is a good thing, and I have some moves. You know …' Helen's voice dropped, '… sexually.'

'Hels, are you all right?' Henry knocked on Helen's bedroom door.

'Come in!' chirped Elle, arms smugly folded.

'I heard shouting …' Henry pushed the bedroom door open.

'Oh, that was just me being me,' Elle flashed him a smile.

'Okay then. So anyway, if you come downstairs in a bit, Nessy's got something to give you.'

Elle triumphantly lay Helen's prom dress on the bed. 'Babe, trust me, this is going to look beautiful …' and they both pulled on hoodies. Nessy was sitting at the breakfast bar, her legs crossed, hands primly folded in her lap like she wasn't quite sure where to put them. Things seemed to be getting progressively more serious between Nessy and Henry; in fact, according to her mum, Nessy had spent every night there that week.

'Hiya!' she said an octave too loudly, then looked quickly at her coffee cup.

'Helen and Elle, this is Nessy, who you haven't met properly yet,' Henry paused just long enough to furrow his brow at Helen; he still hadn't fully forgiven her for cancelling on him that night. 'Nessy, um … heard you were going to Ship/Wrecked and had some ideas of things you might need.' Henry sat down, seemingly relieved that his speech making was over.

'So, I actually used to go to a fair few festivals, before I met Henry of course …' Nessy blushed in Henry's direction. 'When Henry said you'se were going to Ship/Wrecked and hadn't really been to a festival before, I thought I'd loan you a few bits to help …'

'I didn't know you were into that kind of thing …' Helen looked at Nessy properly for the first time. She had sparkling brown eyes and strawberry blonde hair. She didn't look like a party animal, more like an elf.

'To be fair you don't know much about Nessy yet, Hels.' Henry's arms were crossed now.

'Oh aye, I love a good party me.' Nessy had a soft Glaswegian accent and yellow freckles that spun out in asymmetrical spirals on her face. 'Though Henry's calmed me down a bit …'

'He has that effect on people.' Helen sat on the arm of Henry's chair and pulled his bowling ball-like head into a hug. Henry's arms loosened.

'Anyway, I would consider these bits essentials if you're camping. First of all, I always wear this belt.' Nessy held up an oversized khaki utility belt.

Elle's eyes widened.

'I'll wear that!' smiled Helen.

'I know it's not very glam but you'll be surprised by how many useful things you can put in it: wet wipes, anti-bac hand gel, torch, you can even clip a water flask to it like this.' Nessy mimed snapping on a flask using the caribou clip. 'And, of course, your Shewee …'

'Shewee?'

'It's a portable piece of rubber that you can use to, you know, pee standing up. Like a boy!' Nessy stood up from her stool, tucked the Shewee between her legs and mimed peeing in the shape of an 'N'. 'Anyway, I thought you may not want to use the loos there. They can be a bit …' Nessy cast an anxious look at Elle. 'So, I've put my old one in there, nice and clean! Just in case … And a few other bits and pieces too. You'se girls are gonna have such an adventure!'

# Chapter 27

Helen and Elle's newly acquired backpacks were perched against the front door, ready for Henry to drop them off later that evening. They'd managed to borrow sleeping bags from Henry ('don't worry, mum washed them'), Helen's dad had produced head torches from out of his tool shed ('there, I told your mother these would come in handy') and her mum had made them flapjacks ('now I know you say you won't have much signal down there, but please text me to let me know you're in your tent all right. I'm not sure what kind of people go to these festivals.')

Elle was busy fashioning the fairy wings out of Helen's old prom dress, ('hidden talents babe ...') and Helen was making a very important visit to Nanny G. She knocked gently on the annexe door and waited to be called in.

'Helen, that must be you!' Nanny G's voice sounded stronger, clearer. 'I've been waiting to see you ...'

Helen pushed open the door and saw Nanny G, still in bed but sat much more upright, five pillows propped up behind her. The curtains were open this time, letting the long, low evening light coat the room in an orange glow.

'Golden hour! You should take a picture.' Nanny G's eyes twinkled.

'And how do you know about golden hour Nan, got the dating profile together yet?'

'Well I thought that was it for me, Helen, but now I just might.' Nanny G snapped a ginger biscuit in half and turned down *Love Island* that had been on loop on TV. 'Have you seen this, Helen? Terrible really. Human bear baiting. Like a gladiatorial arena for 'dating' as you would say; but I can't turn it off. It's kept me going, all these young beautiful people falling in love, then falling in love with someone else …'

'Nan … I've got something to show you.'

Helen turned her phone towards Nanny G.

'Oh … my …'

'It's him, Nan. We tracked him down. Well, actually his daughter, Vernon's …'

'Of course she is. Of course …' Nanny G nodded and began folding up a handkerchief. 'Did you say 'we'?'

'My friend helped me find him …'

'Now if I was a little nosier, I'd ask if that friend was anyone interesting?'

'He's interesting, as in an interesting person, just not *Love Island* interesting.'

'Are you sure? Sometimes the greatest romances blossom from friendships.' Nanny G's eyes looked vivid again. The warm evening light made her look younger, Helen could almost imagine the years rewinding off her face and what Gladys looked like all that time ago.

'Well, there's actually someone else whose shirt I wouldn't mind ripping off on Kynance Cove!' Helen allowed herself to smile and wondered if anyone else talked to their nan like that?

'Now who would ever do such a thing?' Nanny G's eyes twitched. 'I had fun once.'

'Well, apparently, the fact that Vernon wrote to you every week was quite special. He was married, Nan. Those children he dropped off were his …'

'Ha, I always knew he had the devil in him … of course that's why he was so attractive …' Nanny G was looking out the window now, her mind far out of the annexe and running across the beach again.

'Yeah, his daughter seemed to think he was a bit of a …'

'Flaming youth. I know. I mean, I knew it, I must have known it deep down … and I don't think I minded. It was just nice to have the dream of him to hold on to. Especially during the war! A bit of light relief.'

'His letters were so romantic though? I don't know. I think I feel bad, Nan? I was really hoping he would still be alive, or would have been single when you knew him, or …'

'… have my name tattooed across his heart?' Nanny G grinned.

'Well, apparently, he named his daughter after two of his mistresses, which is nearly the same?'

For the first time in a month Nanny G giggled. She still sounded like a schoolgirl, and covered her hand with her mouth. She had deep crow's feet from a lifetime of finding things funny.

'So, you're not at all disappointed?'

'Of course not, my dear! I am actually very flattered that my beautiful, talented, granddaughter went to such an effort to find this out for me. I also now can take a copy of that picture, can't I? Good job Grandpa M isn't around to disapprove. I'll put them both together on my mantelpiece.'

'It just doesn't seem to be a very good end to the story.'

Nanny G threw her handkerchief into Helen's face. 'Now Helen, if I can give you just one piece of advice, you mustn't keep thinking that life is like a fairy tale. You were always so good at your writing, lost in your own world, but it isn't the real world.

'Vernon, for me, is a wonderful fantasy. You can't keep being besotted on sight with people forever, it doesn't work! Or at least it works a lot better at sixteen than at thirty-six, and even worse at eighty-six. Now I can't say I was very overwrought when Grandpa

M sat down next to me on the train one day and offered to share his sandwich with me, but he grew on me …'

'I thought you two weren't particularly …'

'Well, he certainly annoyed me like no one else in the world, but I loved him. I loved him oh so very much. All his silly ways and annoying notes. He wasn't always such a stick-in-the-mud. We had our good times … and he was always there. He gave me all my wonderful children … But our romance didn't come in the usual forms. It wasn't love letters, alfresco meals, or dancing in the moonlight. It was there when he pitched our tent in the rain, and I sat in the car under a blanket; when I made him pork chops that he loved and I still despise, too chewy! It was there when he held my hand, and took a little sigh as he passed away. It was all him. Those dreadful sticky notes and all.' A glimmer of recognition passed through Nanny G's eyes.

'You must miss him so much …'

'I do; when I go to sleep it's not running across a beach in the moonlight that I think about. I think about how Grandpa M used to put his arm around me every night. Even if we'd spent the whole evening calling each other nitwits.'

# Chapter 28

As the last of the sunlight receded over the clifftops, Henry's
Landy struggled down the shingle path towards Polveath cove.
Helen strained her ears and could swear she heard the dull thud
of Ship/Wrecked in the distance. Hedgerows bursting with gorse
and briars scratched past the windows, as a slow trail of festival
goers marched down the cliffs. Occasionally, a hand would bang
on the windscreen, 'Oggy! Oggy! Oggy!' then slip back into the
oncoming darkness.

Helen kept scanning the faces in the crowd; she couldn't stop
herself from thinking, 'Is it him?' In her mind, she'd gone over a
hundred different ways she could meet Brody. Would he be there
checking into the festival as she showed up? Would they end up
with tents pitched opposite one another and stumble into each
other in the dead of night? Would she not see him, think all hope
was lost and then just as they were leaving on the last day catch
sight of his car and wave? He would smile back at her, run his
fingers through his hair and …

'Well, we're almost here, are you sure you're going to be all
right, Hels, Els?' Henry sighed, resigned to his older sister's latest
misadventure, as he pulled up the handbrake.

'We'll be perfect, don't worry Henry, thank you for driving

163

us.' Elle straightened her floral crown on her head, and leaned over to squeeze Helen's knee. 'We're going to have a good time.'

Helen and Elle dropped out of the Landy and retrieved their backpacks from the boot. They made their way to the check-in point for the festival which had taken over a disused mine building. A huge neon image of a ship being wrecked blinked above them, and somewhere in the distance, below the hiss of the wind, was a deepening thud of music. The air smelt damp and salty as night formed a blanket of starless darkness around them.

'Cloud cover probably means it'll be a bit warmer,' Helen shrugged.

'Or that it's about to rain …' Elle flicked her braids over one shoulder. 'Hopefully we get to our tent then go get a glass of wine.'

'It might be a plastic cup of wine just to warn you,' Helen winced.

'Dan! Oh my Goddd!' A girl wearing a purple sequined catsuit pushed in front of them.

Helen didn't feel bad about mentally labelling her as a 'girl' as honestly she looked about sixteen.

'Have you got your A-Level results? It was mad!'

Yup. Was Helen really twice as old as everyone else here?

Elle fished out a compact to check her make-up. She was always much less preoccupied than Helen about fitting in.

Inside, the old mine building was lit up by floor lights sending an orange glow up the cobbled walls, casting long shadows from the thin gaps where windows once stood. The ground was uneven, and behind the check-in desks were deep openings in the floor, where you could hear the hiss of the ocean rising up underneath. Helen had always been scared of mineshafts – the fact you could take a pebble and throw it in one, then wait five seconds to hear it hit the ocean at the bottom.

At the back of the mine was a row of desks manned by

overenthusiastic eighteen-year-olds wearing lanyards and giving each other an unnecessary amount of high fives.

'Ladies, welcome to Ship/Wrecked! Can I take a look at your tickets?' The festival guide was clearly one of those relentless cheerful types. 'So let me guess …' His eyes lingered on Elle. '… we're taking you to the luxury glamping?' He zoomed in on the QR code on their tickets. 'Oh … actually I see you're in the tree tents. Wow! Well, you really are in for an adventure!'

Helen did not like the fact that the 'a' word had been used twice that day so far. Until these past few weeks, Helen's sense of adventure had always been strongly overridden by her sense of staying warm, comfortable, and safe.

The festival guide clicked on a torch and shone it down the path ahead. 'You see the signpost next to the Airstreams?' The light shone on a series of retro, silver camper vans. The flags on top of them flapped frantically in the growing sea breeze. A dim glow of lights came through their windows. They almost looked toasty. That was clearly where Brody and Alice would be staying.

'Well those aren't for you!' The festival guide yanked uncomfortably on Helen's backpack and gestured to a winding path in the darkness. 'Head down that way, it's quite steep, so be careful.' He gave a pointed look to Elle's flatform boots. 'Then when you get to the bottom of the valley, you'll see a stream, turn left and go over the bridge. You're tent 107, it will be towards the end of the trail up on the right-hand side. Have fun!'

The way he said 'have fun' sounded a bit too much like 'good luck!'

Helen and Elle made their way down the small shingle path that pulled away from the cliff edge and led them down into the valley. Gnarled trees hung overhead, blotting out any remaining light. Helen flicked on her phone torch and retrieved her head torch from Nessy's utility belt. Elle grimaced as she discarded her flower crown to use the torch instead. The path had the fresh, damp smell of the countryside, fed by cowslip, doc leaves, and

165

nettles that hemmed in the sides of the trail. As they descended into the valley, the stone path dissolved into mud.

'Geez, they could have done with a few more fairy lights down here …' Elle clung to stray branches at the side of the path for stability. 'And how come there's so much mud? It hasn't rained in days.'

'Cornwall,' Helen shrugged and adjusted her head torch.

Occasionally another festival goer would meet them on the path, waving, their hands covered in neon paint; Helen limply reciprocated. 'How about we just get to the tent, skip finding the wine, and eat a flapjack?'

'Great idea Helen, great idea …' Elle struggled across the small stones and watery shingle, negotiating the muddy path like a human Bambi.

After a forty-five-minute trek with backpacks (which was easily harder than any BodyPump workout Helen had recently attempted) they reached the stream at the bottom. Helen swung her head torch to read the wooden sign that hung from a nearby tree, 'wild swim here!' Helen mentally checked off if she'd brought enough towels, bed socks and jumpers. She looked at the black water of the stream – it didn't exactly look appealing. She thought about her legs sliding into the cold water, the slippery pebbles at the bottom, Brody walking around the corner …

Elle squinted to look at the sign with her head torch. 'Tents 90–110, this way,' she said pointing to an unfeasibly dark section of the woods. The tents were individually marked with fluorescent numbered tags hanging from each one. A discordant hum of music reverberated through the trees.

'Okay here we go, 103, 104, 105 … where's 107?'

Helen looked into the darkness, trying to not let the increasing wall of sound distract her. She was pretty sure that from one direction drum and bass was playing, and the other the Vengaboys. Stapled to the tree trunk was another sign saying, '106–110' with an upwards arrow.

'Do they mean we have to climb up the bank?' Helen looked at the steep bank in front of them, strewn with damp fallen leaves, and knotted roots covered in moss. 'Perhaps we should just turn around?'

'We are not going home.' Elle's finger was pointed at Helen. 'Look, we knew this was going to be … well it was always going to be a bit shit. I mean who goes to a festival in the UK anyway?'

Helen knew Elle was going to make that comment.

'But we haven't just got on a train to Cornwall, and trekked down the side of a … a … mountain …'

'… cliff …'

'… whatever … to give up now! Give me a leg up?'

'You mean push you up the bank?!'

'Yeah man, I go first, I'll get a hold of that tree branch, then I'll pull you up, okay?' Elle's ruby fingernails were already groping blindly into the rippling, cold mud.

'Okay.' Helen's hands pushed on Elle's hips as Elle dug her heels into the bank, grappling up the side of the bank to the first row of branches.

'Now take my hand!' Helen could see tiny clods of dirt in Elle's manicure.

Elle pulled Helen up behind her, and assessed that perhaps all of Elle's spin classes and squat racks hadn't been entirely in vain.

107.

They could just make out the outline of their tent in the trees, hovering above them like a damp, green spaceship. Their tent was suspended above the ground in a triangle shape, tied unevenly to the surrounding trees. The website had shown a picture of the tent bathed in sunlight, a happy couple (of course) dangling their legs out of the side of it, like a pair of wood nymphs.

The reality was the tent was pitched at an angle, which was obvious even to someone as un-technically savvy as Helen. When they were inside this meant the heaviest item (their backpacks) slid to the bottom, Helen lay in the middle, and Elle was bunked on top of her like a layer of sediment.

Elle had changed into her lilac tracksuit which already had mud splattered up the inner leg. The bedding the festival provided was damp with dew and their sleeping bags felt highly inadequate. Elle pulled on her 'beauty sleep' eye mask 'for extra warmth' alongside a beanie which Helen was surprised she owned. The wall of sound had now morphed into a genre of music Helen strained to recognise as Psytrance coming from one direction, and techno from the other. The phrase, 'I'm losing it …' reverberated around the tent, repeated endlessly over the thudding base.

'Flapjack?' Helen meekly offered Elle. 'Sorry this is so …'

'No more saying sorry, we're good. I am cold, I am tired of this music, and I need to pee,' Elle said. 'But we're good. Tonight we sleep, tomorrow we find this Brody and I go have a glass of wine with your nan.'

# Chapter 29

Helen was surprised when she finally woke up that it wasn't to the dull thump of music that had mocked her foam ear plugs all night, it was to birdsong. Somehow warm sunlight had also managed to reach them, the outlines of trees dancing in shadow on the inside of the tent.

Obviously, Helen had struggled to sleep. Normally sleep involved a ritual including moisturiser, fluffy socks, and a hot water bottle shaped like a sheep. Washing your teeth by swilling some water around in your mouth, brushing furiously, and then spitting it out over the side of the tent wasn't going to cut it. Elle had also woken up at least three times to pee, which she did by hanging her bum over the side of the tent: and flapjack supplies were already running low.

Helen checked her phone and saw a series of dots where the bars of signal were supposed to be. How was she going to follow Alice, and find Brody, without her phone?

'We have to go to the main site to see if there's Wi-Fi,' Elle yawned; she had put large sunglasses on the second she had woken up, like a reality TV star.

They made the forty-five-minute trek back to the main site of the festival. Helen's thighs were burning: between the lack of immediate food options and morning exercise Ship/Wrecked was currently doubling up as a fitness bootcamp.

The main festival site was in a dusty stretch of valley just short of Polveath cove. At one end was a large main stage where some reggae band was already playing; one guy in wellies and a tie-dye onesie danced by himself in the dust. Multi-coloured circus-style tents dotted the valley, advertising things like 'vinyasa yoga' (Helen now knew what doing yoga blind drunk would look like), 'meditation zone' (everyone was asleep) and there was a wooden shipwreck installation where the Instagram clique were taking turns hanging out of the crow's nest in bikinis.

Bikini plus wellies seemed to be a popular look; there was also a strong contingent of people who considered glitter a substitute for clothing, and the odd person styling out an old pyjama set with an extravagant headscarf in an attempt to look Bohemian.

Helen checked her phone: still no signal.

Elle was holding on to an iced latte in a soggy paper cup made with agave, and three rationed ice cubes. 'Don't worry babe, we'll ask the Instagrammers where the signal is …' Elle strode over to the pirate ship where a group of three people were huddled over something. From the outside it looked like they might be choosing which crow's nest pic was the best from their phones, in reality they were holding a shrew. A real life droopy-nosed shrew.

'There you go little guy.' One of the men stroked the shrew's head and put it into his breast pocket.

'Has he got a name?' Elle leaned against the boat.

'He's not our possession to name, but I'm Aiden.' The tallest guy touched his chest gently. 'Have we met before?'

'If we had, I'm sure I would have remembered. This is Helen and I'm Elle.'

Helen had to give it to her: Elle was still managing to purr out her words on minimal hours of sleep talking to an unwashed-looking guy with mini-dreads.

'Hel and Elle, I like it! Well this is Chug, because he likes giving cuddles and hugs, and this is Fairy.' Aiden gestured limply to his two friends, and patted the shrew back down into his pocket. 'There, there little guy. So have you been to Ship/Wrecked before? Or are we welcoming new people to our community?'

'Nope we're first timers, we're actually desperately looking for the Wi-Fi.'

'Of course you are,' said Aiden knowingly, cupping the pocket where the shrew was.

'Do you know where it is?' Helen felt rude and desperately unspiritual asking.

'The real question is do you want to know?'

'Oh Aiden, stop being so cryptic! It's over by the bell tent.' Fairy jumped in and offered a bangled hand. 'You can also call me Sara by the way. So how are you finding it?'

'It's probably safe to say I haven't really gotten into it yet.' Helen tugged uncomfortably at the sparkling bodysuit Elle had convinced her to wear.

'You have to go with the flow and not resist …' The shrew rolled around in Aiden's breast pocket, a pink tip of tail flicked over the top of the lining, clearly it was having some issues with just letting go.

'What Aiden's trying to say is, it takes time; go get some signal, some good food and if you need anything, find me later.' Fairy turned around and hit a button which illuminated a pair of fairy wings on her backpack.

Elle shot Helen a look that said, 'we should have just asked her first'. Women were always so much cooler than men. Except Brody, Helen thought, except Brody.

Helen and Elle sat on a couple of hay bales outside the Wi-Fi bell tent and watched their phones connect.

Henry: *You left your thermal leggings here. Weather looks all right so you probably won't need them.*

171

Mum: *Darling, I asked you to text when you arrived! Can you please let me know you're okay? I'm worried now! ????*

Sophie: *Wish I was there! Have the best time – send pics! xx*

Ish: *I'm having second thoughts about coming, if you still need a wingman?*

Nanny G: *Don't forget to have fun!*

Then there were Alice's stories from yesterday …

An orange camper van driving down the road towards #shipwrecked.

A looped video of a group of people in matching tiger print onesies jumping out of the back of the van – was that Brody in the background? Helen tried holding her finger to the screen to pause the video, but the two guys of the group were too pixelated to be certain.

Throwing open the door to an Airstream caravan … Helen knew it.

Waking up in bed and throwing a pillow at someone.

A pouty selfie in a 1920s sparkling headdress.

Climbing to the crow's nest in the pirate ship. Of. Course.

Pulling back the curtain on a tent.

Helen looked at the hordes of people in headscarves, turbans and face paint. How was she ever going to see Brody here?

'Wait … wait, there was a sign on that tent!' Elle's finger jabbed the screen. 'Go back!'

Helen replayed the clips. She must be Alice's top fan by now.

'There!' Elle held her finger to the screen to pause the video, and Helen could just read the sign 'Sharing Stage'. 'It was only posted thirty-four minutes ago, come on! We can make it!'

Elle grabbed Helen's hand and they jogged back down the cliff path into the maze of circus tents. Helen could feel her heart beginning to race.

'Geez Helen your hands are sweaty!' Elle let go of her hand.

'I'm sorry I'm nervous, is this outfit okay?' Elle stopped and looked hard at Helen. She licked her finger and rubbed near Helen's eye like she was five years old. 'You had a little mascara smudge, now you're perfect. Perfect Helen! Come on! This is so exciting!' She jogged up to the tent clapping her hands.

Inside, the sharing stage tent was dim, with only small cracks of light coming under the tent lining. Yoga mats and beanbags were scattered across the floor, all looking up towards a small, spot-lit stage. An intense looking man in an open shirt was pontificating:

'A bell stops ringing.

Autumn leaves fall in my path.

I am alone now.'

The poem sounded a bit like the ones Helen used to write to Oliver in school. 'Was that a haiku?' she whispered.

'I don't know,' murmured Elle. 'But it was bad.'

The speaker stepped back from the mic and a flutter of apologetic applause rippled through the crowd.

'It was indeed a haiku,' a softly-spoken man in glasses and a cassock ventured. 'I'm Max Savage, sharing stage's creator and what we're trying to achieve here is people feeling that they finally have permission to be radically honest. It's all about connection: that if we're finally able to speak our truth, then and only then can we be fully understood. You can join the speaker's queue there.' He gestured towards the end of the chain. 'It's pretty quiet at this time of day.'

Elle exhaled slowly, took Helen's hand and marched to the end of the line. They both squinted into the darkness.

'How are we ever going to find him here?'

'We will!' Elle hissed, sidling up to a particularly hairy guy who formed the end of the queue. Helen could see her looking

173

menacingly at the scraggly black hairs on his shoulder. She bet Elle wished she had her tweezers with her right now.

'So what's our plan of action?' Helen nervously pulled the bodysuit away from her hips, it was a bit too clingy on her bum.

'Why don't you go on stage?' Elle folded her arms.

'What?!'

'At least he'll definitely see you there.'

'Elle ...'

'Yes ...'

'This isn't where I imagined meeting Brody ...'

'Well funnily enough this isn't how I imagined spending my day either ...'

Helen winced. She could go on stage, maybe? But what could she say? 'Hi I'm Helen, a desperate single woman looking for ... oh hi Brody ...'

'What do I talk about though? I can't really go on stage looking like this either.' The body suit clung like a second skin to Helen.

The person next to Elle let out a little snort. 'Darling, what you need to talk about is your relationship with that beautiful body of yours!'

Helen did a double take. The person wore a PVC sailor outfit, had dark stubble and mascara framed eyes.

'Honestly darling, if I looked like you, I would take it off!' The line moved forwards and the person gave Elle and Helen a coquettish wave as they stepped onto the stage.

'Hello beauties.' They draped themself over the mic. 'So today on this sharing stage, this place for openness, love and acceptance, I was going to talk about myself ...' they paused for a moment to do an imaginary hair flick away from their grade one haircut 'but then I realised that the world isn't all about me!'

A ripple of laughter went through the crowd.

'I know it's shocking, but it's true. It's actually about how we see each other and the stories we tell ourselves about our own self-worth.' A murmur of agreement bubbled in the dark. 'Just now I was speaking to the most gorgeous woman, well apart from me *obviously*,' they did a little curtsy, 'who didn't realise just how beautiful she was.'

Helen's heart thumped louder in her chest.

'Please can you welcome to the stage … my new friend!' The person reached out their hand towards Helen.

'Oh no,' whispered Elle as Helen was dragged on to the stage to a round of applause.

Helen adjusted her utility belt awkwardly. The stage lights made it hard to see anything past the front row: where some people were sleeping, others kissing, some were in a deep conversation about the positive impact of cuddling on your oxytocin levels. None looked remotely like Brody or Alice. There were no tiger jumpsuits or sequined flapper caps. Thank. God.

Behind them a screen lit up. On it the camera focused steadily on Helen, particularly on her low-cut bodysuit. Was this being filmed?!

'Don't you think she looks beautiful?' A huge cheer erupted from the crowd. 'Now obviously this isn't my area of expertise but that skin, those, dare I say it, cheeks?' They gestured towards Helen's bottom to loud hoots from the crowd. 'Oh my, my, my! So what's your name?'

The mic swung uncomfortably towards Helen.

'I'm Helen …'

'A classic name … So Helen, can you do me a favour tonight? First of all, can you just tell the crowd that you are beautiful?!' The crowd roared as Helen struggled back a lump in her throat.

'Sure, I'm Helen and I'm beautiful.' Helen could see Elle's head was in her hands.

The cheering got louder still. Some of the sleeping people shuffled away, probably to the meditation tent.

'Was that really so hard?' The person batted their eyelids at her. 'The problem, my lovely friends, is that we're told day in and day out that we're not beautiful. That if we don't look like some perfect, preened, and undoubtedly heavily filtered picture on Instagram that we are somehow not worthy. And we are worthy!' They held the mic up to the crowd. 'Repeat after me! I am worthy.'

'I am worthy,' chanted the audience.

'I am beautiful!'

'I am beautiful!' the crowd parroted back.

'I am enough!'

'I am enough!' Was Helen saying this too? What had got into her?

Max Savage stepped into the front row and pointed at an imaginary wrist watch.

'Helen darling, I fear our time on this stage is drawing to a close, before we depart, is there anything you'd like to say? Any love you feel like you want to share?'

I guess she could say something? Elle shrugged, her eyebrows two centimetres higher than they usually were.

'Thank you …'

'It's Marty … or Martina depending on my mood …'

'Thank you Marty. Well, first of all I want to thank everyone here today for being so … so … fabulous.' The crowd cheered. 'I also want to thank my best friend Elle for getting outside her comfort zone and coming with me to Ship/Wrecked; it's already been an experience. I also want to thank Brody for the best last first date, I hope to see him again soon …'

'Romance isn't dead people!' Marty grabbed Helen's hand and lifted it up like she'd just won the Grand Prix. People were standing and clapping. Elle's mouth was hanging open, as Helen wobbled off the stage. She looked nervously towards her armpits. Would sweat show through the bodysuit?

'You don't need me to tell you, you've got sweat patches.' Elle shook out her hair.

'I really don't think he's here …'

'No shit,' laughed Elle. 'But seriously Helen, since when did you get such big *cajones*?'

176

'I don't know … maybe it was your pep talk yesterday?'

'Don't forget to give Marty some credit too.' Elle waved goodbye as they stumbled outside of the tent, blinking into the light.

Outside in the sunshine, Helen doled out wet wipes from the utility belt. 'This thing is actually really useful.'

Elle's eyes narrowed. 'You know what Helen? I was expecting you out here crying about not seeing Brody, and instead you're talking ugly fashion accessories. This is real progress. Perhaps …'

'I'm getting over him?' Helen shrugged, and instead of that leaden feeling she expected in her stomach, she felt nothing. Well, she felt a little tired, and hungry, but the emotions she expected to find just weren't there.

Elle stood on her tiptoes and waved her phone in the air. 'Well that's all good because I've just seen a story that Alice is down by the main stage …'

'Where?! When?'

'Five minutes ago! Right at the front unfortunately, like she's actually enjoying it.'

Helen tightened her utility belt and took Elle's hand. 'Okay let's queue-jump.' She really was a new woman.

The band on stage had changed to one fronted by a female singer wearing peacock-coloured leggings, a face full of glitter. The crowd had thickened. Crowds usually made Helen nervous. A mess of people all squeezed together. Women in floral crowns and men in faux fur coats slung over their bare chests lilted to the music. All the germs, the bodies, and the noise. With the crowd compressed to the front, Elle was slinking her body sideways and stepping through gaps in the crowd before they snapped shut again.

'Anyone ever told you, you would have made a good rugby player, Elle?'

Elle turned towards her confused and mimed 'I can't hear you'.

A small guy brushed next to Helen. She could see the beads of sweat dripping down his face. He was wearing a heavy coat that he opened to reveal little plastic packets and bottles. He gestured Helen closer, eyes wide and jaw clenched. Helen of course had never tried (whisper it) drugs. Well okay she'd often had a little too much wine, but that wasn't really the same. There had been no dark alley purchases, all night parties, or being cool at uni. The words 'higher state of consciousness' sounded a lot like a gateway to just being unconscious. Who knows what they mixed with that stuff? Helen shuddered at the thought of putting that into her body. She didn't even eat food that was a day before its sell-by date.

Helen shook her head and the man with the glassy eyes closed his hands into the prayer position and went back to dancing. There was a sharp tug to her arm. Elle held her by the arm and pointed upwards at the stage. Behind the band was Alice in her flapper cap, flashing a lanyard at a security guard and then slinking behind the dark curtains at the back of the stage. She was followed in by two other girls in cut-off shorts, and sequined bralets; and two guys in patterned waistcoats and fedoras. One was wearing Ray-Bans. He turned towards the crowd before slipping behind the curtain.

The blurred image Helen had carried around of him in her mind came snapping into focus. It was Brody. The expanse of time that had existed between them snapped shut. It could have been last night that he was holding her on the cliffs.

'Thank you so much, lovely creatures.' The singer finished. 'I've so enjoyed playing for you and with you today, but now I'm going to go hang out with my friends.'

The crowd roared into applause, as the singer slipped behind the backstage curtain, and a pint of beer came sailing down over Helen's head.

# Chapter 30

'I can't believe he's actually here! Do you think any of those women was his girlfriend?'

Elle rolled her eyes as she undid her boots and put her feet into the stream, shivering at the cool water. 'Is there any soap in that belt?'

Helen went through her pockets and chucked a miniature shower gel at her. 'I'm serious, what do you think?'

'I think they looked like a group of friends, going backstage at a festival, to somewhere much more fun than where we were ...' Elle sniffed the ends of her braids. It was going to take some time to get the smell out.

Elle was annoyed as security would emphatically not let her pass without an access all areas lanyard, no matter how much she negotiated. Also neither of them had realised that at festivals ('UK festivals babe, not all festivals ...') it was customary to chuck your drinks in the air as you clapped. Helen and Elle had been coated in a mixture of fluids they identified as cider, Jack and coke, and, quite possibly, raspberry Slush Puppie.

As they'd imagined, the shower situation wasn't great. One had become an impromptu water park for a group of guys dancing in and out of the shower calling it a rain dance. Helen didn't like splashing. Another had a pile of soggy clothes bunched up around it, like an oozing carpet. The last one had a queue of over twenty people waiting for it. So they'd retreated back to the campsite to wash in the deserted stream.

Elle was up to her waist, wading through the clear water, shivering. 'You know this is actually quite nice. Refreshing!' she said rubbing shower gel around her bikini. 'You should come in!'

Helen waded in up to her ankles. The water was cold but not unpleasant. She could see the small pebble bottom. She did a double check to make sure no other festival goers were around and peeled off her dress.

'That's my girl! So tonight we're going to dress super-hot … don't pull that face Helen! And we're going to get you your man …' Elle tossed the miniature shower gel back at Helen.

The sky was clear that night, leaving a smattering of stars, and a full moon to cast white light along the path to the main festival site. Someone had also considerately added flaming torches to the pathway. Wasn't that a fire hazard? Elle swigged from a water bottle of rosé wine, and handed it over to Helen. Helen felt a warm buzz from the alcohol, and anticipation rising in her stomach. She fidgeted with the wrist straps of her butterfly wings. Could this really be it?

She actually felt, well, ready. She didn't feel nervous, at least not as nervous as she thought she should be. Anticipation sat like a warm tingle in her stomach, and hadn't yet spilled into waves of anxiety. She was safe. She actually looked good. Guys walking by on the path had cast appreciative looks, and not just at Elle.

The main site swarmed with happiness.

People sat in huddles painting one another's faces, sipped each other's drinks, and embraced strangers with the long hugs normally reserved for friends. Helen took another long swig of wine: maybe this wasn't so bad. She fitted in just fine. Maybe she should rename herself 'elf'?

A pair of fairy wings blinked; it was Fairy? Gosh, was Helen

180

actually feeling social? She hoped they'd rehabilitated the shrew in the woods. Fairy, Aiden, and Chugs were sitting on some logs by the side of the main bonfire, which seemed to be the Hyphen nightclub of the Ship/Wrecked festival. Music hummed in the air. Could Helen feel herself dancing? Did she actually want some more wine? She took the water bottle to her lips.

Floating towards the wings, Helen walked to the main bonfire. Orange light cracked and reflected off the glitter on Elle's face. A shadow passed her in the half-light, and turned towards her and smiled.

'Helen?'

'Brody?'

Brody lifted up his hands using his 'guess so' gesture.

'You looked like you were daydreaming again …'

'I know – I was just thinking …'

'Thinking …'

'That I never imagined seeing you here.'

# Chapter 31

'This is wild! It's actually you!' Brody smiled so widely the faint lines around his eyes creased into crow's feet.

He looked just how Helen remembered him: he had the same green eyes, the same slight stubble … she inched a step closer, the same woody, inviting smell. Unconsciously she tensed her tummy muscles, and rolled her shoulders back. She couldn't stop smiling, for a while there was a long pause as she drank him in. Brody's eyes wandered from her prom dress wings, to the glitter around her cheekbones, her navel …

'I didn't think I'd ever see you again …' Did Helen actually feel that was true? Had she always secretly expected Brody to be too good for her? To have another better girlfriend? For her to just be a footnote in his life?

From Brody's reaction it didn't seem like he was stowing another girlfriend away somewhere. As his eyes lingered on her, she realised he hadn't been looking at Alice that way. He was only looking at Helen.

'I know I was going to message you after we met, but then …' Brody's words hung in the air.

'Connex. I know. It was so …' Devastating, unfair …

'Random. I know, it was also funny. The one time I'd done the internet dating thing and that happened. It just showed me again that I'm not supposed to put my persona online …'

Helen chewed over Brody's words. She wouldn't have exactly described Connex's server failure as 'funny', nor did she take it as a signal that all social media and online dating was bad, though maybe it was?

'Hey, anyway you should meet Alice. She was the one who set up my original profile, so I have her to thank for matching with you …'

Helen's heartbeat slowed. Alice was just a friend. He did want to match with her. He just didn't like being online any more than was necessary because he's smart, present, *mature* … and now they were finally meeting in the perfect way. In real life, by a bonfire, at a festival. It was romantic. There's no way they'd lose touch again after this … Maybe even tonight … Helen caught her breath. She was imagining kissing Brody. Would he lean in tonight and kiss her? Would they finally be back together? Would she know everything was going to be okay as her lips pressed up against his?

'Alice! Alice! Come here, there's someone I'd like you to meet.'

Alice turned around wearing her glittering headdress. She was definitely the woman from the train, and definitely intimidatingly good-looking.

'Alice this is Helen and …'

'I'm Elle, I don't think we've met?' Elle held out her hand to Brody and Alice.

'So nice to meet you!' Alice's arms were around Elle, and Elle was hugging her back.

'Wow, an English person who likes to hug!' Elle gasped, holding on to the embrace with Alice.

'Of course babe! And you're Helen?' Alice leaned in to hug Helen, her headdress felt cool against the side of her head.

Alice changed when she spoke. It was hard to keep her

cemented in Helen's mind as some kind of Ice Queen when she smiled so much you could see her gums.

'So how do you know this loser?' Alice shoved Brody and then hugged from the side. A little like how Helen would hug Henry.

Helen noticed her mind rapidly updating the image of Alice she had in her head. From Instagram, Helen had imagined Alice to be the kind of stuck up, popular girl who would have invited everyone at school to their party except Helen and the kid with the lisp. Instead, she seemed really … nice?

Helen and Brody exchanged glances. He was definitely looking at her differently.

'Well this is where I owe you some credit Alice, do you remember when you set me up with that Connex profile a couple of months back?'

'Of course, I only used photos I'd taken of ya, because all of your ones …' She touched Helen's arm. 'You wouldn't have matched with him babe if you'd seen what he was going to use.'

Alice took a long swig from a flask and offered it to Helen. 'Here you take it, I've had enough for now …' The alcohol was strong and bitter, Alice clipped the flask onto Helen's utility belt. Helen tentatively held the bottle in her hand.

'Anyway, the day after, I matched with Helen. We had a really nice date …' Brody looked sideways at Helen. 'Well, I really liked it at least …'

I really liked it too, Helen mouthed silently.

'Then there was the whole Connex server failure and we lost contact. In fact, I think Helen still has a pair of my Havaianas!'

Elle bit her lower lip and smiled conspiratorially.

'Perhaps I should just take your number now to stop that from happening again?' Brody turned to face her, she could see the definition of his chest underneath his waistcoat.

'Sure.' Helen handed over her phone hoping her hands weren't sweating again.

'So we've got a little posse going over there …' Brody gestured to what Helen could vaguely make out to be his group of friends sitting on some rugs and cushions, '… if you'd like to join. If you don't have other plans of course?'

'We were just going to meet some friends, but we got a minute.' Thank God Elle had fielded that one.

They sat down with Brody's group of friends on the rug. Their features were all more defined by the campfire: warm cheeks, and glowing eyes. Helen took a long satisfying sip from Alice's flask, and then alcohol burned down the back of her throat. Helen felt like she was in a movie, one that was so much more beautiful and vibrant than her real life. She didn't want time to slip by, she wanted this to be her forever.

Alice was sitting next to Elle and soon Helen could overhear 'babe you are not serious!', 'you are making me laugh!', 'that is so true!' They would be best friends by the end of the night if Elle had anything to do with it.

Brody and Helen sat side by side on a rug slightly away from the group. The glow of the bonfire backlit Brody in orange light, and cast his features into heavy shadow. Helen's heart rate quickened, being with him at night like this, it felt like anything could happen.

'You're shivering …' Brody gently touched Helen's arm. 'Would you like my jumper?'

'Are you always trying to give me your items of clothing?' Wow, where did this new confident Helen come from? It must be that drink she'd been sharing with Alice. She felt a warm buzz as she spoke, she was barely even registering the cold.

Brody pulled his jumper off, revealing a flash of toned abs as it went over his head. 'Okay I'm just going to be a gentleman and give it to you …' Brody handed the jumper to Helen, who hesitated. 'Don't worry I don't feel the cold …'

Helen snuggled into Brody's jumper, bathing in his scent, their eyes met, and wandered over each other's faces. Brody inched closer to her on the mat, and his arm fell behind her, like he was about to embrace her. Like she was his girlfriend. Helen was taking him all in, she wouldn't forget a detail this time.

'So what have you been up to since we last met?' Please don't say you've met someone, or left the country, or turned into a monk, Helen prayed.

'Everything the same and nothing the same, I guess. I told you I run a company, right?'

Yes, I went to your office party and can absolutely never meet your CMO again, thought Helen.

'Well, it's called True Materials and is in a really good space, we closed off a round of investment just before we met actually, so that means we can stay focused on the mission a few years longer, and there's a bit of interest to buy the company already. The team in London has been great, incredible …' Brody was lovely, Nicky was just a bit bitter …

'So I've been able to take a step back. The team is so experienced, honestly they're better than me at running it. So I've been to a few new places. Took a quick holiday in Tulum, have you been?' No, but I saw your picture there on Alice's Instagram, thought Helen, feeling slightly guilty, like she'd just rummaged through Brody's sock drawer.

'I haven't but my friend Sophie just got engaged there …' Helen waited to see if the information would register with Brody; did he see himself getting married one day?

'Oh good for her. Well, you should definitely go sometime. It's beautiful, and such a cool community there.'

The word 'you' stung though Helen knew it shouldn't. What was she expecting – it wasn't like he would propose to her after meeting her twice in his lifetime? Or suggest they go together sometime, that would just be weird. But who was this 'cool community'? Had he even thought about her?

'Did you ever try to find me?' Oh god why was Helen always so intense? As soon as the words left her mouth, she felt her cheeks burn. She tucked her face into her shoulder, maybe he wouldn't notice.

'I guess not … I mean, don't get me wrong, I *really* liked our date, but I didn't have your contact details, and when Connex went down, I just took it as a sign that it wasn't meant to be.' Brody's eyes lapped over Helen's face. 'I *was* going to message you though, so we could plan our second date.'

Did he sound sincere? Helen wasn't sure. The alcohol had morphed inside her and the balance shifted again. The warm buzz had faded and left a slanting feeling in her stomach, like the world had tilted a little on its axis. Did she feel nauseous?

'Why? Did you try to find me?' Brody smiled, and took a long swig from his hip flask as he now watched her intensely.

Helen's mind raced, was this the part where she was supposed to be authentic and honest. 'Tell him the truth! Just be yourself! It's okay to be vulnerable!' she heard Marty's voice egg her on. 'Absolutely do NOT mention you thought of him once since that day!' she imagined Elle saying. Her eyes drifted over to Elle who gave her a quick look of 'are you okay?' Yes of course, nodded Helen. Of course I am.

'I wouldn't exactly say that …' Helen shrugged trying to pull herself around to being flirty and light and not 'so when are we getting married again?' serious.

'Babe!' Elle moved to sit down next to Helen thankfully breaking the awkwardness of the moment. 'I'm just gonna go backstage with Alice real quick, you'll never guess, she's currently writing for Long Foolish Summer.'

'You love that band!'

'I know, so I'm gassed I get to meet them. Is that all right?' Elle dropped her voice slightly.

'Of course! I'll be right here, have fun!' Was she starting to sound like everyone's mother?

Brody knelt down next to Elle and put his arm around Helen's shoulder. 'I was actually hoping you'd take a little walk with me?

There's such a cool view just past the main stage.' Brody looked right at Helen. 'You can trust me, remember?'

It was like the record of her life had just skipped back several tracks and she was swimming in the past. Here she was, alone with Brody, him wanting to take her to some viewpoint, were they about to kiss again? Helen pulled herself up slightly unsteadily onto her feet and linked arms with Brody. Isn't this exactly what she wanted to happen?

She saw Elle and Alice in this distance slipping behind the black curtain at the back of the stage. They were already holding hands like BFFs. Brody led Helen down past the main stage and around the bend in the cliff. The moonlight was dancing off the shingles on the path, and grew ever brighter, as they walked out towards the sea. Helen looked down at the inky water beneath them on the cliff path; the dull roar of the ocean rippled through her, and she pulled Brody's jumper closer around her. Perhaps this would help her to sober up.

'So you haven't told me much about the life of Helen since we last met?'

'Well there's not much to tell …'

'Does that mean there's so much to tell?'

'Kind of … well my nan got quite unwell …'

'Your nan …' Brody paused. 'I remember, Nanny B?'

'G … but she's fine now …'

'I'm happy to hear that, it must have been stressful for you …' Brody sounded like someone she'd met at a party for five minutes who was trying hard to empathise with her, but couldn't quite conjure up the real emotions. They just hadn't known each other long enough, something wasn't connecting.

'Anyway work is okay, I've got some good new ideas for the business …'

'Happy to hear you're not putting yourself down about that anymore.' Brody offered her a small high five. Helen reciprocated.

'And that's about it …'

'Sounds like there's some pieces to the story missing there?'

'Maybe …'

'Maybe I just have to spend some time getting to know you better again …?' Brody's hands were around her waist, circling downwards. She felt a tingle running through her body, almost paralysed by just how much she wanted him.

'Maybe …' Helen murmured as Brody pulled her in to kiss her. As she shut her eyes her head swam, and her body felt limp. She really had drunk too much. Brody pulled away.

'Not feeling too good?' He held her by the shoulders now and looked into her eyes. Helen pulled her head up to make eye contact with him.

'This is so embarrassing …'

'Woah, not embarrassing at all!' Brody's eyes were filled with warmth, his hands still rested on her shoulders. 'You don't know Alice all that well yet, but her drinks are lethal!'

The word 'yet' reverberated happily around Helen's head.

'Look, would you like something to help you sober up?' Brody pulled his pendant up from around his neck and unscrewed the lid. Inside was a little spade covered in crisp white powder.

'Oh no, I'm fine …' Helen broke away from his hands. Her mind trying to pull itself into focus, like she'd just stepped off a merry-go-round.

Brody turned towards shore so he wasn't facing the wind. 'I don't do it much, but sometimes it's pretty fun.' He cupped his hand to his face and snorted the powder. 'I also have …' He patted down his coat pocket. '… this, if it's more your style?' He produced a tiny plastic bag with what Helen would have (wrongly) identified as having brown cane sugar in it.

'No, I'm good thank you …' Helen felt her arms folding across her body.

She couldn't believe that Brody actually did drugs. Perhaps she shouldn't be so square? Lots of people took drugs and they were at a festival and he did have cool friends who were in bands.

'And this is exactly why you never hung out with the cool kids', a voice at the back of Helen's mind hissed.

Was this a 'deal breaker'?

Could she date someone with such a different lifestyle? He seemed normal, he didn't look like that guy in the crowd with the glassy eyes.

A gust of wind came strongly off the ocean, and it hit her. 'I just don't know him yet …'

It was like she'd got two pieces of the Brody puzzle in her hands and created the whole picture. She'd spent so little time with him, less time even than with Ish. Why was she thinking about Ish right now? The path ahead spinned.

'Helen, Helen, are you okay?' Brody was helping her down the side of the cliff again, her feet rolling on the pebbles beneath her. 'Sorry you were too cold to go up there. Sometimes I get an idea in my head for something and don't really think it through … I guess I was just trying to recreate a moment?'

'The moment when we first kissed on the cliffs?' Helen fished for the words out of her mind and strung them together with tremendous effort.

'That's the one. It was nice …' Brody pulled her in again to kiss him; she tasted something acrid and bitter in his mouth. Helen pulled back.

'So if Connex hadn't gone down, would you have messaged me?' Why was she asking this again? Her brain was reacting too slowly to stop the words coming out of her mouth.

'One hundred per cent.'

'And we would have gone on another date …?'

'In London, yep, maybe back to Fix 126 for an iced coffee.'

'And then …?'

Brody took a step back and put his hands in his pockets. 'Well I don't know. I have to admit I didn't have much more of a plan than that …'

Helen squinted at him, swaying slightly on her feet. A Jenga brick slid. She took another long sip from Alice's hip flask. Her hands clumsily unscrewing the bottle, and clipping it back onto her utility belt.

'I guess I've just slipped back to being focused on my work, then there's so much going on in life, it's like I'm at this really exciting time where I'm just making so many cool new connections, you included of course …'

Helen flinched. Connections, plural?

'… so it wouldn't be congruent for me to make too many promises or future plans. It's just not where my head space is at right now.' Brody's hand rested on her shoulder again. 'Is that okay, Helen? Are you okay?'

The tower tumbled. Lights from the festival spun around her. She held on to Brody's arm and breathed.

'Helen, babe are you all right?' Elle was pushing her way through the crowd, waving furiously at Long Foolish Summer and Alice. She turned to Brody. 'I'll take it from here.'

# Chapter 32

'Babe, babe are you okay?' Elle was hurriedly sitting Helen down on a log by the bonfire. 'You drunk a little too much huh? It's okay, I got you.'

'How was the band?' Helen talked with her eyes closed. Was the festival spinning more if she kept them open?

'We'll talk about them later. I want to know about you! How was Brody?' Elle had unclipped Helen's utility belt, and was foraging through the pockets.

'He offered me drugs.'

'Wow. I can't say I saw that coming. So not really your style then?' Elle paused to watch Helen, slumping back onto the log. 'Look, I'll just get you a bottle of water and I'll be back in two minutes. Don't move, okay?' A rare tone of panic had entered Elle's voice. Her hand felt warm where she touched the side of Helen's face. Helen watched her jog over to the nearest kiosk and set about pushing into the queue. She tried to focus on Elle's golden braids, but kept losing sight of her in the crowd.

She felt really nauseous. She'd have to lie down on the floor. Helen pulled off her utility belt so she could lie flat on her side, and began absent-mindedly picking through its pockets, stopping just short of the hip flask. She wasn't going to drink anymore, she needed to think clearly.

Her fingers ran across the far pocket, and she felt cellophane, how come she hadn't noticed these before? From the belt she produced a small bag of chocolates, they looked homemade. Food would help to sober her up. Thank you Nessy! She was going to have to get to know her more when she got back home.

Helen allowed herself to pause for a moment to think about her childhood bedroom, the familiar smell of the dusty radiator, her old lumpy pillow, Nanny G, a hot shower …

She popped a chocolate into her mouth, it tasted … a little off. She would show Nessy how you had to melt chocolate when she got home, over a pan of boiling water, she'd probably put these in the microwave or something.

'Helen, what are you eating?' Elle squatted down next to her, the light from the bonfire bouncing off the curve of the water bottle. She tore open the chocolate bag, sniffing them, then taking a tiny bite.

'It's okay Elle, I'm not worried about my weight or anything like that … I feel … I think I feel attractive.'

Elle's hand went to her forehead again.

'Helen! It's not about eating … you're beautiful … but I don't think these are normal chocolates …' Elle's hands were around her face and she seemed to be making the same silent prayer action that her mum often made whenever Helen mentioned a new man's name. 'Fuckkk!'

Elle wrapped the rest of the chocolates up and jogged over to hurl them in the nearest bin.

'They weren't that bad, Elle!'

'Helen, my love, here have some water, drink, drink.' Elle was pushing the water bottle to Helen's lips. 'My love, I'm going to explain this now whilst you still understand me. Those aren't normal chocolates; they have mushrooms in them …'

Helen furrowed her brow, struggling to attach this piece of information. They had tasted a bit … woody?

'Magic mushrooms Helen, thank God you just had one …'

Helen raised up two fingers.

'Fuck!!! Okay, well it's fine, maybe they are not so strong, but just if you start seeing things, I don't want you to worry okay. You're my girl, I've got you, and I won't let you out of my sight.'

Elle pulled Helen in for a hug. Helen saw the glow of the bonfire over Elle's shoulder, the flames were brighter than before. They flicked up to the sky like mad tongues licking the air. Pulsing in time with the music.

# Chapter 33

Helen was staring at the main site of Ship/Wrecked but something wasn't quite right. Her legs felt unsteady on the ground beneath her, like she was walking on a giant trampoline. Like every step she could either disappear into the floor or spring towards the stars. The sky twinkled more maniacally and the lights on the pathway were throbbing bright and white.

Elle was holding on to her hand. The warmth from her fingers felt intense. She kept saying things to Helen but the words slipped by without making any sense. 'Just stay close to Elle, she'll look after you,' a dim corner of her mind kept repeating, but was drowned out by the blackout that had fallen across her other thoughts.

She could see the bonfire (they'd made it bigger?) in the distance and she was sitting down, Fairy, Aiden and Chugs were there. Fairy's wings were in a heap on the floor, twinkling. Helen couldn't stop looking at them, and followed the sequence of lights off, off, off, on, on, on. Small fingers brushed the side of her hair, Fairy was looking at her in her eyes. Her face felt so close. Was she going to kiss her? No, she was talking to Elle.

Focus Helen, focus Helen …

Focus. That's what Brody had said? That he liked to focus.

But he didn't. He didn't want to make 'promises or future plans'. That sinkhole feeling in her stomach again. Her mind fluttered.

'I think it's best if we just try to create a peaceful, loving environment for Helen to experience this in.' Aiden stood over her, the hairs of his jacket bristling like a wolf.

'She doesn't want to experience this, she needs this to end!' Elle's hands were on her hips.

'Orange juice will help her to sober up, I think.' Fairy's voice really did sound like a fairy, it was light and delicate. Like she was singing. Like sleigh bells.

'No, orange juice enhances the trip!' Chugs was talking now. His mouth pulled open into an exaggerated O shape.

Chugs was a portmanteau of cuddles and hugs, Helen remembered that. Had she and Brody kissed again? They had. The cliffs. She remembered his face and how it hung half in shadow. She shivered.

'Babe, I'm going to be gone for a few minutes; it's going to feel like I'm gone a long time but I'm not leaving you, okay?' Elle was in front of her, warm and safe. Then she got up and left. The space where she'd been sitting felt cold and oppressive.

Why was she leaving her? As Elle moved away, she left a contrail behind her of orange air. It's okay, she says she's coming back, the voice in Helen's brain remembered. I just need to stay here.

Helen pulled her knees into her chest. She just had to focus. No, not that word again. That reminded her of Brody. Brody. She could smell sea air again. Where were they this time? They were back at Hell's Mouth; the sun was setting and Brody was wearing his pendant? He was. It was glinting menacingly around his neck. He leaned in to kiss her, and she felt the strength draining from her legs. She was leaving her body. She was stuck to him like a long shadow on the ground. Who was she anymore?

'Helen! Look at this love …' Fairy was back in front of her. Where was Elle? Fairy held out her wings in front of her. 'Just look at this and think about people you love.'

Helen tried to focus on the twinkling lights, on, on, on, off, off, off. They were beautiful, and out of their shapes came Nanny G's brooch. The lilac butterfly she always wore, reflected at her. Nanny G. Memories washed over Helen of sleepovers at Nanny G's old house. The smell of fritters in the kitchen, making a puzzle on her dining table, walking across the cliffs in the starlight. Nanny G flicking Grandpa M with a dishcloth, Grandpa M pinching Nanny G's bottom. Chequered tea towels. Stained glass …

'You all right, babe?' A dark voice.

Aiden? No. Chugs? No. Fairy? No. Where were they? Helen turned her head and it felt heavy on her shoulders, there they were dancing, close but not close enough …

'You want a drink?' The voice again. In front of her was the man with the glassy eyes. She watched slowly as a bead of sweat drifted down his cheek, to his chin, and hung like a droplet in the light. He sniffed loudly.

'You want to go somewhere to lie down? Yeah I think you do …' His arms slipped under Helen's; she was being pulled up. She didn't want to be pulled up. She tried to let her body sink into the floor again, but it wouldn't comply. She was too light, like a balloon.

She could feel his hands, sticky, under her butterfly wings. His breath was hot and sour.

'Helen!' Another voice. 'Back off mate.'

'What's your problem?' Bad breath too close.

'Does she look like she wants to go with you? That's my problem.'

The arms loosened and were drifting off.

'Helen? Yer going t' be all right.' A hand was touching hers lightly, like she was a small forest creature.

# Chapter 34

Helen blinked her eyes open, and saw green walls undulating. The shadows of leaves danced in the sunlight that had turned the light in the tent aquamarine. Helen looked down at her hands: her eyes focusing on all the lines that crossed them. That was her life line, her fortune line, her love line …

'Helen! Are you okay? Here, have some water.' Elle's braids brushed against her face.

Elle knelt next to her in the tent, and handed her a bottle of water. Helen hesitated for a moment then brought the bottle to her lips and sipped. It was water, cool and revitalising as she drank.

'I was so worried about you! What do you remember?'

'Brody.'

Elle grimaced.

'I remember not liking Brody. I remember Fairy's wings. I remember … I was alone and then there was a man who … what happened?' Helen clutched at her clothes expecting to touch her old prom dress. Instead she was in Elle's lilac tracksuit.

'I shouldn't have left you alone.' Tears were filling in Elle's eyes and she started flapping her hands to her face furiously. 'I just wanted to meet that band … I'm so angry at myself. No, I'm so angry at him. Both of them.'

Helen reached out to hold Elle's hand. 'It's okay. It was me. I wanted to be alone with Brody and I shouldn't have drunk so much.'

Elle squeezed her hand hard. 'Don't be ridiculous love! You should be able to drink as much as you like, wear whatever you want, without … Rank. I'm so glad he was there to help.'

'Who?'

'Ish … You don't remember?'

'Ish?!' Helen's mind jogged back through what had happened. She was by the bonfire. She'd met Brody. She'd met Alice …

'We met Alice, she was really nice …?'

'Yeah she was a cool girl, though I wish she hadn't given you her flask to drink …'

'Then you went backstage to see Long Foolish Summer … and I went to the cliff tops with Brody … and he wasn't the same …'

'Maybe it's less that he's changed, more that you got to know him better.' Elle shook her head like she was removing a bad memory from it.

'And I was upset and I went through the utility bag and ate …'

'Two mushroom chocolates …'

'I actually think it might have been three …'

Elle made a sound that was half-laugh, half-cry. 'And you were wasted …'

'I was really wasted …' Helen nodded.

'And I went off to get you an orange juice, as that was meant to help you sober up …'

'Doesn't it make you more … high?'

'Don't go telling me you're the expert now!'

Helen shook her head. No. That was one experience she wasn't going to repeat anytime soon.

'Anyway, when I got back, Fairy, Aiden, and Chugs were all off dancing …' Elle shook, her voice straining back anger, '… and I told them to look after you! Instead it turns out some nasty, pathetic man tried to take you … Like what is this? What year do we live in that guys think they can …?'

'Then Ish saved me.' The pieces in Helen's mind swirled back together. The creepy guy with the sweaty face receding. Ish sitting next to her. Warm and glowing. Patting her hand. Waving one long arm and calling to Elle. Them carrying her back down the woodland path to the tent. The trees beginning to glow green in the dawn sunlight. The throbbing lights along the path. Happy, safe feelings.

'Where's Ish now?' Helen scanned the tent.

'He thought you'd be hungry, so he's gone to buy us takeout at the main campsite.'

# Chapter 35

Clothes had erupted over Helen's bedroom floor. Mud splattered backpacks were ripped open leaving a trail of leggings, organza butterfly wings and glitter. So. Much. Glitter.

The disbanded Shewee was slumped against the utility belt, its pockets unzipped in fury by Elle several hours earlier. Helen really needed to talk to Nessy later. Definitely before Elle did.

'Oh Helen, what have you done to your dress?' Her mum picked up the shreds of Helen's midnight blue prom dress from the pile of clothes and held it up against her body. 'You wore this? Like this?!'

Her mum's chosen way to express her affection for Helen was often to fuss. Fuss that she needed to have a haircut, to do her homework, to get an ISA, and especially to hurry up and get a boyfriend …

She hadn't been surprised at all that they had ended up fleeing the festival, and was now actively pretending to be helping them unpack, loitering, desperate to hear exactly what happened, and who exactly was that tall man in their back garden …

'I bet Helen looked almost as beautiful last night as she did when she first wore that dress to her prom?' Elle went into a charm offensive. She didn't look like someone who hadn't slept.

Helen's eyes twitched, briefly remembering not having a date for that stupid prom, Lucy Wheeler prying her with a discreet bottle of Malibu, and throwing up when she got home. Some things never changed.

'Well you must let me know if you need me to do any washing.' Her mum started to walk backwards out of the room, somewhat mollified, scooping up clothes as she went.

Henry walked in. His mass taking up most of the door frame.

'You all right, Helen … I was really sorry to hear about … Nessy wouldn't have wanted …'

'It's okay Henry, it's not Nessy's fault …'

Elle's eyebrows flinched.

'I think she was trying to be nice …' Henry shrugged.

'It was a nice … gesture. How much effort she'd put into that utility belt …'

'The hand sanitiser was very useful.' Elle flicked her eyes up to create an expression that restrained itself from a scowl.

'Anyway you're home now. Nice fellow you've got with you too.'

Helen felt herself blushing. 'You mean Ish?'

'Yeah, he's out in the garden now chatting to Nanny G.'

Helen flicked back the curtain in her bedroom window. Nanny G was sitting in a large wicker chair in the middle of the lawn; Ish was telling her some elaborate story, his arms waving in the air, Nanny G was laughing. She offered Ish some of her (was that alcoholic?) drink, he took a sip, though Helen knew he was teetotal. On the way back from the festival Ish had insisted they stop at McDonalds to get an apple pie and strawberry milkshake for Nanny G as 'all old ladies love 'em'; and his gesture seemed to have worked wonders.

She hadn't got the full story out of Ish yet: there hadn't been a moment, Elle had always been around. Why and how did he show up?

The first thing Helen really knew was that Ish had stumbled back to the tent that morning with four bacon rolls, 'eat two Hels, ya need the salt ...' like he'd been there all along. She was glad he didn't bring quinoa this or acai that. Bacon was good. He was wearing an outfit cobbled together from his YouTube videos: a top hat from his Jack the Ripper look, a Sir Walter Raleigh cape, and a plague doctor mask that Elle immediately insisted he threw out. Other than that, and the lack of sleep, he looked ... well, he didn't look bad. Helen had found her half-open eyes drifting down across his brown skin, and unexpectedly defined chest ...

'He's just a friend.' Helen shook her head. Why was she always justifying herself?

'All right then, anyway I'll leave you girls ...'

'Women ...' smiled Elle sweetly.

'... to finish up and I'll see you later ...' Henry slumped out the door.

Helen flopped back onto the bed and looked up at the ceiling. 'Elle?'

'Uh-huh?' Elle was tackling the remnants of her braids with a tangle teaser brush.

'In what kind of alternative reality are we in where you and Ish are hanging out with Henry and Nanny G?'

Elle paused and met Helen's eyes. 'The kind where the lead singer of Long Foolish Summer has followed me on Instagram ...'

'Isn't that just another day in the life of Gabriella Estevez?!'

'... and where Brody has just sent you a WhatsApp.'

Helen snatched the phone out of Elle's hands:

Brody: *Helen, I lost you last night! Let's try to avoid doing that for a third time ... coffee next week?*

'What do I say?'

'I'd think about whether you want to say anything at all.' Elle was definitely scowling now.

Helen sighed; wasn't this exactly what she'd spent the past few months hoping for? No, it went beyond hoping: finding Brody had been all she could think about. She'd chased after trains, gone renegade at a festival, and now he was right here and she didn't know what to do about it.

Her feelings swirled inside of her in a confusing mess. Was it because Brody wasn't the perfect guy anymore? That God forbid he had some faults? Was this why Helen was really single: that she couldn't accept anyone, and always focused on the negatives? Brody was smart, handsome, cool, successful, yes a little bit of a party guy ... and did he know what he wanted? Last night it didn't sound like it, but if he didn't want anything serious why bother messaging her the next day? Why did he say he wanted his last first date? It didn't make sense. Her dehydrated brain couldn't connect the dots – and then there was Ish.

Even Helen had to be honest with herself here: Ish definitely *liked* her. As Elle had been at pains to point out. 'Love, you're *loco* if you think this guy doesn't like you, and even crazier if you don't like him too,' she'd hissed at Helen whilst Ish helped Henry load their backpacks into the Landy.

The fact he had driven hundreds of miles to find her, and come to her rescue (again) meant he liked Helen. The evidence was stacking up: that bar he took her to was far too nice for casual drinks, he'd walked her home, abandoned his own work to go and track down Vernon ... he was doing everything right, and she was confused. Her mind flashed back to his bare chest in the tent this morning, the brief thought of 'what if Elle wasn't here?' But they were just friends, right?

There was no doubt she liked how gentle he was, how much his stupid games made her laugh until her cheeks hurt, how he didn't care too much what other people thought ... But if they kissed, and they kept spending so much time together, what would that all mean? Wouldn't that feel quite like a relationship?

'So what about Ish?' Elle shook her hair out into tight ringlets. Helen winced. 'I am serious Helen, that guy is not just boyfriend material, he's husband material, and that is coming from *me*, and you know I ain't getting married anytime soon.'

'I know … I know he's …'

'… he's?'

'I just don't know, it feels like a big step … and even if something did happen how would I introduce him to everyone?'

Elle lunged a pillow at Helen's head, stood up and pulled the curtains open. 'Babe, he's already done that for you!'

Ish was stood talking to Helen's family, her dad had temporarily stopped fussing about the mud stains they'd left on the carpet, her mum was busily talking about this being the best time of year for roses, Henry's arms weren't folded, and Nanny G was eating the last of her apple pie.

# Chapter 36

As the light coming through her window shifted from yellow, to gold, to lilac, Helen's brain felt like it was catching up with the day. She'd had a shower (and despite Elle's protestations) was wearing her comfiest tracksuit bottoms and finally felt ready to leave her room. She hadn't responded to Brody … yet. Not because two days at a festival had morphed her into the kind of woman who coyly played games, but because she just didn't know what to say.

In truth she felt like she couldn't say what she really wanted – that she was surprised that's what his pendant was, that she was disappointed he'd left her when she clearly needed help, that her feelings had or maybe hadn't changed … How were you supposed to put that into a message?

Helen lay back on her bed and listened to the shower running in the room next door. Elle had been in there for at least twenty minutes. There was a knock on her door.

'Hels? Can I come in?'

Somehow she'd also successfully avoided Ish all day. Showering aside, she'd essentially hidden in her room, relying on her mum to bring her rounds of tea and toast, and hoped she could avoid any kind of honest conversation.

'Yep!' Helen pulled the scrunchy out of her hair, and flicked the lamp on. Though she didn't really understand why she was suddenly worried about lighting.

'How're ya feeling?' Ish had had a shower too, and sat awkwardly at the end of the bed in Henry's XXL jumper. He'd rolled the sleeves up, his firm arms half gesturing towards her. 'Not my best look.'

Helen was about to say she didn't look that great either, but bit her bottom lip instead. The pause in their conversation stretched out for what felt like an eternity. Why did it suddenly feel so awkward? Had Ish's hand moved a few inches closer on the bed?

'Ish?'

'Yup.'

'Why did you come to the festival?' Maybe this was one time when blurting her words out made sense.

He pulled his hand back. 'I came to see you … can't really be anything but honest about that, it's a bit obvious now, isn't it?' Ish scratched the back of his head.

The words seemed to fall from the air like lead. Helen's heart started beating faster.

'Now I know you may not feel the same. I know you came to see that other guy … And honestly when we met that night, I wasn't sure how I felt about you either …'

Helen frowned. Ish was itching his ear now.'I mean it wasn't like … there wasn't a spark when we met right?'

'More like a creepy guy in a brown beanie … and nice guy with a blister plaster …' Helen shrugged.

'… and a yellow bike. But as we spent more time together, I dunno, I felt something click. When we were driving over to find Vernon …'

'Seven dinosaurs!'

'Yep … when we were sitting together in that garden bar … and I thought "Ish you need to back yerself more," I realised that here was someone I actually liked, and got on with, and … you're gorgeous by the way …'

Helen blushed hard.

'… and I thought if I didn't try to see ya at the festival that might be it: you could meet, who was it? Brody? And then I'd have missed my chance.'

'I still don't know how I feel about Brody …'

For a millisecond Ish's facial expression tightened, then relaxed again. 'I know and that's all right too. You don't owe me anything.'

'Well you did save me twice already …'

'I think I just have good timing … well apart from not meeting ya three months ago, before you met Brody, that's a bit unfortunate that …' Ish's dark brown eyes looked down, he half-smiled, and cleared his throat. 'Also, just because I fancy ya doesn't mean I don't want to be yer friend, you know, if you don't feel the same. I still wanna help with your work, and chat to your nan …'

'She's the best, right?'

'Well she has stiff competition from Grandma R in my family but yeh she's a good'un. Knew she'd like the milkshake.'

'You know how to make the elderly ladies go wild.'

'What can I say? I know my market!'

'Ish?'

'Yup?'

'You know I don't know what I want right?' Helen felt herself tense: was she even making sense? Did she sound like Brody? She'd always wanted a guy to just come into her life, and for once be clear about what he wanted, and now the opportunity was sat two feet away from her and she wasn't taking it. But something was holding her back and Ish was about the last person in the world she wanted to hurt …

'I know, and that's also okay.' Ish's eyes locked with Helen's. Her hand crept towards his on the bed, just as Elle walked back into the room.

# Chapter 37

Helen's keys jangled in her front door, as she shoved her oversized backpack into her studio apartment. The mud splattered bag looked out of place among the old factory walls of her studio, she poked a tuft of fairy wings back into the front pocket. Cornwall seemed like a long way away. She picked up her mail off the floor: there was a depressing student loan annual statement, a flyer for Alabama Fried Chicken's new vegan burger, and a thick, cream envelope. Helen tore gently along the seam:

> Dear Helen,
> Sophie & Frank would like to cordially invite you to their engagement party at the Hilton Metropole at 7pm on Saturday 27th July.
> Please RSVP no later than Monday 22nd to Sophie@sophie-andfrankswedding.co.uk
> We look forward to you joining us to celebrate!

Underneath the writing was a gold embossed image of a phoenix and a dragon interlinked in a heart shape.

Helen waited for a physical reaction, but the knot in her stomach didn't come, nor did the sickly feeling of being left behind. She actually felt happy; if anyone deserved this happiness it was Sophie, and Frank wasn't so bad either. She marched into the kitchen to pin the invite onto her fridge with a star-shaped magnet: at this rate of chirpiness, she'd be taking out a subscription to Soul Cycle next.

The journey back from Cornwall hadn't quite felt the same either. She hadn't pressed her face up against the cool window pane, shovelling chocolate into her mouth, trying to resist googling Brody.

She'd in fact been tagged in a surprisingly flattering picture of herself on stage with Marty (or @martixxxx as he was known on Insta) and got a lot of nice comments. Only some were about her bobs. She'd even got a like from Jonathan out of the blue, though he stopped following her when they broke up. It was good to know she wasn't the only one checking in on her ex.

Elle had been absorbed in a long exchange with Rex, the lead singer of Long Foolish Summer, which had made for an excellent distraction, as Helen watched her strategically leaving him left on read: *Sorry I thought I'd responded to this!! Sure, I could do next week x*

Helen on the other hand, had finally written back to Brody:

> Helen: *Sorry I thought I'd responded to this!! Sure, I could do this weekend? X*

(Elle may have helped her a little bit with that one.)

> Brody: *How about tomorrow? I can take you for our first Fix 126 coffee date? And you can finally make friends with Bean xx*

Helen held the screen up to Elle so she could read. Elle rolled her eyes. 'Guys are always like that.'

'Like what?'

'Our first blah, blah, blah. Meet my dog, blah, blah, blah. Men always get you all excited at the start, like they're planning to marry you, and trust me babe they just want you to *like* them. It doesn't mean what it sounds like it means. Just take it with a pinch of salt my love; actions babe, not words. Brody's still got a long way to go before you should like him.'

Normally Helen would have felt a crumpling feeling as Elle burst her Brody bubble, but something inside her had changed. Rather than feeling annoyed that Elle wasn't being supportive, she was starting to think that Elle was probably right. She wasn't going to spend two hours getting ready to meet Brody, she wasn't going to cry all day if he cancelled, and she was even starting to think that the perfect guy (much like the perfect pair of jeans) probably didn't exist.

So they were going to meet tomorrow, and the thought of her and Brody's second (or was it third?) date had neatly swept Ish out of her mind. Elle had been probing her on the journey home about what she was going to do about the whole Ish thing, and Helen was beginning to concede that it was indeed becoming a thing.

She couldn't neatly pigeon-hole Ish anymore; he wasn't just some guy she knew, or even a friend, something new had crackled between them yesterday. Not to mention the gooey look her mum had got in her eyes when Helen actually brought home a man … But he wasn't Brody. He wasn't smooth (Helen winced at using the word) like Brody. Or suave like Brody. She couldn't imagine swanning into some party and everyone being impressed that her boyfriend was so cool like Brody. But should that even matter? Why did she, of all people, suddenly want to be cool? She was obviously shallower than she thought.

Something about Ish almost scared her. Well not scared her like brown beanie, or the guy at the festival, but intimidated her. Like if she was going to walk through that door, would that be it?

The idea of being with Ish felt like it spelt the end of something. It wouldn't just be a kiss at a party: it would be the end of slouching around her apartment, the end of messages on Connex, the end of Jonathan, the end of Brody …

Perhaps Helen didn't hate being single after all. She folded up the envelope into her hands, and threw it into the bin, wishing she'd kept Brody's Havaianas after all.

# Chapter 38

For the first time in her life Helen was fashionably late, as opposed to anxiously early. For once she hadn't caught the bus fifteen minutes earlier than necessary, hadn't spent ages figuring out a perfect outfit (though the yellow maxi dress did look really nice on her), and certainly hadn't nervous peed two times before Brody arrived.

The weather was warm in London, and Shoreditch glowed with the vibrancy of a city in high summer. People sat on the doorsteps of cafés, arms slung around one another, sipping cider at lunchtime. Hipsters cycled past, with their shirts open, Ray-Bans flashing in the sun. It genuinely looked like no one had a proper job, or because it was twenty-five degrees, not one they were actually going to turn up to do. Completing the festival atmosphere, there was an impossibly long queue for iced lattes at Fix 126 on Curtain Road.

Helen edged down the queue, feeling extremely rude, and apologising more than was strictly necessary; expecting to see Brody up ahead with coffees in hand. But there were no Havaianas, no Bean the dog lapping at a water bowl. She was definitely casually late, this meant Brody was late-late.

The thought that he was also late for their first date drifted like a cloud across her mind. She checked her phone: no message from Brody, and the one from Ish still glared at her from her WhatsApp, unresponded to since last night. Why did she never have the right words to say? She knew she needed to get back to Ish, but she couldn't right now. Not whilst the date with Brody was occupying so much of her mind. She just wasn't a juggler. How anyone managed to date two, three, or more people at a time, she didn't know. It sounded stressful, a bit like …

'Helen?' A strong firm hand touched her shoulder, and she felt a shiver trickle down her spine in response.

'Brody?' Helen spun around, pleased to feel her maxi dress rustling around her legs like a damsel in a romantic movie.

'You look amazing!' Brody stroked a hand through his sandy hair. 'Sorry I'm late, we had a very exciting board meeting.' Brody paused for dramatic effect. 'It looks like I'm going to be able to exit True Materials! Oh and this is your new buddy Bean by the way.' Brody lifted up Bean, who was flopped over his forearm, like a rag doll.

'Oh wow, congrats!' Helen felt herself lunge into a hug that Brody wasn't quite expecting. For once his body felt more stiff than strong. Helen rebounded back off him like she'd hit a force field. 'So what exactly does "exiting True Materials" mean?'

'Well, firstly it means coffee is on me! Secondly, that I may be pretty busy over the next month or two with our lawyers …'

Of course he would have his own lawyers. Of course he was going to be busy. Any idea of them actually spending time together regularly folded itself away, embarrassed, into a corner of her mind.

'Can we have two iced almond milk lattes please? And the gluten-free chocolate brownie for the lady.' Brody smiled at the barista, and Helen could swear it made her blush.

He tapped his phone down to pay, picked up their coffees, and casually pulled out a bench for Helen to sit on. Helen perched down gingerly and folded her hands primly in front of her,

her body language somewhere between scary job interview and debutante.

'That sounds amazing, I'm so happy for you. You must feel so proud?'

Brody put Bean down gently on the floor. The dog turned around three times under the table, then started determinedly licking something on Helen's foot. She suspected it might have been the vegan chicken nugget remnants from last night.

'Well it's not all good news; they'll probably try to make me do an earn-out for a couple of years, so we'll have to figure that out …'

'Earn-out?'

'It's when you have to work at the company that acquires your business for a certain amount of time, it's like they're also buying you as "human capital".' Brody used inverted commas with his fingers and shook his head. 'But I want to avoid that. The last thing I want is to be an employee at a big London company for the next two years: this could be my opportunity to really travel. You know I've never worked for someone else? I bet you must be the same?'

Helen's head swam latching onto all the new pieces of information. Brody was selling his company? I guess that meant he was technically even more successful, but it also sounded a little like humble bragging? Had he just spoken about himself for the first five minutes? Also he wanted to travel? For how long? That wouldn't be with her right?

'No, I mean, yes, I've never had a "real job".' Helen winced to find herself mimicking his inverted commas with her fingers over the words 'real job'; it wasn't like she was anti-establishment. If anything, she was totally conventional, and the whole freelance thing had really been an accident born out of being utterly unemployable. 'So where do you want to travel?'

Helen shook her hair out over her shoulders, and leaned over to take a long sip from her straw. Maybe if she channelled Elle, she'd start to feel more comfortable? She started to realise how she never really felt comfortable when Brody was around. She felt … on edge? Like she was being judged (though of course she wasn't) and that if she said the wrong thing, or wore the wrong outfit, that his attention would fly away from her, leaving her like a forgotten house plant on a dim window sill.

'That's a big question.' Brody leaned back in his chair, did he like being interviewed? 'I guess I'd like to start in Europe, skiing in Slovenia, that would be incredible this winter, if I can get things tied up …'

Of course he would like skiing. Helen stirred her iced latte with her straw, watching the cubes of ice disappear into the whirlpool she was creating.

'… then maybe down into Croatia, Montenegro … I've always wanted to backpack through Transnistria.' Brody leaned in, conspiratorially. 'That's not even a recognised state, it's meant to be wild …'

Backpacking through an illegal country, what could go wrong? Helen inwardly rolled her eyes, and noticed the pendant glinting out from under Brody's T-shirt.

'It sounds like quite the journey …'

'You're coming with me, right?' Brody's eyes met Helen's and her heart skipped a beat. Brody held her gaze for a moment too long like he was watching for her reaction.

Helen pushed Elle's words to the front of her mind. 'Travelling the world with you, blah, blah, blah, yeah right!'

'I'll have to check my schedule.' Helen braved a flirty smirk – how she came up with that quip she would never know.

This wasn't at all true of course. If Brody was really asking her to travel the world with him, that would be something; but she sensed it was just words he was saying because he liked to watch the effect they had on her.

'Damn, you got me …' said Brody as he leaned across the table and slipped his hand into Helen's hair pulling her in for a kiss. Was he enjoying this? The uncertainty? The game?

Their lips touched, and Helen inwardly rippled with excitement, or was it just plain old anxiety?

It didn't matter; her body reacted to him like a bad habit; she wanted to lean into his smell, tingling. She felt her skin harden as he pulled her closer, but should she really be kissing him like this in public? It was a bit embarrassing ... the queue of people ...

Helen pulled back, Brody's fingers tangled in her thick hair, nearly dislodging a hoop earring.

'You know the festival ...' The words popped out of her, like they'd been barely contained since the last time she'd seen him. With Brody her radar was starting to feel off, like she couldn't quite pin down exactly who he was, and at this stage she just needed to know.

'Yeah that was awesome, *wild*, especially bumping into you again ...' Brody's voice was smooth, but Helen noticed he sat back on the bench now, and pulled Bean up onto his lap, sort of like a Bond villain.

'Do you do that often? You know ... out on the cliffs?'

'*She asked me if I do this every day, I said often ...*'

Wait, did he just answer her with a song lyric?

'No I'm serious, I know I'm maybe a bit ...' Helen stopped short of apologising for being too square, too serious, too uncool. 'But I just wondered if that was, well, normal extracurricular activities for you?' she pressed.

Brody slightly shifted his body weight. 'I guess, like lots of people, my friends and I go out, and we have some healthy fun, all in moderation obviously ...'

Healthy fun? Wasn't that cycling or yoga? Now Helen was leaning back. 'Obviously ... and when you're going travelling, is that going to be to Columbia for a month?'

'Bogotá is great actually ...' Brody sniffed. 'Latin America is worth a good six months I think, I'll have to add it to my itinerary. Is it on your bucket list?'

217

'Well it better be, if I'm coming with you right?' Elle would kill her for saying that.

Helen paused, the slippery feeling of excitement (anxiety?) within her was hardening into a new tougher emotion. Was she angry with him? Why was she angry with him? Was it for the flippant suggestion she came with him? Or at herself for believing it for a millisecond? What about her work? Her family? Her friends? Why was she in such a rush to give all that up, to pack her bags and be giddy with excitement for a round the world trip with a guy she barely knew? For a guy who didn't even mean what he said anyway?

The problem was Brody didn't think like that, he didn't actually think about her, he thought about what words would sound good for him to say.

'You're amazing Helen …'

'… but?'

'I think we need to wind it back a few steps. We've only just met again, and I can't make any promises about where I'm heading, at least until this deal is done. Then who knows? Anything could happen.'

'And one of those possibilities is we end up skiing together in Slovenia this Christmas?' Even Helen knew this would never happen, not least because she was never going skiing ever again.

'Well I always spend Christmas just with my family …'

From her extensive research into Alice's Instagram, Helen knew that was a lie.

'But who knows? I like to stay present, I don't think it's good to project too far forward into the future. Especially, well you can probably tell what I'm like? When I commit to something, I really commit to it. I'll end up spending all my time on it, kind of like True Materials …'

Apart from the fact your employee told me you were never around …

'So I just like to take my time, before I dive in.' Brody kept speaking slowly but Helen noticed his eyes tracing towards the door of the coffee shop.

'I guess before I "dive in" ...' Helen was finally using inverted comma fingers ironically, '... I'd like to know you're at least open to this going somewhere, and aren't planning on leaving the country ...'

'Well I don't want to make you any promises Helen, but that's actually because I care too much about you to mislead you ...'

Helen snorted into her iced latte so much there were bubbles in it.

'But who knows? As I said, anything could happen in the future, if it's meant to be ...' Brody leaned in again, but his words faded out, like her ears were refusing to listen to them.

Helen paused, allowing Brody to wash over her. The sandy hair was the same, the trademark smirk, but something was missing, that wasn't going to come back. Perfect fantasy Brody had melted into totally-average-flaky-guy Brody. She quickly pulled on her shoulder bag.

'Instead of me waiting to find out the answer, how about I tell you right now it's not meant to be.'

'Helen?' Brody gazed up at her as she rose to her feet. He looked at her differently this time, not with his normal, confident, steady gaze, but with watery adoration; all because she had thrown the pen in the bin, instead of signing on the dotted line. This is what it must feel like to be Elle. Is that really what he wanted? Someone to say no to him? Someone to chase? No, a challenge, but one that he could ultimately win ...

Helen walked out of the door into the bright sunshine, hearing the satisfying sound of the swing door shut behind her. She half expected Brody to chase after her, but then remembered the real Brody wasn't actually that romantic. He was probably checking his emails right now, smoothing down his hair, and acting like nothing had happened.

She looked around her, a woman with a septum piercing was

arguing with a guy in tortoise shell sunglasses. There was a faint hum of bass from some long forgotten afterparty in the distance. The tarmac glowed in the heat, and she felt just fine. There was no gaping pit in her stomach, no Jenga block falling, just normal life marching on.

Helen started back for home and opened her phone:

Ish: *Hels, I know we just got back yesterday but what do you think about filming this week? Rumour has it you make a great roly-poly (I hope Nanny G wasn't confused when she told me that!) and we could make our Victorian cakes collab? No pressure if not though x*

Helen: *Technically roly-poly is a pudding, not a cake but other than that it sounds fun … Friday? xx*

# Chapter 39

Sophie: *All fine over here, just manic with party preparations and dance lessons\*.*
*\*Frank has some 'interesting' ideas about things he'd like to do at the engagement party.*
*I didn't know he was that creative?!*
*Anyway I'll reveal all this Saturday! Can't wait to see you guys!*
*@Helen also dying to know how the date went?*

Helen: *I either acted in a way that was crazy …*
*Or empowering …*
*I feel it's a fine line?!*

Elle: *It is …*
*What happened?*
*Also @sophie dance, wow! I like how we're not even having to wait to the wedding for this.*

Helen: *Okay so …*
*I'm actually quite proud of myself.*
*Brody was late (not great).*

*Then just spoke about himself.*
*Then told me he's off travelling.*
*Invited me along (of course).*

Elle: *Please.*

Helen: *I know!!*
*He didn't mean it …*

Elle: *Obviously …*
*Getting you gassed, then letting you down …*

Helen: *And so I walked out on him.*
*That's right, I, Helen Pines actually ended a date with an*
*eligible man.*

Elle: *No babe, a weak man.*
*I'm proud of you.*
*And just you wait … he'll be back.*

# Chapter 40

Brody: *Helen, great seeing you today.*
*Look, I've been thinking that as sexy and smart as you are,*
*that we're better off as friends? Don't be a stranger x*

# Chapter 41

Helen woke up again that morning and waited for the sinking feeling to hit: to have a flash of remembering that it was definitely over (not that it *technically* ever began) with Brody, and that she was alone. Every day that went by since their last date, she expected to feel the dip of disappointment in her stomach, but the feeling never came. Instead she felt fine, just like herself. Maybe even better than ever.

She was solidly on the healthy granola, bought kombucha (still horrible) instead of lattes at her local coffee shop, and allowed herself to feel almost excited about seeing Ish later. Helen laid out everything they would need for their YouTube collaboration video: foil, greaseproof paper, a rolling pin, and her cutest apron that made her 'bobs' look big.

The past few days felt different. For once she didn't have Spotify blaring out 'hits of the 2010s' that made her feel old and young all at once; she was happy to potter around in silence. Since she walked out of Fix 126, and had left Brody on read: the constant chatter in her head had stopped. It didn't feel like she'd lost someone, she felt peaceful. She'd even started writing blogs again.

The first night she'd got home, she'd felt almost on edge, brimming with nervous excitement. Normally at this stage of working out a romance was definitely over, she'd be ordering greasy takeout and pondering whether wine on a Wednesday was acceptable. Instead, she felt fresh, like something in her was glowing and new.

After the date, Elle and Sophie had raced onto a group call with her, and as she was recounting the details (even the awkward bits) she felt good. She didn't say, 'I always end up falling for commitment-phobes,' she didn't cry (not that there was anything wrong with that), instead she felt, well, victorious; like she'd slain a dragon. Okay not a dragon (too violent), more like a ghost of something that had trailed her around since … Helen paused and leafed back through her memories. Then it was there: it wasn't since she met Brody.

It was since Jonathan got engaged. No – since Jonathan had made some excuse about needing time to work on himself, then casually popped up on social media with a new girlfriend and no explanation. That's when it started.

The irony was, back then she wouldn't have dared to confront Jonathan about his bad behaviour; in fact, she'd actually resisted telling him what a scumbag he was because she didn't want to ruin the chances of them getting back together at some mystical point in the future. She actually believed that he would saunter off with another woman, then return to her in a fit of remorse, and they'd live happily ever after, because, of course, that would solve everything. So instead of telling Jonathan exactly what she thought of his underhand, slippery infidelity, she'd spent the following months in a haze of cheese toasties and YouTube videos with titles like 'The one thing you should never say if you want to get your ex back'.

Slowly the pain of Jonathan disappearing had morphed inside of her, away from white hot anger and gut clenching misery, into a dull background ache, that only flared up when she saw his stop on the tube map, or his profile on Instagram. Okay, when she checked his Instagram. Admitting is the first step as they say.

Then there was the news he was engaged, and Brody turned up at the perfect moment. Suddenly Jonathan only got second billing in her mind, Brody became all important; the plaster that covered the pain she'd been lugging around with her since Katy's perfect heart-shaped face appeared on Jonathan's social media. The diamond engagement ring burning into the image of them in Kenya.

The irony was, now the plaster was off, Helen didn't feel the pain anymore. She didn't miss Jonathan; in fact she was weirdly grateful that someone else had taken his issues off her hands. She didn't really miss Brody either. The idea of meeting the perfect man was nice, but maybe that was just for the movies.

Helen's buzzer rang.

She smoothed down her apron, and opened the front door. Ish stood in front of her in his top hat and cape, thrown over a tracksuit.

'I didn't really know what to wear.' He shrugged, and opened his arms for a hug.

She hesitated, then stepped forwards, locking her arms under his. Yes, he was a lot taller than her, but it didn't feel as awkward as she thought it would, snuggling in. As she tucked her head in under his chin, and breathed in Ish, slowly she softened.

'Are ya all right, Hels? You're sort of err, slumping?' Ish twitched his shoulder to check she was still breathing.

Helen straightened up. 'Sorry. I mean not *sorry* but ... do you want me to put your cape down somewhere?'

She took his cape over to her coat stand and realised that she was avoiding making eye contact; every time she met his gaze, she flinched and looked away, like she was staring into the sun. Even Helen noticed the little bubbles of excitement rising up in her that she was trying to squash. The comfortable chumminess that had always existed had shifted out of place, and something else was there instead.

'So this is where the magic happens!' Ish walked around her

kitchen table wading through the awkward silence. 'What on earth is this?' Ish picked up a curved cylinder.

'It's a spiralizer …'

'Of course, I use one of these all the time!'

'I thought you were a dab hand domestically, Ish?'

'I know my limits …' Ish's hands were on her table, and this time his eyes looked right into her. 'So, I was thinking for the video that we could set it up right here …' he said gesturing to the middle of the room like a movie director. His voice sounded deeper than normal, confident.

Ish pulled a Canon camera out of his backpack, and started snapping a tripod together. He directed the lens out towards Helen's large picture window, capturing her kitchen table in the foreground.

'Maybe if you just stand there,' Ish waved for her to walk into the middle of the shot. 'It makes a nice scene, see?'

He took a still then flipped the camera monitor towards her. Helen walked over and looked at the image.

'I like it!' Helen's body language in the picture was a little slouched (she quickly rolled her shoulders back) but how Ish had framed the shot was actually quite nice. Sunlight was falling through her hair and onto the kitchen table, making it look more mahogany than plain old brown.

'Good. So how do you normally like to do this? Shall we work out how we're going to fit together … or just go for it? I mean, do you plan what you're going to say or just sort of freestyle?' Ish looked relieved to have finished talking.

'I'm more of a freestyler personally, though I've done a little preparation this time.' Helen pulled a jam roly-poly out of the oven. 'Here's one I made earlier!' She placed the roly-poly in the middle of the table, cut a slice, and poured a jug of oozing custard over it.

'You'd be good on Bake Off Hels …'

'Or Blue Peter, I'm very PG like that.' Did Helen just wink at him?

She turned the camera on and nudged Ish into the shot. 'Seeing you take your first bite is good content!'

Ish pulled a spoon out of a ceramic jar on Helen's table and dug in. 'I'd like to say @helenbakes roly-poly vintage cake …'

'… pudding,' Helen corrected.

'Pudding, sorry. Is enough to turn me from being vegan. But we're here today to look at another slice of Victorian life …'

'… that was a terrible pun!'

'If you'd been watching my channel, Helen, you would know I'm *renowned* for my terrible puns, and my lit rhymes, speaking of which …

*'The Victorians' diet wasn't so bad,*
*With eels, sprats and herrings to be had.*
*They invented the real Sunday dinner,*
*And compared to us, were often thinner!*
*If you were poor, it was bread and gruel,*
*This nasty food was your only fuel.*
*But rich folks ate a lot of cake,*
*Which Helen here is gonna bake!'*

Ish delivered the rap in his usual style, moving erratically around the kitchen, up close into the camera lens and finishing off by doffing his hat to Helen.

Ish switched the camera off. 'Was that all right? Sort of what you were thinking?'

'Totally average …'

Ish's large eyes flicked down. 'Oh.'

'… for a YouTube megastar, I mean! You're annoyingly talented, I need to have stronger material like that to stand out.' Helen's eyes met Ish's for the first time that day. A long second passed.

'I actually like ya channel ye know? I reckon if we can just improve your thumbnails and titles a bit, the crowds will come flocking back.'

228

'So no need for me to suddenly become good at improv or rapping? Buy a push up bra?'

'I wouldn't think so, no. You've got a nice persona, very ... natural, and likeable.' Ish turned his back to Helen, and fiddled with his camera lens. 'So how's your week been anyway? How's yer guy?'

'He was never really my guy.' Helen re-tied her apron strings. 'It's more like he doesn't exist ... I mean he *exists* ...'

'... as in, has objective reality ...'

'... but I just don't think he's the right guy for me.' Helen stuffed her hands into her apron pocket. 'What about you? How's the dating life going? Are you on any apps?'

Ish smirked. 'My bio reads, "*more woke than bloke*".'

'Are you serious? How have we not matched?!' As usual the words came out of her mouth before Helen could sort and edit them. She blushed so hard she wondered if she matched the jam roly-poly.

'Their algorithms obviously need some work ...' Ish's voice trailed off as he wiped a napkin under the brim of his hat.

His deep eyes looked steadily at her. She inched closer. She could see his chest gently rising and falling beneath his tracksuit. The intensity crept up on her in a wave of heat. She could almost feel individual springs of hair standing on edge like there was static electricity in the room.

Her eyes couldn't find a comfortable place to rest: they went to her feet (why was she wearing bed socks?), the door, the table, the camera, the fridge ...

'Looks like you've got a fancy party comin' up?' Ish picked Sophie's engagement party invite off the fridge door. 'Your best friend, right? The one with the ... the guy who's a bit ...'

'Boring? Well not boring, just ... he's quite steady I guess?' Helen paused. 'Yes, it's Sophie and Franks' engagement party tomorrow ...'

'Nice venue!'

'You know it?'

'Went to a stage magician convention there once ...' Ish slid the invite back onto the fridge.

'Want to come with me?' Helen squinted as if she'd just detonated a bomb.

Ish reciprocated like a startled cat, desperate all of a sudden for personal space. 'It's tomorrow?'

'I know it's quite last minute ...' Helen's hands kept rummaging through her apron pocket like all the answers were in there.

Ish scratched the back of his head. 'Well, I had some plans ...' His eyes caught Helen's again. 'But you know I like a bit of spontaneity ... and I can actually scrub up quite well ...' Ish adjusted the drawstring on his tracksuit.

Helen turned away now, it was the only reliable way to control her facial expression. She smoothed down her apron. Deep breath. She turned back towards Ish and scooped a large soothing bite of roly-poly out of the bowl, leaning over a tad more than was strictly necessary to show off her apron. She teased the spoon towards him, and as he leaned in, fed herself the bite. Sticky jam went on the side of her mouth.

'Be careful, Hels, that's our only prop.' Ish took a piece of kitchen roll and gently dabbed her face.

'So shall we keep filming?' Helen clung on tight to the last remnants of her professionalism.

'Let's keep filming.' Ish straightened his hat back onto his head, and moved to switch the camera on, just brushing Helen's fingers as she did the same.

# Chapter 42

Brody: *Yo!*

# Chapter 43

)

Sophie: <u>*Just a quick note about the party tomorrow, sorry to be*</u>
<u>*pedantic but can you be punctual, Frank's planning something!*</u>
*Also how was filming, Helen?*

Helen: *It was nice …*

Elle: *There have got to be more details than that?*

Helen: *Nothing happened yet, but I did invite him to*
*Sophie's engagement party tomorrow!*

Sophie: *'Yet' is the word I'm paying attention to here ;-)*
*@Elle, are you also going to bring a plus one?*

Elle: *Maybe …*

Sophie: *What's his name, I'll add him to the guest list.*

Elle: *I'll see how I feel about him in the morning.*

Helen: *Too cool @Elle ;-)*

# Chapter 44

'Helen!' Elle strode towards Helen down Edgware Road, her coat flapping open, the lights from kebab and hookah shops bouncing off the gold sequins of her dress.

Helen tried to leverage her clutch bag to pin down her dress, which was billowing out slightly as the 414 to Maida Vale rumbled past. It was all a bit Marilyn Monroe.

'Where's Ish? I thought you guys were coming together, no?' Elle gave Helen a tight hug.

'Where's Rex?' Helen smirked. She knew Elle had been having a passionate Instagram flirtation with the lead singer of Long Foolish Summer since they met at the festival, but the thought that a famous person would actually be coming to Sophie's engagement party at the Hilton Metropole was too weird.

Helen had obviously had a little creep on Rex's Instagram: he was tall, with bleached blonde hair that stuck out at a strange angle. His face also looked carved, like he had walked out of a video game. Whilst he was all a bit GQ model for Helen, she bet him and Elle would look really good together.

Elle pulled her hair over her shoulder and started smoothing it down. 'I decided I wanted to come solo.'

'Why?'

'It's still early days my love …' Elle had taken out her compact mirror and was examining her eyelash extensions, '… and some things are better just experienced with friends, you know? But come on, where's your guy?'

It was just like Elle to deflect, she wanted all the gossip in your life, but revealed very little. Helen suspected that the day she knew Elle was serious about a guy would be the day that she got a wedding invite.

'He's not "my guy" … at least not yet. I don't know, I just want to make sure this time, and I didn't want to lead him on …' Helen was really using inverted commas a lot these days.

'Love you are not "leading him on" by allowing him to share a lift with you here.' Elle shook her head.

'Do you think I'm just attracted to emotionally unavailable men?'

'Do you like Ish?'

'I am definitely liking him more and more …'

'Well Ish is definitely emotionally available, so if you like him, you're probably okay my love. I mean the guy is coming right along to your best friend's engagement party and not getting cold feet thinking you want to hurry up and get married …'

'I wouldn't mind getting married one day …' Helen batted the wistful look out of her eyes and tried not to focus on how lame she must have looked.

Elle rolled her eyes. 'Do you want to know a secret?' She leaned in and linked arms with Helen.

'What?' Helen accepted her arm grudgingly.

'I actually think Ish is pretty hot …' Elle caught Helen's eye.

'No way!'

'Yes … and I go further, I think he's actually hotter than Brody.' Elle's almond brown eyes looked into Helen's, waiting for a reaction.

'What?!'

'Let me explain … Brody has this too cool, too pleased with himself look you know?'

'And Rex doesn't?' Helen gave Elle a playful nudge.

Elle barely flinched. 'You will see babe, you will see … but as for Ish, he's actually confident you know? He's kind of masculine, I like that he doesn't have to constantly tell you how great he is …'

'Like Brody did …'

'Yeah man, it might be impressive on date one, but that's gonna get boring. Ish, he's cool and actually a good-looking man. Like when he brought us breakfast that time, and his chest …'

'He has a good body.' Helen thought back to the morning in the tent with his smooth brown chest, the line that led down his hips.

'Big dick energy for sure …'

'Elle!'

'What! It's the truth and you know it is …'

'Are we objectifying him?'

'Maybe just a little.'

They walked together arm in arm (Helen suspected this was partly for physical support as Elle's high heels couldn't have been comfortable) to the hotel entrance. It was a huge, grey block of windows and concrete. They twisted through the lobby, ignoring leering stares from foreign businessmen. Sophie's party was downstairs in an Asian themed bar area. Tufts of bamboo sprung up out of low red sofas, and shoji doors decorated the walls. It looked a little bit like a club they would have tried very hard to get into five years ago.

Mr and Mrs Wu were standing stiffly at the front of the room welcoming guests, whilst Frank's mum and dad looked like they had started early on celebrations; Mrs Edwards' fascinator sat lopsided on her ginger curly hair. Chinese lanterns had been added on a string overhead, and there was a pile of oranges and Chinese cakes on a stand.

'They look pretty good actually …' said Helen, gravitating towards the desserts and pinching a glass of champagne from a waiter along the way.

As usual her mind was giving her helpful diagnostics of exactly how she felt in this moment: right now, she was thankful that the sense of anticipation/anxiety (anxipation?) wasn't too overwhelming. Her hands felt a little sweaty around her champagne glass, but that was okay because Ish probably wouldn't notice, unless they held hands?! Helen shook the thought out of her head, and reminded herself it was just Ish.

There was a distinct crackle of emotions in her stomach though. Not quite like she was about to go down a rollercoaster (never again), more like she was about to walk into a surprise party for herself. Wait, was that narcissistic?

'Hels!'

Ish was walking over. Helen felt her stomach muscles reflexively tighten. Her hands really were a bit sweaty, where were the napkins? Ish was wearing an all-black suit, and looked … well he looked a lot different to when he was in one of his costumes.

'He's *hot*,' Elle whispered to Helen as she sauntered by with a wink.

'Hi.' Helen smiled as she waved Ish over.

'How's it going? Looks like a good party.' Ish plucked a glass of champagne from a passing waiter.

'I thought you didn't drink?'

'Nanny G got me back into it!' Ish shrugged and smiled.

Helen found herself struggling to smile back. Something had changed between them. An intensity cracked in the air now, and suddenly every small movement, every word she said, hung heavy with meaning. She could almost feel the heat that was radiating between them. She tucked her arms close to her sides: stepping any further into Ish's space felt like it would start a chain reaction that she wouldn't be able to stop.

The sound of a microphone buzzing on filled the room. Helen

236

and Ish swapped glances and turned their attention to the front of the bar where Sophie, Frank (wow he really looked loved-up) and their parents had lined up to face the crowd.

'Thank you so much for coming here today to celebrate our betrothal ceremony …' Sophie smiled and caught Helen's eyes in the crowd. She was wearing a lucky red dress.

'She looks so beautiful!' Elle had sidled back up against Helen.

Next Frank took the mic.

There were many things Frank was probably very good at, but Helen braced herself that speech-making probably wasn't one of them. In all her months of knowing Frank, she'd yet to prise a really good conversation out of him. She knew he loved Sophie, and that was really all that mattered, but she wasn't sure she could be with someone quite so … Anyway, she was glad Ish had so much personality. Not that Ish was *her* Frank or anything like that! She needed to stop thinking like that. Early days … early days …

Helen shuffled from side to side on her feet, and took a long swig of champagne, as Frank took the mic from Sophie's dad and stepped towards the front. Was he tipsy? He didn't really look entirely steady on his feet. His tie had been loosened, exposing his chest that was dialling up to a shade of bright red under the bob of the overhead lights and Chinese lanterns. Frank gave a loud 'ah-hem' into the mic: this was going to be bad.

'May I start with a toast, to my enigmatic father-in-law-to-be Mr Wu!'

The crowd obliged by raising their glasses. Helen took another long swig, she hoped they were doing top ups.

'Thank you so much for attending our special day, without all of you here, it wouldn't be the same … but it would be cheaper!'

Elle's eyebrows twisted out of shape and Ish conjured up a laugh that sounded more like a cough. Helen gave him a look of apology, which Ish returned with a shrug.

'In all seriousness, I am so happy to be here today with all of you and my glowing wife-to-be …'

Sophie smiled awkwardly, and leaned into the mic. 'Don't get too excited Mum and Dad, I'm not pregnant!' She turned to Frank and mouthed the word 'glowing' before handing the mic back.

'Oh of course, "glowing" … well I mean … you look beautiful as always.' Frank shuffled his cue cards. 'On my way here today to our engagement party …'

'It is quite cute how much he loves her, no?' Elle whispered to Helen. 'Though we both knew this was gonna be *awkward*.'

'I kept reflecting on all the *steps* we took to get here. I was very grateful that Rupert and Hugo convinced me to stay on for those extra drinks after our office Christmas party so we ended up meeting, and that all that extra whiskey helped me to summon up the courage to approach you.'

The crowd let out a collective 'awww'.

'I remember us dancing together that night, and thinking even back then how I never wanted to let you go …' Frank sniffed quickly, and gave himself a shake. 'Sorry – I didn't think this would make me so … emotional.' Sophie reached over and squeezed his hand.

'He's got hidden depths,' Helen hissed under her breath to Elle. Even she was feeling quite emotional, but that might just have been the champagne.

'Which reminded me of how my own father and mother met …'

The crowd turned their focus to Mr and Mrs Edwards who stood on the side lines, Mrs Edwards' rather outlandish purple fascinator bristling in the air-con.

'Uh-oh tangent …' winked Ish.

'Not many people know this, and I very much hope that my parents won't mind me relaying their story, but I'd like to tell you how Jane met Ian, all those years ago. My parents met before the age of dating apps, at a roller disco, when my mum fell on the floor and my dad held out a hand to pick her up. Rumour has it that 'Hot Stuff' by Donna Summer was playing at the time!'

Genuine laughter rippled through the crowd.

'And far away in a distant corner of the world …'

Sophie leaned the mic towards her. 'It was actually Raffles hotel, Singapore …'

'Thank you, my love … anyway a young Mr Wu saw a beautiful British air hostess. Speaking no English …'

'And she no Mandarin,' Sophie corrected.

'He communicated with her in the only language he knew they had in common … dance!' Frank glanced at Mr and Mrs Wu, the latter of which towered over her husband. 'Which is why today, I thought it was only fitting to honour this ancient …' Frank winced, '… courtship ritual with our very own "dance-off".'

Everyone was quiet now.

'I know this is a tad unconventional, but, as Sophie knows, I do like to sometimes push the proverbial envelope …'

Elle and Helen swapped confused glances. Frank was the most boring person they knew.

'So it is my delight to encourage you to grab a partner, and join in our celebration of partnership through dance … and of course Sophie and I will be leading the way with a little taster of what you can expect at our wedding!'

The first few chords of 'Hot Stuff' blared out the room's speakers. The crowd parted like the Red Sea and an increasingly flushed Frank led Sophie into the centre of the room.

'Poor Sophie …' Helen flinched seeing her friend, tottering onto the dance floor, forcing a smile to the crowd.

'This must have been what all those dance lessons were about?' Elle pushed onto her tiptoes for a better look.

Sophie's red dress shimmered as Frank led her across the floor. 'Frank and Sophie's First First Dance' appeared on the screen behind them. The main lights dimmed, and multi-coloured spot-lights danced across the floor.

'Oh God,' Helen winced. Was it even possible to feel this embarrassed when it wasn't you?

'I think this will be all right ya know,' smiled Ish.

'What makes you say that?'

'Just give it a chance.' Ish briefly squeezed her hand, and Helen felt a rush of warmth through her.

Sophie turned away from Frank and started stalking off the dance floor.

'Is she upset?' hissed Elle.

'Sophie?' Frank called out.

'Tell me about it, stud!' Sophie spun around as 'The One That I Want' blasted out of the speakers.

Elle gasped.

Sophie was striding towards Frank. Frank's tie was in her hand. She playfully pushed him, he twirled her, there was shimmying.

'I have to say I never thought I'd see Sophie slut dropping,' Helen giggled.

'Would it be unfeminist if I said I thought it suited her?' Ish smiled.

'Is that Sophie's mum and dad joining in?! Wow, her dad can really move!' Elle's folded arms dropped to her sides.

Mrs Wu's hat came flying off as Mr Wu led her through a complex series of turns, flicking her down into an unfeasible drop considering their height difference.

'Quite amazing spinal mobility for a woman in her sixties too …' Ish mused clearly loving every minute, '… and that's obviously how Mr Wu pulled her.' Ish paused and turned towards Helen. 'Want to give it a shot?'

'Give what … dancing?! Oh no, I'm no good at dancing.' Helen's head was shaking involuntarily.

'Don't make me tell you off for saying you're not good at something again.' Elle pushed Helen into Ish's arms. 'Besides, I seem to remember many years ago in Hyphen you pulled out some serious moves, and that's by my standards.' Elle smiled.

A man walked up to Elle and waved a diminutive 'hello' to signal 'do you want to dance?' Elle shrugged and strode onto the dance floor. Mr Enthusiastic tossed his suit jacket over the back of a chair and followed her obediently onto the floor. It was about as awkward as when a politician dances on to the stage at their party conference to show you just how cool they are. Elle seemed unfazed and was doing something very interesting with her hips in time to the music.

'Elle's always so confident …' Helen murmured, swaying vaguely along to the music.

'Shall we … ya know … try?' Ish extended his hand towards Helens. 'I would ask you if you trusted me, but that sounds a bit like a line.'

'Is now really the right time?'

'Yeah of course, unless, I mean, if you'd rather wait?' Ish studied Helen's face and his hand retreated back into his trouser pocket.

Somewhere deep inside of her, Helen gave herself a tremendous kick. The protective shell she'd been carrying around with her felt heavy. Did she really want to be anxious, uncertain Helen forever? No, tonight was going to be different. She felt herself heat up, butterflies exploding in her stomach.

'No, I'd rather not wait anymore.' Helen forced herself to make eye contact and took one step onto the floor. She could see Elle had already untangled herself from guy number one, and was now politely dancing with someone's uncle. 'Uptown Funk' blasted onto the speaker, and the over-thirties crowd burst into movement.

Ish beamed at Helen, and went spinning into the centre of the dance floor. Hang on? Since when could Ish *dance*? Helen saw Elle glance at Ish over the middle-aged man's shoulder and wolf whistle.

Ish strode back towards her, agile and lythe, suddenly his

limbs didn't seem too long for his body anymore. If anything, he looked ...

'... is that?'

'Did a bit of hiphop back in the day ...' Ish stepped forwards perfectly in time, his arms and legs extending out. It was all quite Jason Derulo.

His hands took Helen around her waist, he pulled her closer and she was moving along with his rhythm. She was dancing ... with Ish?!

Fuck.

The room blurred. She was moving. No, they were moving together and it felt ... good ... natural. She could maybe do this after all?

Mr and Mrs Wu, Sophie and Frank, Elle and guy number three, all faded into the background; Helen just felt her heart beating progressively harder in her chest. She pushed the thought of having very sweaty hands out of her mind.

'Helen ...'

'Yes?' Her voice sounded suddenly huskier for some reason, almost sexy? Her hand reached out automatically, and touched Ish's shirt button. He was breathing heavily too.

'Are you okay?'

'Better than ever ...' She felt her body slowly melting into his.

Ish moved closer in towards her now, she held herself against his chest for balance, and was surprised by how good he felt. They danced faster and faster, spiralling into the centre of the room. How were her feet keeping up? How were her feet not hurting?

This is what it must feel like to be a great dancer, Helen thought, as she felt the attention of the room on her, burning into her, and she responded by dancing harder. Her body was on fire, her hips moved, and the voice in her head was silent.

Perfectly there, in the present, with Ish, noticing how he was radiating too. Shining before her. She breathed through every moment, like she needed to catch on to the split seconds of pure excitement racing past her. The song was finishing …

'Hold on,' Ish whispered, and he dipped Helen into a backbend. Did they call it a cambré on Strictly?

She held on tighter around his back, her hand finding its way to touch the skin on his neck.

'Helen …'

'Yes?'

Ish took a deep breath. 'Can I kiss you now?' He blurted the words out.

'You didn't have to ask …' Helen slowly answered, studying Ish's face like she'd only just met him.

'No Helen, you always have to ask.' Ish was confident again, and pulled her up to his lips.

Sometimes time seems solid and concrete: like when you're waiting in a queue for the doctors, on hold to HMRC, or taking a train journey to Cornwall after your boyfriend breaks up with you. Other times it runs through your fingers like water, and just when you want to catch the individual, perfect moment in your hands, it runs right by you.

Helen wasn't sure how long she'd been kissing Ish for, but she knew it started out tentative, their lips barely grazing each other, then slowly deepened. The song faded out, until she was in another time and place, as if her body, disconnected from the world around them, already knew his. His hands were in her hair, and she tilted her head back to receive him deeper.

His intensity faded into smaller, lighter kisses, and she found herself fighting for them back again, letting her body relax into his arms.

Slowly, like she was coming out of a deep sleep, she became aware of being in the room again. The notes of the next song became gradually more pronounced, it wasn't the same one that was playing when they started kissing. Helen flicked her eyes open and saw the small dotted lights on the ceiling, then Ish's kind, beautiful face looking at hers. He relaxed his hold and Helen returned to her feet. Gradually she took in the room around her. They were in the middle of the dance floor, and people were facing them?

'Ladies and gentlemen, Ish and Helen!' Frank announced on the mic, and the crowd exploded into applause.

Ish squeezed Helen's hand, and then they started to applaud right back.

# Chapter 45

Helen rattled her keys into her apartment door, why weren't they working?! Okay it was probably the two (or was it three?) extra glasses of champagne she'd poached.

Ish and Helen had danced more that night; time went quickly and dizzily by. Soon Elle was making her excuses to leave, giving her (and Ish) a big kiss on both cheeks before she ran off into the night, messaging furiously on her phone. Helen and Ish kept finding themselves in the same place together: shaking hands with Mr Wu, getting their coats together, moving towards the door. There was an unspoken language between them that night, and like an ocean current they were pulled together in the same direction.

They'd stumbled out onto the Edgware Road together, hand in hand, kissing, stroking each other, happy, so happy. A passer-by called out 'get a room!' and Ish had flagged down a black cab. He held open the door. Sophie mimed for Helen to message her as she waved them off.

'The Kingsland Road please!' Helen called to the driver with surprising confidence. I guess this meant …?

She wasn't sure, and couldn't concentrate. Her head and heart were fizzing, like she wanted to hurry up back to her apartment, and yet stop to enjoy every second as it was passing. That's really when it started. It was the end and a beginning. The end of days feeling lonely, down, ignored. The belief that she couldn't be loved, that she'd always be let down, was being swept out of her mind; her fears had shrunk into shadows of their former selves. Now a precious new moment in time had opened up: one where she knew everything had changed. Not just in the present, where she felt Ish's hand pressing firmly into hers, but in the future and in the past. The story she'd lugged around with her of being terrible with men, that she'd never find love, was evaporating like a fine mist. Instead, everything she'd done whilst she was alone felt necessary to bring her to the place and time when she wasn't.

The dizzy buildings of central London unfolded into the ramshackle array of hipster bars, graffiti and fried chicken shops of East London. Helen leaned into Ish more as they went hurtling over a speed bump. Her apartment was just down the street.

'I'll just make sure you get home safe,' Ish nodded, though they both knew that he wouldn't be carrying on to his own apartment.

'Do you perhaps want to come up for just one more drink?' Helen offered, knowing full well she only had one lonely half-drunk bottle of gin in her cupboards.

'Yes sure.' Ish blinked at her, his tie slightly undone.

Now they fought their way into her apartment, kissing as they moved down the hallway, kicking off their shoes. Helen made herself pull her body away from him: somewhere in her mind, she had to actually make Ish a drink, otherwise … Well otherwise it meant Ish was just there because …

'So, gin?' Helen optimistically pulled the mostly empty bottle from the back of her cupboard and threw open the fridge door. 'And tonic!' She announced triumphantly seeing a flat bottle of tonic water hiding at the back of her fridge behind some gherkins.

Ish was leaning against her kitchen table, just like he had yesterday afternoon, though his presence felt loaded with intent now. 'You've got some grapefruits?' Ish handed her some fruit from the bowl. Helen wasn't one hundred per cent about how long they'd been there.

'Great, I'll make gin and grapefruit cocktails,' breathed Helen, trying overly hard to be composed. 'Can you put on some music?'

Of course, a drink and music made everything more civilised. Helen struggled some ice cubes into the glasses.

'Some music: okay I can do that.' Ish started shuffling through John Mayer (too smoochy), Goldfrapp (too intense) and INXS (too old-fashioned) before playing some Drake.

'Shall we sit down on the sofa?' Why did Helen now need to narrate everything they were doing? Worst of all she was doing it in her overly polite voice, the kind her mum used when guests were unexpected.

Ish sat down next to Helen on the couch. Helen put her undrunk cocktail down onto the floor, and reached back towards Ish, feeling a burn of urgency to kiss him again.

He reciprocated with even more intensity as Helen's fingers began pulling at his shirt buttons. His fingers grazed her arms, as his shirt fell open. He really did have a nice body. She stood up, pulling her dress off over her head, wriggling it over her shoulders, throwing it onto the floor, and dislodging her cocktail. She would think about the dry cleaning tomorrow.

'Wow …' Ish paused, admiring her, '… sorry I probably shouldn't have said that.'

'Is this okay?' Anxious Helen questioned, whilst confident Helen straddled Ish, touching his toned shoulders.

'Yes, I mean if you're okay, I'm okay?' Ish breathed heavily.

'I'm okay …'

Ish slid Helen's bra strap down.

'I mean I probably don't just see you as a friend anymore …' When were words ever going to learn to stay put and not fly out of her mouth?

'Me neither,' said Ish as he caressed her shoulder. The heat rising within her.

'… and you won't judge me if we, you know …' Awkward Helen, so awkward.

'No … No!' Ish pulled Helen's bra straps back up. 'Sorry I got caught up in the moment but …' Ish grabbed a nearby dirty tea towel and held it over her bra. 'I like you Hels, so ya know whether it's today, next week, or never, it's all the same to me …'

Helen giggled. Her hair dangled over her face, just brushing his bare skin.

'Okay well maybe sometime in the near future would be nice, but I'm in no rush …' Ish's hands rested on the sides of her hips. She wanted more.

'I know, I know you're not … but I think I might be …' Helen let the towel drop and pushed her hips down to touch his, his head rolled back, as she grasped at his belt buckle. '… what … Ish?!'

'Yes …' He sat up blinking.

'You never told me you have a …'

'A what?'

'… you have a really big … you know …'

Ish smiled, and pulled Helen closer again. If only she had known it could feel that good, she wouldn't have waited so long.

# Chapter 46

Helen blinked her eyes open to the scene of destruction that now categorised her apartment. A knocked over tumbler had spilt G&T into a puddle on the floor, as a lowly slice of old grapefruit had rolled towards her rug. The sofa was … well it was broken. There had been a moment when … well … she must have been holding on to it quite tight, and it obviously couldn't withstand the pressure.

It wasn't even 10 a.m. and she was blushing.

She looked back over to her bed, and realised she was also very naked, and in her bed, equally naked, was Ish snoozing softly with a pillow over his head. She normally hated sleeping next to anyone else (Elle was a real fidget in that tent) but with Ish it was easy. She'd had a long dreamless sleep, and somehow arrived the next morning, with a man in her bed. It was a little bit alarming; she looked at him like some alien life form that had strangely appeared in her apartment. What do you do with one of those? Well apart from the obvious?! Helen smirked again, she was starting to develop a really dirty mind.

She pulled on her favourite fluffy dressing gown and shut the bedroom door gently behind her. Pulling a spoon from the drawer she took a large mouthful (oh Helen stop it!) of peanut butter to help her hangover, and began throwing pieces of kitchen roll onto the floor. She picked through her handbag that had been thrown into the corner of the room, and checked her phone.

Elle: *Err someone tells me that you left with Ish @Helen. Need all the details xxx*
*Also hope you had a brilliant night @Sophie, you looked beautiful!!*

Sophie: *I had the best time, thank you both so much for coming.*
*Ps nice dance moves Helen!*

Helen: *I'm awake!*
*And Ish is here with me …*
*Well he's still in bed asleep …*

Elle: *I knew it!!*

Helen: *How come you're up?*

Elle: *Going for brunch with Rex, I think he feels like he missed out …*
*But more importantly how about you??*

Helen: *Well let's just say you were right …*

Elle: *Always ;-) But about what specifically this time??*

Helen: *Big dick energy.*
*2 hours!!!!*
*I'll tell you more when I see you xxx*

Helen pulled out of the chat and quickly glanced around the room to make sure Ish was still sleeping and he absolutely hadn't seen her write that.

> *Hi, it's now 3 a.m. and we've heard banging in your apartment for over an hour. I don't know why you feel now is an appropriate time to be doing 'DIY' but please bear in mind we need to be up in four hours. We can hear EVERYTHING.*

Helen bit her lower lip, that must be number 41.
Finally, she saw a message from her mum:

> *Hello darling, just wanted to see how Sophie's engagement party went? Please send her our congratulations. Did you meet anyone nice?? Xx*

Her mum's messages always contained a distinct undercurrent of anxiety, which is where Helen must have got it from. She started typing a response:

> *Yes it was nice, Sophie looked beautiful in her dress. Nothing much to report …*

Helen deleted the message and started again.

> *I had a great time thanks, you'll never guess what but I ended up going with Ish, he stayed over and …*

Delete!

> *It was nice, thanks Mum! Ended up going with Ish, and we had a really nice time. Will call you later to tell you all about Sophie's dress xx*

'Cuddles?' A low voice called out from her bedroom.

Helen put the phone back into her handbag and padded towards the bedroom door, slipping out of her dressing gown as she walked back in.

# Chapter 47

Brody: *Hey, haven't spoken in a while and thought I'd see how your week is going?*

# Chapter 48

Nanny G was propped up at a table in The Boat Shed café. Currently her food groups had dwindled down to ginger biscuits, semolina and the occasional glass of warm port. Despite her mum's protestations that she wasn't having enough macro nutrients, Nanny G didn't seem to care. Her arms were thinner now under her pink cardigan, and she had a constant wistful look in her eyes, like the wind was going to blow her away any day now, to a distant time and place.

It was Ish's first *official* trip to meet Helen's family as her boyfriend, and he'd clearly had no idea what to pack. He was wearing hiking boots, a ski jacket and an orange beanie, like visiting the countryside was akin to mountaineering. He seemed happy here though, probably because his presence was welcomed like that of a foreign dignitary by Helen's mum. She had bought all his favourite foods, presented him with cooked vegan breakfasts every morning, and been merrily doing all his washing. Yes, it was deeply unfeminist, but if it made her mum happy, it probably wasn't all that evil. Helen's dad had also been almost pleasant, holding himself back from intervening as Ish finally got Alexa up and running for them.

She hadn't seen too much of Henry, probably because he'd

finally moved out, five minutes down the road, into a cottage with Nessy. They weren't even thirty, and they seemed so much older than Helen: they had two rescue cats, a welcome mat, and a herb garden undergoing construction.

Helen turned to look out over the bay. It was low tide, exposing a sheet of shimmering sand down to the ocean. She couldn't believe it was Easter already, and that the cliff tops were slowly turning from brown, to green, to golden gorse, and purple heather. It was nice to have some sunshine again, though winter hadn't been its usual gauntlet of depressing TV romcom marathons, and awkward, 'so have you met anyone yet?' questions at Christmas parties.

Ish had spent Christmas up North with his mum (they were uncannily alike, right down to their love of 'I Spy') and Helen had been happy to spend it with her family. Rather than dodging all questions romance, she'd regaled her mum with stories of the Christmas stocking Ish had made her ('so thoughtful!') and how he'd been helping her get her work back on track ('see isn't it nice to have someone so supportive?')

Helen thought back to all those other Christmases. The ones where she saw returning home by herself as some kind of failure, like she hadn't met her annual target for finding a boyfriend. Where she went for long, dreary walks on the stormy cliffs, and sullenly dodged talking about her life. Perhaps she hadn't needed to spend all those days worrying about being single: so many Christmases had gone by where she had poked her Christmas pudding around her plate, her stomach in knots, living in sheer terror of being alone forever.

Looking back, she could see that fear for what it was: good old-fashioned anxiety, finding something to be anxious about. Anxiety that was in cahoots with every blog she read, that contained some vague threat about her ovaries. Anxiety that had messed with her ability to enjoy all those moments being with herself, a tidal wave that had receded from her life as a new chapter sprung open.

Even if she hadn't met Ish, or in fact hadn't met anyone at all, she knew life didn't really need to be like that. Elle loved being single so much she was having a hard time giving it up, even when an impossibly successful and handsome rock star was falling over himself trying to get to know her. Sophie was also finally back to girl's nights out and glasses of wine, after thoroughly establishing that Frank was going absolutely nowhere.

Single life could have probably been a lot better if she'd been able to let go, have fun, and some faith that she'd meet someone. (Of course, if she'd have realised how good being in love could be, she also probably wouldn't have stuck it out quite so long with the Jonathan's of this world. To think she could have spent all that time with her friends, dancing around her studio apartment in mismatched underwear, rather than worrying about boys … it would have been a revelation.)

Not to say, things between her and Ish hadn't been good, really good. Thinking about their relationship, there actually wasn't that much to report. There had been absolutely no incidents of him walking out on her, standing her up, or telling her she was absolutely amazing … but he just wasn't ready, yet. From the moment they'd woken up together after Sophie's party, things had just clicked. She didn't even fret that he wouldn't call the next day, because he'd 'got what he wanted' or anything like that.

In fact, he'd been back over later that night, joking about how he was going to get behind on his editing soon, with a grab bag of Maltesers and a new sci-fi show on Netflix he wanted to watch. Suddenly they were sharing box sets, friends, pin codes to their phones, house keys … Ish was an open book, and after a month of 'dating' he casually told his mum on the phone he'd call her back because he was out with his girlfriend (!) which made Helen suppress a scream.

Ish was totally straightforward, no confusing mess of 'what are we' conversations and dashed hopes. Yes, she wished she'd known sooner this is what love (he'd maybe said that too, as they were falling asleep together one night) was all about. That love was easy, not difficult. But then again, if she'd have known that any sooner, she wouldn't have met Ish. So it all had worked in the end, much better than she thought it could.

'So who wants cream tea?' Ish's raw, gluten-free diet had fallen to the wayside since meeting Helen. 'Or a pastry?'

'It's past-y! And yes please, I'll have one,' Helen smiled and pre-emptively loosened her knotted shirt as Ish sauntered over to the counter.

'I like that one you know …' Nanny G smirked.

'By one, do you mean Ish?'

'Yes, yes I do. He reminds me a little of Grandpa M you know? He's got such *joie de vivre*!'

'I thought Grandpa M was a little, well, you know …'

'Curmudgeonly? Well, yes, he was in his old age, as all old men are by the way, but when we first met, he wasn't like that. He was always …' Nanny G waved her hands in the air trying to catch the right word. '… so much fun. We laughed together, before we started laughing at each other. I also knew he wasn't going to be one of those men who promised the earth and then promptly disappeared …'

Like Brody, Helen thought.

'… like Vernon! Oh he was good-looking, but not to be trusted!'

'Are you getting some flashbacks being back at Kynance Cove again?' Helen flashed Nanny G a wry smile.

'Well now that would be telling! But it's good to have some memories at my age …'

'Oh Nan! Don't pretend you're not on Instagram again, eyeing up all the younger men!'

'And Connex …'

Helen dropped her spoon.

'… promise me not to tell your mother!'

Helen giggled: she hoped she could be like that when she was ninety.

'So what have I missed?' Ish sat down at the table and handed Helen her pasty. He emptied his out onto a plate and pulled off a piece of buttery crust, handing it to Nanny G. 'There, I know that's the bit you like!'

Nanny G daintily unfolded a handkerchief from her pocket, put the crust on it, and began slathering it in butter.

'Well I do have something to tell you …' Nanny G borderline flirted with Ish these days (she told Helen it helped to keep her young). 'Today there's an exceptionally low tide …' She checked the diamante watch that hung loosely around her wrist, '… so if you go for a nice walk on the cliffs, you should get quite a lovely view …'

'You're being very cryptic, Nan!'

'Oh am I?' Nanny G gave one of her trademark secretive looks, the same Helen bet she had on her face as she walked back from meeting Vernon, all those years ago.

'What do you think Hels? Sounds like fun?' Ish was already tying his boots, and stuffing the last corner of his pasty into his mouth.

'Yes, okay let's walk, Nan are you okay to wait here?' Helen pulled a beanie over her head, as the wind still ran cold along the beach.

'Of course, I'll wait here, I've got plenty to do!'

Helen noticed Nanny G surreptitiously slipping her mobile phone out of her pocket, as they walked out of the door of the café. Ish was particularly trepidatious about puddles and walked gingerly across the wet sand.

'You're wearing hiking boots, Ish, you'll probably be okay.'

'I'm just not like those rugged men of your past Helen, I like warm toes.' Ish pulled her in for a side hug. 'Not that there's anything wrong with Cornwall, but it is freezing down here!'

Like Helen, Ish was naturally wary of anything involving hiking, heights and getting wet. Especially waves. They were quite compatible like that.

The beach looked so similar today to a year ago, it felt like it could have been yesterday. Walking across the same beach, it was like her mind was running a split screen: Brody lightly touching her on her arm, as he postured in his Ray-Bans, to Ish, who kept grooming himself for tiny bits of seaweed.

She remembered the feeling so well, of hoping and waiting for someone to carry you off on some adventure. Back in the Brody days it was like she didn't want to be Helen anymore. Brody was an escape hatch from herself. Sometimes she thought back about Brody. The memories of him no longer needed to be ring-fenced in her mind as something special and sacred: Helen looked at them differently now. Like a balloon that slowly deflated, her image of Brody had shifted. Yes, he was obviously a charming guy, but was he ever genuine? Would he have messaged even if Connex hadn't broken, or would he have got swept away to some new horizon? When they met up again in London that time, the magic she thought was between them had evaporated like a rock pool in sunlight.

He still messaged every now and again, but this was one person Helen was going to be rude enough to leave on read. 'Archive that chat babe!' Elle's voice (and wagging index finger) came back into her mind.

There was no comparison really between Brody and Ish. Not because one was self-obsessed, and the other giving. Not because Brody liked to party, and Ish's idea of vice was chocolate cake. Not because one was all talk, and the other surprisingly talented in the bedroom. But because one was her breathing, laughing, (and today shivering) real-world boyfriend, and the other was a perfect fantasy she had created in her head.

Ish ducked as a seagull dipped past.

'They're probably interested in your pasty crumbs,' Helen said, brushing flakes of pasty off Ish's coat.

'You don't get this up North! And I'm guessing there's no tram to get us up that?' Ish's hands were on his hips as he looked up to the cliff path above them.

The shingle path wound up around the cliff edge, at an incline that no Stairmaster could match, touched by the silvery light of spring that was just getting warm.

'But if we don't go up, we won't get to see the view, or the moor ponies, or get a sprig of heather …'

Ish gave her a look.

'Heather's Nanny G's favourite,' Helen shrugged.

'All right, but only because it's you and Nanny G pulling at my heartstrings.' Ish walked behind Helen and helped push her upwards by the small of her back. 'You can call this manoeuvre an IPA: Ish power assist!'

'Very useful for hills!' Helen laughed and slumped into his hands more. They circled up the cliff edge, bent double against the wind as they ascended. The beach, and the sea, shrunk into miniature beneath them. From the beach the sea always looked murky and grey, but from up here it was brilliant jade, with frothing surf bashing the cliff face.

'See, isn't it beautiful?' Helen breathed deeply, out of breath, her cheeks flushed in the cool air.

'It is …' Ish conceded and pulled Helen in for a kiss, her hair whipping the sides of their faces in the wind. There was still a fizz between them, a grappling to get closer, an urgency to be together.

'Come here it's more sheltered …' Helen took Ish's hand around the corner, where some boulders clustered around the cliff edge. They provided natural shelter, and she didn't think many other people would be up there today, so maybe, just maybe … She unzipped Ish's jacket to feel the warmth of his chest with her hand.

'Helen?'

'Henry?'

Helen spun around and readjusted her beanie. Nessy stood with her arms wrapped around her, a long white scarf out like a wind sock in the breeze. Henry had his arms folded in annoyance, and he was, he was on one knee …

'What funny timing!' Nessy said brightly.

Helen did a quick double check: no ring on finger, but distinct bulge in Henry's side pocket; a very different kind of bulge to the one in Ish's …

Ish zipped up his coat, and tugged his jacket down a few more inches. 'So this looks err … sorry Henry.'

'It's fine …' Henry huffed.

'Sorry Henry, we didn't even know you were here today.' Helen took Ish's hands and they respectfully shuffled back a few feet. 'Don't let us interrupt you, just carry on like we're not here!' Of course, Helen, because that's entirely possible.

Henry furrowed his eyebrows, took a deep breath, and looked at the ground:

'Vanessa Elizabeth Curly, since the moment we decided to make up a cover story about matching on Connex, I knew you were the woman I wanted to be with. You are so much fun to be around, and I know I need more of that in my life …'

Helen nodded along solemnly. Henry took a deep breath into his barrel chest.

'… you're an excellent mum to Sticky and Fudge, look after me, and are also totally out of my league. In fact, there are a million reasons why I want you to be my wife …'

Henry produced a ring box from his jeans, and opened it to reveal a simple, beautiful, solitaire diamond.

'… so will you marry me?'

'Of course!' Nessy bounded over to Henry, who quickly stood up and swung her around in his arms.

Henry had gone the same shade of beetroot that Helen did whenever she was overwhelmed. Was he actually crying? Helen didn't think she'd ever seen Henry show that much emotion. Nessy was of course near hysterical, as was Helen, and Ish was wiping his eyes furiously with the corner of his sleeve.

'Mum is going to go crazy when she hears the news!' Helen grabbed Nessy and brought her in for a hug, as Ish patted Henry on the back, '… imagine a wedding next year …!'

'… and grandbabies!' Nessy squealed, and Henry shrugged. 'I mean not that life is all about getting married and having babies …'

'But it's still fun to plan,' nodded Helen.

'Here guys get in for a photo?' Ish pulled his phone out and kneeled down to get the best picture of them arm in arm, with the sea behind them. 'Gotta remember a day like this!'

Henry looked both deeply uncomfortable with so much attention, but also deeply happy. The way he looked at Nessy …

'Okay this is too much … we have to go and tell Nanny G!' Helen was doing a little dance on the spot now to warm up in the cold sea breeze.

'And get some drinks in.' Nessy clapped her hands together, and Henry nodded.

'See that wasn't that awkward, was it?' Helen smiled and gave Henry a big hug.

'Just how I imagined it.' Henry rolled his eyes and gave Helen an unprompted kiss on the forehead.

'So what are we thinking … red, white, bubbly?' Ish was shivering.

'Oh definitely bubbly,' said Nessy and linked arms with Henry for support as they set off back down the side of the cliffs.

Ish and Helen also linked arms and followed them down.

'A bit uncanny that …' ventured Ish.

'I know right, almost as if someone had planned it.' Helen gave a little shake of her head.

'Well when you're ninety I suppose you have to do something for a laugh.'

'I think Nanny G probably has more fun than we think,' Helen smiled at Ish, who took an unusually long pause before speaking again, his eyes set straight ahead of him.

'So ya know yer nan, and yer mum, and yer dad of course …'
Ish dropped his voice now, as Henry and Nessy broke out ahead
on the path.

'Yes?'

'They like weddings, and all that kinda thing?'

'Yes …' Helen smiled coyly into her coat collar, also looking
straight ahead. '… any special reason you're asking?'

'Nope none at all.' Ish took Helen's hand firmly now, as they
walked back down to the beach.

# Chapter 49

Brody: *Just wanted to let you know I sold True Materials!
Too late to get you that plane ticket? ;-)*

# Chapter 50

Helen sat on the train back to London, watching Ish struggling to put her (admittedly slightly full) case into the top luggage compartment. He lumbered down the aisle towards her, clutching a sharing size bag of Twirls in his hand. Helen hadn't seen him making any strange green shakes in a while, she was a bad culinary influence like that.

Ish brushed some crumbs off the radioactive blue coloured seat, and slumped down next to her, his too long legs awkwardly resting against the tray table. He automatically propped out his arm for Helen to slide underneath and snooze against his chest for the journey. She had a bad habit of falling asleep on him in such a way that managed to give him pins and needles. He'd gently have to shake her off an hour later.

Ish opened up a heavy tome of a book and rested it against one knee. He was vehemently against Kindle. Helen now knew the source of his wise comments (and historical raps) came from a voracious appetite for reading: he'd read standing up brushing his teeth in the morning, when he paused at traffic lights on his bike, and even after they … Well, that was also nice, Helen was asleep so fast afterwards that she didn't get annoyed by the flick, flick, flick as he turned the pages.

This would be the last week she was spending in her bachelo-rette apartment, her and Ish having both agreed that it was silly to keep paying rent on two separate places, ten minutes apart from one another. So his flatmates were moving out, and she was going to move in with his house plants, and the samurai sword. Although the BJJ mat would definitely have to go.

They'd talked about a lot of things they could do together: should they remote work from Cornwall? Do a joint video series with a travel theme as a tax-deductible excuse to go on a world tour? They could start in Europe, then go to Asia? Their YouTube collabs had been surprisingly popular, but ironically Helen wasn't as glued to likes and followers as she had been. Though it was nice to have more than a month's rent in her savings account, her moods weren't that closely correlated to how many likes she got. Instead she was successfully channelling her anxiety into planning potential itineraries for their travels. Ish had already made them a shared google docx of their savings goals, which was probably the most grown-up thing Helen had ever done.

Ish was always helping like that. Lightbulbs had been replaced in the run up to her moving out, he'd organised a man and a van, and had been very patient when it came to turning out her under the stairs cupboard. (Helen had made an impassioned argument as to exactly why she was never throwing her butterfly wing prom dress out.)

As the brown removals boxes started piling up in her hallway, she felt like she was slowly packing away an old, beloved identity that she'd slowly grown out of: the stupid faux leather leggings that were a mainstay of her girls' nights out, the sangria jug that was slowly getting less use, and all the self-help books she'd bought with best intentions but never read. On the other side, single life no longer felt like the austere, scary place that it had done when she was actually single. It was no longer something to fear, to hide, to avoid at all costs.

It was like a good old friend who she was gradually losing

contact with. She felt like she could blink her eyes, and be back to that life again: jangling the keys in her front door, cursing the wine she drank, the guy she kissed, the yoga class she skipped. Like it was yesterday, she would be skidding across her floor in her sweatpants, listening to Destiny's Child, a chicken satay stick in hand. She would be calling Sophie about a disastrous date; or Elle would flop down on her sofa, throwing her stilettos onto the floor. The memories of single life weren't depressing, they were perfect. A beautiful episode of her life, that she would look back and smile about when she was ninety. She'd probably end up saying, 'those were the days'.

The hard and lonely times of wondering (and worrying) if she was ever going to meet someone were slowly drifting out of focus, like they were being carried away on some strange tide. They'd been replaced with a slow crunch of nostalgia for all the memories she'd made, and the woman she'd become, from the time she'd spent alone.

# Epilogue

@helenbakes

A blender, whisk and food processor spilled out of Helen's suitcase with the broken wheel. The location was tagged as Heathrow Terminal 5.

*Having a few issues packing #highqualityproblem #wheresmypassport*

@sophiewuwu

Sophie had taken a mirror selfie of her petite frame dwarfed by a huge baby bump.

*Last day before mat leave – we'll see you on the other side xx*

@elleshhhxxx

Elle was backstage somewhere, a men's leather jacket draped over her shoulders, red plastic cup in hand. An access all areas lanyard hung around her neck, she had a coy smile.

*Here for a good time, maybe a long time, but that would be telling ;-)*

Lots of women had commented underneath her picture with the broken heart emoji.

@martixxxx

Marty/Martina had just got their toenails done. A pair of incredibly well toned legs stretched out against a leopard print couch.

*Don't expect to see any more of me today xxx.*

(@dk113 had already made several admiring comments about what he could do with his pennis if he got the chance.)

@aliceimagines

Pikes Bar in Ibiza. Alice wearing a wide brimmed hat, black sheer maxi dress and holding an espresso martini. Gaggle of cool friends all tagged. Brody takes one step off the side of the pool, about to hit the water below, smiling, his pendant swinging around his neck.

*Ibiza with these creatures. #wedidntmakeourflight*

@truematerials

Nicky Fox leaned backwards against a brick wall, her arms folded across her chest in a black turtleneck.

*True Materials is excited to announce our new interim CEO will be our all-star former CMO Nicky! Behind the scenes Nicky has been working hard to keep creating the True Materials vision, and we're excited for this #newera in our leadership structure.*

@henrynnessy

Nessy's strawberry blonde hair was flying around her face in the Cornish wind, Henry huddled over her like a physical barricade. She flashed a perfect smile and an even more perfect solitaire diamond ring to the camera.

*Can't stop sharing these pics from our engagement!! Thanks for the snap @ishtory. I love you so much H xxx*

@jonathanplease

Jonathan's back was to the camera, overlooking a sunset, in some remote and dusty country that he'd been so enigmatic as to not tag. A solitary Harley Davidson was propped up on a nearby wall.

*Some things are for a reason, others for a season, on to the next chapter.*

@nannygstagram

Nanny G raises a small crystal glass to toast the pictures of Grandpa M and Vernon on her mantlepiece. (Wait ... is that a man's slippered foot in the background?)

*Don't mourn a lost love: you get more than one in life. Just like when you've run out of Buck's fizz, only to find a box of Snowballs at the back of the cupboard. Keep looking on to your next adventure.*

@ishstory

A silent beach with palm trees that dip into the water. It's sunset as the sky has turned orange. Ish's palm reaches into the frame, a ring in his hand.

*I hope we can make every day as good as this one.*

# Acknowledgements

I'd like to thank all the good friends and bad dates that inspired this book.

Special thanks to Nanny B & Nanny M who the character Nanny G is based on. Nanny M genuinely fell in love with Vernon during the war, and I have used transcripts of their real life love letters in this book. The memory of their romance stayed with Nanny M until her final days.

Thanks as well to my mum, dad, and wider family for always supporting me. As well as to Suzie and Ian for providing me with a beautiful place to write in, and to my husband for doing a lot of childcare whilst I wrote this book.

Finally, thank you to all the single people out there who are courageously searching for their last first date.

Dear Reader,

We hope you enjoyed reading this book. If you did, we'd be so appreciative if you left a review. It really helps us and the author to bring more books like this to you.

Here at HQ Digital we are dedicated to publishing fiction that will keep you turning the pages into the early hours. Don't want to miss a thing? To find out more about our books, promotions, discover exclusive content and enter competitions you can keep in touch in the following ways:

### JOIN OUR COMMUNITY:

Sign up to our new email newsletter:
http://smarturl.it/SignUpHQ

Read our new blog www.hqstories.co.uk

🐦 https://twitter.com/HQStories

📘 www.facebook.com/HQStories

### BUDDING WRITER?

We're also looking for authors to join the HQ Digital family!
Find out more here:

https://www.hqstories.co.uk/want-to-write-for-us/

Thanks for reading, from the HQ Digital team

If you enjoyed *The Last First Date*, then why not try another delightfully uplifting romance from HQ Digital?